Early Modern Actors and Shakespeare's Theatre

RELATED TITLES

The Hand on the Shakespearean Stage, Farah Karim-Cooper

Shakespeare's Theatre and the Effects of Performance, edited by Farah Karim-Cooper and Tiffany Stern

Early Modern Acting Companies and their Plays in Shakespeare's London, Siobhan Keenan

Shakespeare's Acts of Will, Gary Watt

Early Modern Actors and Shakespeare's Theatre

Thinking with the Body

Evelyn Tribble

Bloomsbury Arden Shakespeare
An imprint of Bloomsbury Publishing Plc

B L O O M S B U R Y
LONDON · OXFORD · NEW YORK · NEW DELHI · SYDNEY

Bloomsbury Arden Shakespeare

An imprint of Bloomsbury Publishing Plc

Imprint previously known as Arden Shakespeare

50 Bedford Square	1385 Broadway
London	New York
WC1B 3DP	NY 10018
UK	USA

www.bloomsbury.com

**Bloomsbury, Arden Shakespeare and the Diana logo are
trademarks of Bloomsbury Publishing Plc**

First published 2017

British Library Cataloguing-in-Publication Data
A catalogue record for this book is available from the British Library.

ISBN:	HB:	978-1-4725-7603-3
	ePDF:	978-1-4725-7605-7
	ePub:	978-1-4725-7606-4

Library of Congress Cataloging-in-Publication Data
A catalog record for this book is available from the Library of Congress.

Cover image © The British Library Board C.31.c.49, 'Over the head of the
Horse' from *The Vaulting Master*, William Stokes, Oxon 165

Typeset by Fakenham Prepress Solutions, Fakenham, Norfolk NR21 8NN
Printed and bound in Great Britain

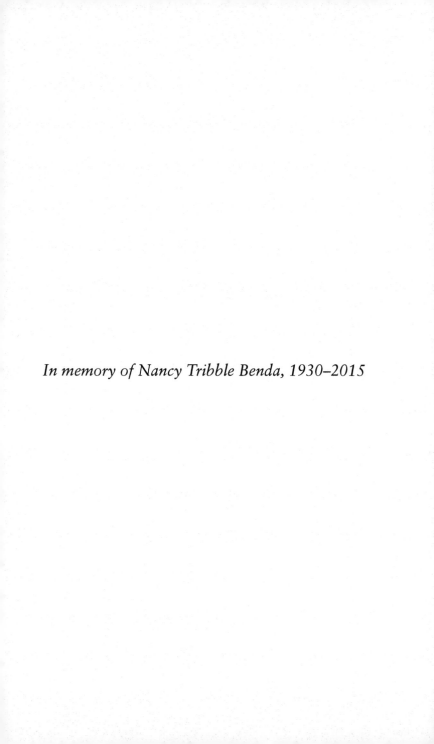

In memory of Nancy Tribble Benda, 1930–2015

CONTENTS

ACKNOWLEDGEMENTS

My debts in writing this book are many. I thank the Royal Society of New Zealand Marsden Fund for its generous support of my research. I spent 2013 researching this material at the Folger Shakespeare Library as a long-term Mellon research fellow. Although I have worked at the Folger many times, 2013 was an especially joyous and productive time there, for which I thank the Fellowships Program Manager, Carol Brobeck, as well as 'fellow fellows' Katherine Booth Attie, Dennis Britton, Pamela O. Long, Kevin McGinley, Paul Menzer, Julie Park and Denis Romano. Others at the Folger who helped me think through my work include Kathleen Lynch, Gail Kern Paster, David Schalkwyk and Michael Witmore. Thanks are also due to the Early Modern Conversions Project, at which I presented early work on this material; I am especially grateful to Paul Yachnin for including me in the project and to Steven Mullaney for inviting me to present my work at the University of Michigan.

John Sutton of Macquarie University has helped me more than I can say, and I would also like to acknowledge Doris McIlwain's influence on my thinking about skill. Audiences at 'Memory Days' held at Macquarie University and at the University of Otago have helped me to refine and clarify my thinking about skill, embodiment and expertise. The members of the Shakespeare Association of America seminar on 'Skill' provided a wonderful forum and sparked ongoing conversations, as did the contributors to the *Shakespeare Studies* Forum on 'Skill'. I also thank the audience at the University Pennsylvania Med/Ren seminar for their patient and insightful comments; I am especially grateful to Zach Lesser and Marissa Nicosia for the invitation. Other colleagues who have helped to shape the book include Gina Davis, Farah Karim-Cooper, Roslyn L. Knutson, Lois Potter, Henry Turner and Penelope Woods.

I would like to thank Andrea Gammon of the Stratford Festival for organizing my trip to interview fight directors and actors, including Ruby Joy, Brady Ruby, Geoff Scoville and Sarah Topham. Daniel Levinson was very generous in opening his studio, Rapier Wit, to me. I also thank Casey Kaleba for his discussions of stage combat with me, and for his tolerance for my inept attempts to learn the art.

Margaret Bartley has been a patient and supportive editor. I also thank the readers at Bloomsbury Publishing for their helpful comments. Thanks are also due to Emily Hockley.

Sarah Entwistle has been an enormously skilled and helpful research assistant. I am so fortunate to have her support. I also thank Karen McLean. I am fortunate in my colleagues at the University of Otago, who have listened patiently to numerous redactions of this topic. These include Dave Ciccoricco, Nicola Cummins, Simone Drichel, Jacob Edmond, Thomas McLean, Chris Prentice, Shef Rogers, Anne Feryok and Paul Tankard.

Some of the material in this book is a much-revised version of material that originally appeared in my chapter on 'Skill' in *Early Modern Theatricality*, ed. Henry Turner (Oxford: Oxford University Press, 2013), 173–88. It is reproduced by permission of Oxford University Press.

The Houghton Library at Harvard University provided the image for the cover photograph of a plate from Will Stokes, *The Vaulting Master* (London, 1641).

And, finally, I thank Timothy Mixter and Emelia Hillis Mixter for helping me see it through.

1

Introduction

Simon Jewell's box

Suffering from the plague, Simon Jewell made his last will and testament in 1592. A sharer in the Queen's Men Company, Jewell reveals the intertwining of his personal and professional affairs.[1] Jewell meticulously recorded the substantial sums for apparel and other necessaries for touring that he had paid out to the company, which were owing to his estate. He also noted what he owed to others: four pounds to Mr Fletcher and five to Mr Mathews, 30 shillings to Mr Brookes for a pair of velvet hose, among others. He also made a number of bequests: to Robert Scott he gave his black coat lined with taffeta; his wife received his livery suit, presumably to sell; and to Robert Nicholls he bequeathed 'all my playing things in a box and my black velvet shewes'.

Sadly, Jewell's box is lost. This book aims to reconstruct that box, conceived both literally and metaphorically. What was in such a box, and how might it differ from the boxes of today's actors? Up through the mid-twentieth century, it was not uncommon for actors to own trunks of acting equipment – they might have in them props such as daggers or swords, costumes, wigs or false beards, perhaps musical instruments.[2] Today it would be unusual for actors to haul their own gear around with them; once cast in a play, actors rely upon the company for costumes and properties, which follow an overall look or design decided by the director, in consultation with other specialists, within the constraints of the budget. Today's actor is not expected to bring with her a particular set of material objects. But in another sense, of course, all actors bring their boxes with them – the sum of their experience, their training, the past roles that they have played, their physical and mental preparations, as well as specialized knowledge such as fight experience and training, musical accomplishments, knowledge of dialects and so on.

What might have been in Jewell's box? The will of Augustine Phillips of the King's Men, made on 4 May 1606, gives us some idea of what may have been inside.[3] Amongst many monetary bequests to 'hired men' of the company as well as to his 'fellows' (including Shakespeare, Christopher Beeston and Henry Condell), Phillips bequeathed to his 'late apprentice' Samuel Gisborne 40 shillings 'and my mouse Colloured veluit hose and a white Taffety dublet A blacke Taffety sute my purple Cloke sword and dagger'. In addition, he bequeaths to his current apprentice, James Sandes, a 'Citterne a Bandore and a Lute'.[4] These were valuable bequests. We know from Henslowe's diary and Alleyn's inventory of costumes – and indeed from Jewell's will itself – that special costumes were purchased and owned by the company; Jewell calculates that he has paid out £13 6s 8d for his 'share of apparel', thus making its total cost the vast sum of 80 pounds.[5] The records of Henslowe and Alleyn show that some actors had their own garments in addition to company-owned apparel; Jean McIntyre, noting the relative 'paucity of women's clothing', suggests that adult actors to whom boys were apprenticed may have owned some female garments.[6] 'Taffety' suits and purple cloaks would have been valuable personal property, which could have been used both to outfit the player for a role and to provide capital (there are examples in Henslowe's diary of actors buying, selling and pawning garments). Items such as hangers or carriages for a rapier could be seen in the category of fashionable apparel as much as tools, and it is very likely that Jewell's box might have contained a rapier with its accoutrements. Other playhouse wills, including that of William Shakespeare, bequeath swords. The possibility that a sword and dagger were in the box is bolstered by two of the outstanding debts Jewell mentions: Mr Mathew's five pounds and Mr Fletcher's four. As Hanabusa has established, these men were fencing masters; the relatively large sums owing to them indicate the commitment to the art of defence that must have been a vital component of skilled practice on the part of the accomplished actor.

The box, then, may well have contained expensive clothing suitable for the stage, swords, hangers and girdles, daggers, musical instruments and other specialized equipment such as dancing pumps. Our hypothetical box accords well with the enumeration of the skills of the early modern player as recorded in *The Rich Cabinet*, probably written by Thomas Gainsford:

> Player hath many times, many excellent qualities: as dancing, actiuitie, musicke, song, elloqution, abilitie of body, memory, vigilancy, skill of weapon, pregnancy of wit, and such like: in all which hee resembleth an excellent spring of water, which growes the more sweeter, and the more plentifull by the often drawing out of it: so are all these the more perfect and plausible by the often practice.[7]

To a modern eye, this list might well seem like an indiscriminate mix of proper actorly skills and specialized physical or athletic abilities. Particular physical abilities such as fencing, dance and agility might be helpful marketable skills for actors, and they are often specified in casting calls for certain kinds of roles – for instance, calls for Tybalt in *Romeo and Juliet* and Laertes in *Hamlet* list stage combat experience as essential. But skills such as these are seldom seen as integral to the individual preparation for a role. In modern productions, stage combat and dance are overseen by fight and dance choreographers, who create convincing displays using actors who may well have very unequal levels of skill and training.

However different contemporary and early modern actors may be, both work within *distributed cognitive ecologies*. As I have written elsewhere,[8] early modern players coped with seemingly overwhelming cognitive loads as they dealt with the constant demand of the purpose-built playhouse system for new material. It was often said that players could only have managed by using stock practices or routines, pandering to the groundlings, and so forth. But a model of distributed cognition can help us see that they succeeded by creating and embedding themselves within physical, social and material smart structures. These structures included the playhouse itself, governed by shared conventions of movement across the stage; cognitive artefacts such as the part and the plot; the strong social bonds fostered by the system of sharers in the playhouses; and the regimes of training and education that undergirded their practice. Playing companies were in fact building such structures as they went along, in an instance of cognitive niche construction: 'organizing our physical environment in ways that enhance our information-processing capacities'.[9]

Distributed cognition posits that a complex activity such as performance is spread, smeared or extended across mechanisms such as attention, perception and memory; the experience of training as it is sedimented in the body; social structures and the material environment. Another way of describing this concept is as a 'cognitive ecology', which emphasizes the *interplay* of internal cognitive mechanisms and social and physical environment.[10] Cognitive ecologies are dynamic, changing to accommodate new circumstances: some systems will place more or less weight on internal mechanisms, on central control or on particular forms of cognitive artefacts and social systems. Such an approach lends itself to a variety of historical and theoretical approaches to performance. It predicts historical change and variation as new configurations of material and social practices emerge. For example, technical innovations in theatre such as lighting and sound boards in turn trigger fundamental shifts in how actors move in a space, therefore altering rehearsal practices and in turn generating new ways of engaging audience affect and attention.

A model of distributed cognitive ecologies is a particularly rich framework for studying skill, which links mind, body and environment in intelligent action. Skill is a property of biological, neurological, social, historical and material forces, and is best viewed through an approach that can keep each of these areas in play. One such framework is the emerging sub-discipline of 'neuroanthropology', a promising approach to cross-cultural and cross-historical pictures of skill. As Greg Downey, one of its most prominent practitioners, notes:

> The study of embodied knowledge and its development in bodily practices suggests that gaining bodily skills requires more than 'knowledge', involving changes in physiology, perception, comportment, and behaviour patterns in unsystematic, diverse modes. Embodied knowledge from this perspective appears more complex, less systematic or susceptible to structural account, than typically modelled.[11]

This approach to thinking with the body takes account of complex interactions among internal cognitive processes, embodied skill building, technologies and environments to ask how skill is inculcated, appraised, transmitted, valued and evaluated. The study of skill entails examining the training and the plasticity of the nervous system with habituation and practice; the role of attention, memory and perception; and the extension of the body through a range of instruments and objects, including tools, treatises and social and material practices such as apprenticeship, enskilment and enculturation.

I argue that such models can usefully supplement and modify approaches derived from critical and social theory. The 'bodily turn' towards the end of the last century has been extremely important in drawing attention to the body as a product of history and ideology rather than a natural category. Yet much work on body and embodiment in the early modern period neglects skill as a category. The influence of the early Foucault often resulted in emphasis upon violence done to bodies and discourses of inscription and subjugation rather than skill, performance, training or pleasure. As Barbara Ravelhofer has observed of Foucauldian-inflected scholarship on early modern dance, such orientations do not fully account for the ways that a body can become an 'active producer of its social meaning'.[12]

A highly influential model of the relationship between structure and the body has been that of social theory, especially as articulated by Norbert Elias and Pierre Bourdieu. Such studies have demonstrated the myriad ways that the body is shaped through implicit (and, more rarely, explicit) forces and cultural codes. In contrast to some social science literature that sees skill as primarily the property of the individual, social theorists such as Bourdieu attempt to account for embodied practices as produced by the larger cultural field, or 'habitus'. Bourdieu defines habitus as 'systems of durable, transposable *dispositions*' operating largely out of anyone's conscious control: 'It is because subjects do not strictly speaking, know what they are doing that what they do has more meaning than they know.'[13] Bourdieu's rich account of the ubiquitous implicit social shaping of culture has been enormously influential, but its account of skill is not fully developed. Bourdieu argues that:

> [in] treating the body as a memory, [societies] entrust to it … the fundamental principles of the arbitrary content of the culture. The principles em-bodied [*sic*] in this way are placed beyond the grasp of consciousness, and hence cannot be touched by voluntary, deliberate transformation.[14]

Placing 'voluntary, deliberate transformation' of the body and of the central nervous system 'beyond the grasp of consciousness' leaves skill difficult to explain. Downey has suggested that Bourdieu's concept of the habitus, whilst providing a careful account of the social shaping of the subject, places a kind of 'black box between input and output' that occludes 'a careful examination of how the body acquires knowledge and the nature of this bodily knowing'.[15] Greg Noble and Megan Watkins's brilliantly titled paper, 'So, How did Bourdieu Learn to Play Tennis?', nicely pinpoints the neglect of what they term 'bodily attention' in this model, particularly the relationship between agency and embodiment. Observing that Bourdieu was an accomplished tennis player, they argue that the concept of habitus easily explains why he should wish to attain the 'acquired capital' of skill in this sport, but cannot provide a full account of the training and practice needed to acquire and hone skilled play in tennis. Because Bourdieu wishes to argue against the rational actor model of social theory, he stresses 'the unconscious nature of the habitus, [and] largely abandons the important question of consciousness'.[16] Habitus was meant to be a dynamic model, but it can instead be employed in a 'deterministic', static and problematically 'unconscious' way.[17] As Noble and Watkins suggest, turning attention to the complex mechanism of training could allow a more nuanced understanding of the relationship between subject and structure, a 'distinction between habitus, or what the body is disposed to do, and bodily capacity, or what the body could do under different circumstances'.[18] Training 'involves both speaking to the body and speaking about the body'.[19] Both dance and tennis require 'body work' to 'produce bodies with capacity'. A 'feel for the game', in Bourdieu's famous phrase, 'is developed over time, and is only acquired through enormous application.'[20] This emphasis upon capacity and training is a useful modification of Bourdieu's model; Noble and Watkins argue that constraints create the conditions for work and change: 'Rather than construe habitus simply as constraint, we need to think of habitus as also entailing capacitation.'[21] While social theory is indispensable at one level of any analysis of skill (for example, in the role of cultural capital and status in the practice of rapier fighting versus the native sword and buckler tradition), it fails to fully account for other levels, in large part because its propensity to privilege social structures neglects the purposeful, mindful training of the nervous system and body that marks skilled practice.

I attempt to steer a course between theories of rationalist models of skill and expertise and those that simply flip the binary, instead privileging an ill-defined account of bodily intelligence. My use of the term 'distributed cognitive ecology' may give the erroneous impression that I favour what some might call a cognitivist or fully rational-actor theory of skill. But a distributed model of cognition rejects the idea that cognition is located in the head, with the body simply along for the ride. 'Cognition' is often equated with rationalism and propositional logic, but ultimately cognition is simply thinking, conceived of very broadly to encompass remembering, feeling, dreaming, making our way through the world – skilful activity of all sorts.

The account of skill I favour, then, seeks a middle way between the models offered by existing debates on expertise, which tend to anchor themselves at either pole. The first of these is associated with K. Anders Ericsson, a psychologist at Florida State University, who has been studying the nature of expert performance for several decades. Ericsson's model stresses the 'expert's representation and memory for knowledge'.[22] In this model, mere experience is not sufficient: 'All the paths to expert performance appear to require substantial extended effortful practice.'[23] Ericsson's work was popularized in Malcolm Gladwell's bestselling book *Outliers*, which put forward the so-called 10,000 hour rule, the hypothesis that ten years of deliberate practice in a domain was necessary to attain true expertise.[24] This model tends to stress declarative knowledge and conscious control. Ericsson and others in this tradition, including Roger Chaffin, who has written influential accounts of musical expertise, argue that a 'detailed, overarching cognitive framework constructed and consolidated over the course of many hours of practice'

– otherwise described as a 'declarative roadmap' – is the essential element in expert performance.[25]

While Ericsson's work has been highly influential, it has been seen as excessively dependent upon conscious control. The best known of these challenges has been mounted by Hubert Dreyfus, working within the phenomenological tradition. Dreyfus argues that only relatively inexperienced performers rely upon cognitive roadmaps such as those described by Ericsson and Chaffin; instead, he claims that the true marker of skill is best described as 'mindless coping'. Repudiating the top-down approach of Ericsson and Chaffin, Dreyfus asks, '[C]an philosophers successfully describe the conceptual upper floors of the edifice of knowledge while ignoring the embodied coping going on on the ground floor; in effect declaring that human experience is upper stories all the way down?'[26] That is, his model might be described as 'body up' rather than 'mind down'. For Dreyfus, highly developed skill is less a result of cognitive rule-following than it is a form of 'absorbed coping'.[27] Indeed, Dreyfus argues, as performance improves, the cognitive roadmap can be abandoned in favour of an embodied engagement with the world that emphasizes flow and the 'switching-off' of conscious monitoring.

As Wayne Christensen, John Sutton and Doris McIlwain have suggested, such an account has intuitive appeal; the idea of flow resonates with experiences of fluid performance in such domains as sport, debate, acting and dance.[28] But this is only a partial account of what it might mean to think with the body. As Sutton and Geeves argue, the wholesale rejection of 'mindfulness' in skilled activity is an overreaction to 'ultra-cognitivist intellectualist or rationalist theories'.[29] Simply reversing the dichotomy sells short the fundamental intelligence of skilled action.

It is this space that I am exploring. Christensen, Sutton and McIlwain describe this middle way between mindless coping and full-scale planning as 'Mesh'. In this model, 'high order control plays a key role in virtually all action – not just action that involves explicit reasoning … expert awareness will be selective, highly shaped to task demands, and may often "roam" or "float" as it flexibly and anticipatively seeks out important information'.[30] So when, for example, a cricket player says that 'in batting you have to be mindless', he is referring not to the absence of thought, but to a certain deployment of attentional resources, 'employing sophisticated forms of attentional control and self-regulation'.[31] So too for the actor, who must banish certain forms of thought and harness others. This quotation from Ralph Richardson nicely encapsulates the nature of the 'meshed' thinking of the expert actor:

> You're really driving four horses, as it were, first going through in great detail the exact movements which have been decided upon. You're also listening to the audience, as I say, keeping if you can very great control over them. You're also slightly creating the part, insofar, as you're consciously refining movements and perhaps inventing tiny other experiments with new ones. At the same time you really are living, in one part of your mind, what is happening. Acting to some extent in a controlled dream ... . Therefore three or four layers of consciousness are at work during the time an actor is giving a performance.[32]

The key to expertise is managing these layers of attention in real time. It is absolutely correct that certain forms of conscious control or 'disruptive attention' will indeed impede flow and cause one to lose control of one or more of these horses. But experts differ from novices not just by *accumulating* experience, but through training themselves in how to allocate attention; they learn to employ 'instructional nudges', little maxims that reduce weeks, months, years of embodied experience to a heuristic. Such approaches permit a brief distillation of an entire practice to be remembered 'on the fly', refocusing rather than disrupting flow.

I argue that early modern actors who cultivated the seeming miscellany of mental and physical skills ascribed to them built a form of *kinesic intelligence* that undergirded their entire practice. The concept of kinesic intelligence, built upon a foundation of training and practice in demanding practices such as fencing and dance, helps to explain how early modern players could produce plays despite a minimum of group rehearsal time. Mindful bodily skills such as gesture, dance and swordplay were crucial forms of kinesic intelligence honed by the early modern player within particular cognitive ecologies of skilled practice; they taught not simply the skills themselves but an entire way of being in the world, including wit, timing, grace and skilful coordination with others.[33] Fencing treatises emphasized that the art moulded the body and mind: the eye, the foot, the hand and the judgement were said to walk together.[34] Similarly authors of dance manuals insisted upon the mindfulness of their practice. Just as verbal recall was meant to be active and spontaneous, not mere rote repetition, so physical memory for intricate dances required expert 'on-line' intelligence and constant attentiveness to unfolding demands of performance. Thus kinesic intelligence demanded by dance was closely related to the qualities of 'grace' and ease that marked elite performance in the early modern period.

The concept of 'kinesic intelligence' has been articulated by Guillemette Bolens, who adapts the term from Ellen Spolsky.[35] Bolens usefully extends the philosopher Shaun Gallagher's description of bodily schema, which he defines as a largely 'pre-noetic ... system of sensory-motor processes that constantly regulate posture and movement ... without reflective awareness or the necessity of perceptual monitoring'.[36] Gallagher here distinguishes conscious, reflective movement – such as we might undertake when learning how to swing a bat or throw a hammer – from the relatively unreflective actions we perform when, for instance, we adjust our body when picking up an object. Those who spend long hours training the mindful body hone their abilities to lift the pre-noetic to conscious awareness. To capture this ability, Bolens adopts Hubert Godard's term 'postural musicality', which captures the preparation for the skilled movement of the trained dancer: 'A person's kinesic style manifests itself at this specific level of a corporeal organization of meaning.'[37] As Bolens notes, these styles are susceptible to training – that is, the pre-noetic can be brought to conscious awareness, which is above all the job of experts in movement such as dancers, fencers and actors. A full study of kinesis, then, requires examining how 'experience gets under the skin', in Downey's words, who notes that 'Culturally distinct forms of physical education shape distinctive bodies in a literal sense, forging muscles, crafting tendons, assembling sensory systems, and generating physical capabilities.'[38]

Yet, for a variety of reasons, skill has historically been undervalued in accounts of early modern theatre. One reason for this neglect is the general predominance until recently of author-centred accounts of the drama, in which players tend to be reduced to more or less successful function-aries of playwrights. Much has changed in the past two decades, however. Recent company-centred research such as Lucy Munro's work on the Children of the Queen's Revels, Laurence Manley and Sally-Beth McLean's book on Lord Strange's Men, and investigations of the Queen's Men have focused more attention upon the players themselves, their practices and the disparate skill sets fostered by different companies.[39] In addition, new work on theatricality, games, gesture and clowning has greatly enriched our understanding of theatre as a fundamentally material practice, much of which takes place in the interstices of language.[40]

Players trafficked in a wide range of skills. A look at Alan Dessen and Leslie Thomson's invaluable *A Dictionary of Stage Directions in English Drama 1580–1642* affords a glimpse of the range of actions early modern players were asked to perform: 'to use vehement action', 'to make passionate action';[41] to 'enter as affrighted and amazed', to dance an antic;[42] 'to enter as newly come from play';[43] 'to run against the Cage and brain herself';[44] to caper and sing, to chafe and stamp;[45] to sing a catch;[46] to 'make ridiculous conges ... and dance in several postures';[47] to run a coranto pace; to 'dance a jig devised for the nonce';[48] to whip forth their swords; to 'stagger with faintness'; to 'walk by and practice postures'.[49] Actors dance, drive, flourish, flinch, mock, kick, kill, kiss, lament, make signs and pipe.

The very casualness with which such an array of actions is called for gives us some idea of the skill sets that playwrights could routinely expect of the players. At key moments in the plays the discursive action all but ceases, and the players engage in inset skill displays, brief or prolonged. Terse stage descriptions, such as '*Enter Richard and Richmond. They fight. Richard is slain*' or, even more commonly, simply '*fight*', are testimony to abilities that now require elaborate fight choreography. More specialized skills are also called for, as in *As You Like It*: '*Wrestle*', which assumes that the players can credibly engage before an audience likely to have a sporting eye for good wrestling. Pike-throwing is called for in Heywood's *Four Prentices of London*, and vaulting, or at least credible preparation for it, is called for in one of the dumb shows in *The White Devil*: 'Flamineo and Camillo strip themselves into their shirts, as to vault' (Act 2, Scene 2, The Second Dumb Show). The boy players in Lyly's *Campaspe* dance, tumble and sing in quick succession. Boy companies in indoor theatre performed *entre'act* entertainments, especially dancing and singing; the Citizen wife in *Knight of the Burning Pestle* asks the boy whether he can tumble and breath fire in addition to dance (Act 3, Interlude 3: 12–15), which hints at the nature of some of the entertainment on offer as an adjunct to playing.

Many of these stage directions indicate a high level of proficiency and technical ability. Stage directions often indicate extended conflicts, punctuated by pauses for the players to catch their breath: '*He fighteth first with one, and then with another, and overcomes them both*'; '*they fight a good while and then breathe*'; '*alarum a fierce fight with sword and target, then after pause and breathe*'; '*Alarum, fight with single swords, and being deadly wounded and panting for breath,*

making a stroke at each other with their gauntlets they fall.[50]
Some stage directions call for very complex and technical
moves such as '*throws his cloak on the other's point*',[51] '*gets
within him and takes away his sword*',[52] or, more famously, '*in
scuffling they change Rapiers*'.[53] As with the range of technical
fencing skills expected by dramatists, the plays routinely call
for highly technical and varied dances: '*dancing a coranto;
dances the Spanish pavin*'; '*place themselves in a figure for a
dance; dance after the ancient Ethiopian manner*'.[54]

We also have numerous accounts of extra-fictional feats of
skill performed by players attached to companies or travelling
with them. The Admiral's Men was paid by the court both
for presenting plays and for 'activities', as in 1588 when they
were paid 'for two Enterludes or playes ... and for showing
other feates of activity and tumbling'; there is also a record in
Henslowe's diary from 1601 for 'a pair of hose for Nicke to
tumble in before the Queene'. Players visiting the continent
are reported to have been paid both for playing and for feats
of activities, as in the payment of Robert Brown in 1592 for
'qualitiz en faict de music, agilitez et joeux de commedies,
tragedies et histories'.[55] In 1582, Gosson's condemnation of
the playing assumes that the experience comprises much more
than simply viewing a play:

> For the eye beeside the beautie of the houses, and the
> Stages, hee [the Devil] sendeth in Gearish apparell maskes,
> vaulting, tumbling, daunsing of gigges, galiardes, morisces,
> hobbihorses; showing of iuggeling castes, nothing forgot,
> that might serue to set out the matter, with pompe, or
> rauish the beholders with varietie of pleasure.[56]

Here we may have difficulties in interpreting evidence, as there
is little direct account of what shows and feats might have
been performed on the edges of the play (apart from numerous
references to jigs). In contrast, account books detailing payouts
to players at the court and in the provinces tend to be more
specific about precisely what was being paid for. Thus our

assumptions about the differences among companies, or about shifts in taste, could result from the vicissitudes of record-keeping. Did boys, especially the younger boys, in the adult companies routinely offer displays of tumbling, dancing and athletic skill?

Chambers suggests that such extra-dramatic 'feats' were something of a last resort and that players of the 1580s and early 1590s were 'ready at need to eke out their plays by musical performances and even the "activities" of acrobats'.[57] Playwrights sometimes complain in their prefaces and inductions about the preferences of audiences for fights and clowns: Ben Jonson has the Stage-Keeper in *Bartholomew Faire* complain about the tyranny of 'master poets'[58] who eschew the 'sword-and-buckler man'[59] and even refuse to countenance 'a juggler with a well-educated ape',[60] thus satirizing the tastes of playgoers who prefer 'the concupiscence of jigs and dances'.[61] In fact, much of our knowledge of ephemeral skill displays is derived from satire within the drama and paratextual complaints in prologues and epilogues; skill displays often come to our attention only as they are mocked. Ben Jonson and other poet-dramatists encourage us to see the words as the matter, with stage fighting, music, dancing, dumb shows and sounds relegated to ephemeral concessions to popular taste. This is a line of narrative that is repeated by theatre historians. Greg speculated that the large number of calls for fights and clowning in *Orlando Furioso* showed that the play was designed for touring, a point that L. B. Wright echoed in his description of inset skill displays as 'variety entertainments'.[62] Such descriptions smack of disdain towards the provinces that the REED project has done much to dispel. But I argue that reorienting our attention to skill display and to theatre as a form of entertainment, with as many affinities to sport as to literature, helps us to capture a fuller picture of the early modern stage.[63] Attention to skill demands that we abandon such invidious distinctions still made between the proper ambit of drama and so-called extra-theatrical displays.[64]

An ecological model of skill demands that we consider audience expertise as well as the cultural values placed upon certain modes of skill display. The tight connection between expert performance and the aesthetics of skill is attested to by Roger Ascham's *Toxophilus*, which contains this fascinating account of the relationships among skill, aesthetics and spectatorship:

> For this I am sure, in learning all other matters, nothing is brought to the most profitable use, which is not handled after the most comely fashion. As masters of fence have no stroke fit either to hit another, or else to defend himself, which is not joined with a wonderful comeliness. A cook cannot chop his herbs neither quickly nor handsomely, except he keep such a measure with his chopping-knives as would delight a man both to see him and hear him. Every handcraftman that works best for his own profit, works most seemly to other men's sight. Again, in building a house, in making a ship, every part, the more handsomely they be joined for profit and last, the more comely they be fashioned to every man's sight and eye.[65]

Players were in a particularly complex position with respect to skill display, as they were called upon to give a credible emulation of aristocratic skill before audiences drawn from the highest orders of society. As Lois Potter writes, 'Men and women who had spent years learning to fence or dance would be critical of inadequate performance from characters purporting to be royal or aristocratic.'[66] Swordfights on Shakespeare's stage took place between highly trained men who used and carried weapons in daily life and before audiences who were themselves highly skilled viewers, with a sporting eye for good swordplay. Actors today, even those highly trained in fight stagecraft, are in a very different position; much of the swordplay must be carefully designed and overseen by a fight director, while in turn audiences have both little knowledge of the art and possibly unrealistic standards derived from their experience of film. Observing the culturally complex cognitive performance ecology will permit insight into the strategies used to structure and coordinate novel forms of skilled group action.

Induction into any skilled activity, whether as a spectator or a participant, involves developing an 'eye' for it. An everyday example of such training is the work of the sports commentator, whose job it is to educate the audience in the nuances of the game, to train their eyes and ears so that they can distinguish excellent from run-of-the-mill performances, to capture in words the criteria by which, say, synchronized diving is assessed by expert judges. Commentators on sport guide our attention to the tiniest of movements – the boxer has dropped his hands, the fielder has shifted to the left, the diver has bent his legs. Even in the absence of commentators, anyone who has witnessed a high-stakes sporting match amongst a knowledgeable group of fans has experienced the skilled viewing of the spectators – the sense of collective expertise in applauding a skilled catch or bemoaning a botched pass. Such expert forms of spectatorship constitute a form of 'skilled viewing', as Christina Grasseni has described it, through which one learns to discriminate and evaluate.

Grasseni uses the concept of 'skilled viewing' to account for the ways that 'specific sensibilities and capacities ... are engendered through the active socialization of apprentices into structured and shared contexts of practice'. Grasseni conducted her fieldwork in Tuscany, shadowing cattle breeders. These breeders were highly attuned to their cattle, and the ability to 'recognise each of one's cows at sight is a highly respected capacity, the mark of a dedicated herder'.[67] To understand her hosts' worldview, Grasseni realized that learning to look at their cows was a necessity. She observes that 'learning to deal with cows' shapes, to appropriate them in every detail, from every angle, both close-up and from a distance requires a constant training of attention, which begins early on in life'.[68] As an apprentice 'viewer', Grasseni attempted to assimilate the skilled vision of the breeders, a process that 'involves disciplining, selecting, re-interpreting and distancing oneself from one's naïve and undiscerning vision'.[69] Using the work of Tim Ingold, Grasseni refers to this process as an 'education of attention'. The novice-looker again engages in a highly skilled activity that takes him or her from simply gazing to a form of active vision, ultimately resulting in careful fine-grained discrimination of animals that to an outsider look at first simply like a bunch of cows.

The sports commentator offers a model of a rapid, quick and dirty induction into skilled vision, assisted by such technologies of instant replay and on-screen charts and diagrams designed to make visible events and nuances that otherwise escape notice. But truly skilled vision involves education and attunement over time, a practice sedimented in the body. For this reason, practitioners of bodily disciplines develop a particular attunement to these movements, a form of motor perception that underpins appreciation of such skilled activities as dance and gymnastics.[70] As Doris McIlwain and John Sutton argue, 'To the untrained eye, different styles of movement and different shapes are all that is seen when looking at a body. However, when a skilled observer sees a body, she or he sees the sedimented history of a dynamic coupling between body and world.'[71] The briefest of touches – how a hand goes to pick up a weapon, the first turning out of the toe, the dropping of the shoulder or the raising of the chin, the minute relaxing of the knees to work the body into a state of readiness – reveal to the trained observer a lifetime of skilled habits. The 'skilled vision' necessary to recognize expertise is attested to in Thomas Hoby's translation of Castiglione's *Courtier*:

> [M]arke a man that taketh weapon in hande: yf goyng about to cast a darte, or houldyng in hys hand a swoorde, he setleth hym self lightsomely (not thinking upon it) in a ready aptnesse wyth such activity, that a man would seeme hys bodye and all his members were naturally setled in that disposition and without any payne, though he doeth

nothing els, yet doeth he declare hymself unto everye man to be most perfect in that exercise.[72]

This description of 'ready aptnesse' describes the trained body, so practised in its movements that it 'declares' that it is 'most perfect in that exercise'. This seems to be a moment of relative transparency in Castiglione's account of skill. Although the courtiers cannot explain precisely how to achieve this perfection, 'lightsomeness' seems to function as a moment of grace visible and sedimented in the body, not merely that simulacrum of accomplishment that haunts descriptions of skill in *The Courtier*.

Early modern England inherits a variety of skill discourses: skill and the body can be seen as the confluence of numerous, often incompatible, issues that are inherited from classical antiquity and the Christian tradition. These include the Greek admiration for athleticism and the masculine body, the Roman warrior and gladiatorial tradition, the Augustinian suspicion of the flesh and hostility towards brutal sport, the humanist attitude towards the body and the role of physical exercise in education, including medical discourses such as Galen's *De Sanitate Tuenda*.[73] These come together, collide, jostle, within existing skill traditions with their own relationship to status and prestige, within a peculiarly English context.

Skill and the problem of 'languaging experience'

When Rosencrantz and Guildenstern confront Hamlet after the disastrous performance of 'The Mousetrap', Hamlet gives Guildenstern a recorder and asks him if he will 'play upon this pipe'. Guildenstern demurs: 'I know no touch of it, my lord.' Hamlet replies: 'It is as easy as lying. Govern these ventages with your fingers and thumb, give it breath with your mouth, and it will discourse most eloquent music. Look you, these are the stops.' Guildenstern protests: 'But these cannot I command to any utterance of harmony. I have not the skill' (3.2.359–65). This exchange nicely captures the gulf between discursive knowledge as it might be presented in a manual or a prescriptive treatise and the practical demands of any skill domain. Look, says Hamlet, here are the stops; you simply cover the holes with your fingers and blow. As little as we would wish to be likened to Guildenstern, anyone who has ever learned to dance, to throw a football, to play a guitar, to juggle, to bake a cake or to write a poem knows that it is not so simple, that there is a vast difference between replicating the external movements and having the skill to produce harmony. This is of course Hamlet's point – Guildenstern presumes to play upon him as clumsily as he would sound the recorder: 'You would pluck out the heart of my mystery' (3.2.367).

To write about skill is in a way to attempt to 'pluck out the heart' of a mystery, to define and pin down a quality that always eludes precise definition. The salient point about any performance, of course, is its evanescence. Then as now the vocabulary in which skilled action is discussed can be maddeningly vague, as the arts of the body seem to evade the limitations of written language. Maxine Sheets-Johnstone describes this dilemma as the conundrum of 'languaging experience'. The problem is the more vexing when working with historically remote materials, with the evanescent traces of skilled practices that we can catch sight of only in praise, parody or polemic. If contemporary skill confronts us with the difficulties of languaging experience, studying skill in historical context is even more challenging, since evidence is necessarily scattered and incomplete. I endeavour in this book to work with a range of material: the playtexts themselves, read for their absences as much as their language; early modern treatises on skill, which, although they must be read with a sceptical eye, nevertheless represent sustained attempts to language experience for early modern readers; and contemporary research on skill, embodiment and animation, read both for their moments of intersection and moments of collision with early modern concepts of skill.

In the following chapters I attempt a reconstruction of the mindful bodies of the early modern players. Chapter 2 is the first of three chapters that examines the moving, animate body on the early modern stage. This chapter takes up first the art of gesture, long considered to be the pinnacle of the art of the actor. Like the other physically demanding arts I discuss, mastering the art of gesture involved bringing the body into conscious awareness, recognizing and mastering its natural grooves and tendencies and channelling them into an artistic form that had the capacity to captivate an audience. This interlinking of word and hand then provided the basis for the graceful movement of the entire body, such that the mere act of walking becomes an artful practice. Examining early modern treatises on the arts of *action* and comportment in dialogue with contemporary research on gesture and gait, I offer fresh views of crucial moments in Shakespeare's drama by reading through the lens of skill.

Chapter 3, on the art of fencing, builds upon this attention to the mindful body through an examination of the fighting arts and the role of weapons on the early modern stage. Often considered simply extraneous entertainment, skilled fighting on the early modern stage is caught up in debates about the relationship between weaponry and identity. Contemporary research highlighting that human beings are 'a technological species all the way down'[74] has shown how tools and artefacts shape their users, affecting an entire array of physical and mental dispositions. Debates about how weapons such as longbows and rapiers shaped the men who wielded them raged in early modern England, and these debates are in turn given kinesic form on the stage. I survey a range of plays in which fencing plays a prominent role, arguing that both Jonson and Shakespeare intimately linked verbal and physical skill. The chapter concludes with an examination of the character of Edgar in *King Lear*, who is embedded in existing debates about skill and weaponry in early modern England.

Chapter 4 takes up the art of dance, a skill laden with moral, social and ethical significance. The discourse around dance stressed not only the mindfulness of the practice, but also its links to divine harmony. Dance was also the most socially scrutinized and visible of all skills, particularly at elite levels of performance. It also had a complex relationship to the drama in which it was embedded. As Erika Lin writes, 'onstage dances are one kind of theatrical action in which the referential and performant functions come together'.[75] This chapter concludes by examining the relationships among skill, dance and on- and off-stage audiences in *A Midsummer Night's Dream* and *Much Ado about Nothing*.

Chapter 5 first takes up what we might call the 'skills behind the skills' that Gainsford mentions: memory, vigilancy and pregnancy of wit. These skills are at base attentional: 'vigilancy', for example, is akin to skilled attentiveness or anticipation – the ability to attend to more than one thing at once, to simultaneously perform and monitor that performance through a form of meta-cognitive awareness. Although all competent players may well have possessed such skills, they were particularly associated with the clown. However, evidence also suggests that the categories through which we understand early modern drama are skewed towards character and plot rather than the art of variety that was valued in the period itself. I conclude the chapter with analyses of plays that I argue should be considered 'skill plays', including brief discussions of *The Jew of Malta*, *The Changeling* and *Hamlet*.

My final chapter examines kinesic intelligence on reconstructed stages. The case of original practices productions offers a particularly rewarding arena for studying distributed cognitive ecologies within the framework of skill. Original practices may be in dialogue with some forms of past practice, but equally they are simply practices, emergent and evolving, and in dynamic relationship to other forms of contemporary theatre. I examine this relationship between early modern and contemporary skill through an analysis of reconstructions of dance and stage combat.

2

The Moving Body

Things in action sooner catch the eye /
Than what not stirs
TROILUS AND CRESSIDA 3.3.184–5[1]

Action and the art of gesture

Actors are above all experts in movement. From holding out the hand, to turning the head, to kneeling, to passing over the stage, to drawing a sword, to dancing a pavan or a jig, to tumbling, wrestling, vaulting or other feats of activity, the actor's body is above all kinetic. This section of the book takes up the question of the player in motion, attempting to reconstruct the kinesic intelligence of the early modern actor. In understanding kinesic intelligence, Maxine Sheets-Johnstone's term 'animation' is perhaps a more precise way of conceiving of the actor's body than the rather inert term 'embodiment'. She writes that 'when we properly begin our inquiries with animation, with movement, with the quintessential feature of our aliveness, we have no need for lexical band-aids on the order of embodiment. Minds are not embodied. Bodies are mindful.'[2] In her view, the term 'embodiment' is too static a term for capturing the moving body. Actors are not packaged into a role like a paper tucked inside an envelope; rather they animate their character in rich ongoing modulation with their environment. In endorsing Sheets-Johnstone's critique of the term, Tim Ingold writes that:

> animacy and embodiment pull in opposite directions: where the former is a movement of opening, the latter is bent on closure … . We do not [Maxine Sheets-Johnstone] insists, experience ourselves and one another as 'packaged', but as moving and moved, in ongoing response – that is in *corre-spondence* – with the things around us. Of course, we have bodies – indeed we are bodies. But we are not wrapped up in them.[3]

In this section, I approach the question of the mindful, animate body of the actor through the lens of skill and training. In training their bodies, actors build upon what Sheets-Johnstone calls the 'qualitative kinetic dynamics of our everyday lives'.[4] She notes that whilst we easily identify the 'qualitative dynamics' or 'style' of others – their gait, their little tics, their habitual ways of speaking, laughing or carrying themselves – our own 'coordinated dynamic patterns' are often 'sidelined in our awareness', they 'flow forth effortlessly in the sense that we do not have to concentrate attention on our movement'.[5] But this does not mean such movements are entirely sunk beneath conscious notice; even without training, we can identify our own 'kinesthetic melodies'.[6] And those who undertake mindful training of the body – including, among many others, the early modern player trained in the techniques of gesture, the contemporary actor studying movement, the martial artist or the dancer – gain a purchase on their movements that can render them mesmerizingly attractive.

Indeed, in the early modern period, the art of action was described precisely in such hypnotic, quasi-magical terms.[7] Action was seen as a serious and powerful art. In early modern plays, in the wider debates and discussions about the theatre and in treatises and literature on oratory and

sermons, the ability of the skilled actor or orator is likened
to bewitchment. 'By a full and significant action of body',
writes the author of 'The Character of an Excellent Player',
'he charms our attention.'[8] Like a magus at the centre of a
conjuring circle, the skilled actor pulls the audience to him:
'sit in a full Theatre, and you will thinke you see so many lines
drawne from the circumference of so many eares, whiles the
Actor is the Center'.[9] The ability to produce 'significant' or
meaningful movement through the managed body is akin to
sorcery, a reminder that the secret of both the actor and the
conjurer is to manage and direct attention and affect.[10] The
actor is imagined as seizing the eyes, ears and attention of the
audience and directing them through an invisible tether.

Detractors and defenders of the theatre alike imagine a
quasi-physical link between the movement of the actor's body
and the eyes of the audience, a link given weight and heft
through the attraction of animal spirits as they flowed through
the body of the actor into the spectator. Joseph Roach has
written eloquently of the theory of animal spirits that underpinned these views of the power of the stage: 'the spirit moves
the actor who, in the authenticity of his transport, moves the
audience'.[11] Such powers could be used for good or ill. In the
hands of a powerful cleric such as John Donne, these abilities
could be used to move men and women towards God, as
Jasper Mayne describes Donne's effect on congregations who
heard his sermons: 'Such was thy carriage, and thy gesture
such / As could divide the heart, and conscience touch.'[12]

Action comprised both gestures made with the hands and
the larger movements of the body – more generally, it is used
'to signify the physical animation of a speaker, whether on
stage, in the pulpit, in its Christian sense or on the lecturer's
or legislator's podium'.[13] The term connotes the ability to
manage the body and to 'grace' the language of the playwright,
rendering it vivid and present. Descriptions of 'action' and its
importance derive from classical rhetoric, especially the work
of Quintilian and Cicero, and teaching skilled pronunciation
and gesture was a bedrock of the English grammar schools.

As John Astington notes, 'The acquisition of proper pronunciation, clarity of enunciation, vocal emphasis and control, respect for rhythm and pitch, and the accompanying "action" of facial expression and bodily stance and gesture … were all regarded as appropriate educational attainments in the mastering of oratory.'[14] This early practice in oratory formed the substratum of embodied knowledge brought to the stage by the men and boys trained in this system, and the truly skilled among them were able to lift these practices into an art form in itself.

On the other hand, precisely because speakers, including players, could ensnare the eyes of the audiences through their expert action, their art was a potentially dangerous one. If a preacher inspired by God could use gesture to touch the heart of his listeners, so too could an actor inspired by Satan use the same abilities for nefarious ends. In his anti-theatrical treatise *A Second and Third Blast of Retrait from Plays and Theatres*, Anthony Munday notes that 'it is marvellous to consider how the gesturing of a player, which Tully termeth the eloquence of the body, is of force to move and prepare a man to that which is ill'.[15] Resonance between the movement of the actor and the body of the spectator could be dangerous as well as delightful.

Advocates of theatre argued that the ability to 'enthral' the eyes through action and gesture lay at the heart of the art of acting. Players could animate the past and bring it vividly before the eyes of the audience, shaping the viewer and readying him for deeds of patriotism and heroism. Contemporary accounts of actors' skill emphasized this ability above all, often contrasting the static nature of written language to the animation that the trained player brought to the part. In *Pierce Pennilesse*, Thomas Nashe describes the ability of the stage player to take English history off the page and into affective circulation. Referring to Shakespeare's play *1 Henry VI*, which portrays at length the death of the English warrior Sir John Talbot and his son at the hands of the French, Nashe writes:

> How would it haue joyed braue Talbot (the terror of the
> French) to thinke that after he had lyne two hundred yeares
> in his Tombe, hee should triumphe againe on the Stage,
> and haue his bones newe embalmed with the teares of ten
> thousand spectators at least, (at seuerall times) who in the
> Tragedian that represents his person, imagine they behold
> him fresh bleeding.[16]

Nashe contrasts the power of the actor to evoke and manage
shared emotion to the inert accounts of history available
in 'worme-eaten books' and neglected monuments. In his
Apology for Actors, the most complete defence of the art
of acting written in the period, Thomas Heywood similarly
argues that the representation of the past in 'our domesticke
histories' spurs the audience to emulation: 'What English
blood seeing the person of any bold English man presented
and doth not hugge his fame and burnynge at his valor
… so bewitching a thing is liuely and well spirited action,
that it hath power to new mold the harts of the spectators
and fashion them to the shape of any noble and notable
attempt.'[17]

Heywood's claim that lively action could strike an
answering chord in viewers is elaborated in Philip Massinger's
The Roman Actor (1626). Early in the play, Aretino accuses
the tragedian Paris of treason, charging that actors 'search
into the secrets of the time' and 'traduce / Persons of rank
and quality' (1.3.37, 40).[18] Drawing directly from Heywood's
treatise, Massinger has Paris argue that the theatre has the
capacity 'to inflame / The noble youth with an ambitious
heat' (1.3.70–1). In inflaming 'desire of honor' the stage
is superior to philosophizing. Philosophers traffic only in
the written word: they 'with cold precepts, perhaps seldom
read / Deliver what an honorable thing / the active virtue is'
(1.3.78–80). Contrasting inert cold words and the warmth of
action, Paris argues that mere precepts, like the history buried
in Nashe's 'worme-eaten books', do nothing to animate the
audience.

> But does that fire
> The blood or swell the veins with emulation
> To be both good and great equal to that
> Which is presented on our theatres?
> Let a good actor in a lofty scene
> Show great Alcides honored in the sweat
> of his twelve labors …
> All that have any spark of Roman in them,
> The slothful arts laid by, contend to be
> Like those they see presented. (1.3.78–86; 90–5)

Paris imagines audiences engaging in a kind of mimetic mirroring, spurred to reproduce not only the ethical imperative presented, but also the kinesis itself. In figuring spectators sparked to 'emulation', the passage anticipates research on 'entrainment', or the tendency of people to synchronize movements with one another, a point that will be discussed at greater length in the conclusion.

Massinger borrows heavily from Heywood's apology in this defence, particularly Heywood's elaborate catalogue of the range and vitality of theatrical representation. In contrast to printed histories or static images, which are mere 'shadows', Heywood argues that the actor alone fully conveys action:

> A Description is only a shadow receiued by the eare but not perceiued by the eye: so liuely portrature is merely a forme seene by the eye, but can neither shew action, passion, motion, or any other gesture, to mooue the spirits of the beholder to admiration: but to see a souldier shap'd like a souldier, walke, speake, act like a souldier, to see a Hector all besmered in blood, trampling vpon the bulkes of Kinges, A Troylus returning from the field in the sight of his father Priam, as if man and horse euen from the steeds rough fetlocks to the plume of the champions helmet had been together plunged into a purple Ocean: Too see a Pompey ride in triumph, then a Cesar conquer that Pompey, labouring Hanniball aliue, hewing his passage through the

Alpes. To see as I haue seene, Hercules in his owne shape
hunting the Boare, knocking downe the Bull, taming the
Hart, fighting with Hydra, murdering Gerio, slaughtering
Diomed, wounding the Stimphales, killing the Centaurs,
pashing the Lion, squeezing the Dragon, dragging Cerberus
in Chaynes and lastly, on his high Pyramides writing Nil
ultra, Oh these were sights to make an Alexander.[19]

In Heywood's account, the actor's part of speech is the
verb – he walks, speaks, acts, tramples, rides, conquers,
hews, hunts, fights, murders, kills and, finally, inscribes the
pyramids themselves. Through such 'motions', the actor
gains a direct hold over the audience and is able to 'mooue
the spirits of the beholder to admiration'. As Joseph Roach
has pointed out, the animation of the actor kindles a recip-
rocating action in the spectator, a resonance of 'spirits'
that cannot be attained through word or image alone. For
Heywood, action is the *sine qua non* of the actor. He notes
that although rhetorical treatises prescribe that the orator
must be skilled in the traditional disciplines of invention,
disposition, elocution, memory and pronunciation, 'yet all
are imperfect without the sixt, which is Action; for be his
invention neuer so fluent and exquisite, his disposition and
order neuer so composed and formall, his eloquence, and
elaborate phrases, neuer so materiall and pithy, his memory
neuer so firme and retentiue, his pronuntiation neuer so
musicall and plausive, yet without a comely and elegant
gesture, a gratious and bewitching kind of action. I hold all
the rest as nothing.'[20]

These are of course interested accounts, arguments made by
defenders of the stage against its detractors. But they nevertheless capture something of the framework of values that
governed the stage, and the sense of distinctively kinesic intelligence brought to bear by the actor upon his part, as well as
the way that such kinesis reverberates through the theatre to
affect the spectator, a sharing of the animating spirits between
actor and viewer.

Such power is not simply conferred by nature, but is honed through practice and long training in the art of gesture. Recent research by Tiffany Stern and others has demonstrated the importance of individual study of the actor's part in the theatrical economy of Shakespeare's theatre. Group rehearsal seems to have been reserved for especially complex scenes, or was undertaken as part of the master–apprentice system that predominated in that theatre. The primary cognitive artefact of the player was his individual part, which contained only his own lines and his cues.[21] His preparation consisted primarily of private study of this part, during which time he scanned the part for the changing passions on display and uplifted them into his body – moving them from the language of the playwright through his body, and by means of the art of gesture out to the audience. This discipline at its best was no mere mechanical exercise, but a highly trained praxis. So what we might think of as the *absence* of group rehearsal might perhaps better be conceived as the *presence* of a highly effective form of mindful training.

The nature of this praxis is famously articulated in the work of John Bulwer: *Chirologia: or the Natural Language of the Hand and Chironomia: or, the Art of Manuall Rhetoric.* Published in 1644, Bulwer's works are best known for their woodcuts cataloguing a range of hand gestures and their meanings, perhaps giving the misleading impression that the orator merely pastes a gestural form learned by rote onto the appropriate emotion.[22] Such a view, however, neglects the mindful practice underpinning the work of the true gestural artist. As Robert Toft notes, 'orators never considered gestures frozen positions they assumed at certain points in a sentence, but rather fluid motions of the hands, fingers, head, and so on, born from the thoughts and emotions that produce the words they spoke'.[23] Bulwer is primarily interested in rhetorical rather than thespian applications. Nevertheless, although we must be cautious about applying Bulwer's work directly to the stage, this work is a valuable source for understanding the psycho-physical foundations of the art of gesture in the period.

Especially important is the distinction between art and nature upon which Bulwer insists. Like other writers of how-to manuals, Bulwer seeks to raise the status of his subject to an art. In its 'natural' form, gesture is mere gesticulation, the largely unconscious and unstudied movements of the hand in the course of speaking. Those who imagine that they can simply rely upon their natural ability to gesture are sadly mistaken: 'For as for this opinion of ignorant men who think that gestures are perfect enough by nature ... that every one may please himself, observing no rule or admonition of rhetoricians, the daily example[s] of speakers refute.'[24] Certainly some have a better 'natural' ability to gesture gracefully. In defending his practice against those who view it as 'vain and unnecessary art' because the Greeks left no guides to gesture, Bulwer argues that the Greeks existed in a peculiarly rich environment for gesture and thought. Because their region 'by reason of the thinness and purity of the air' was a naturally fertile ecology for 'good wits', they had 'naturally both motions of the mind and body to explain and unfold their cogitations and recondite senses with an incredible facility; by reason whereof they less needed the precepts of this art'. The rich physical and mental infrastructure in ancient Greece meant that the 'artifice of the Hand' was so common that no precepts were needed. In contrast, the Romans, trained in martial rather than mental vigour, found handbooks necessary.[25] The English in particular are gesturally-challenged, as they live in cold environments that slow the hand. Thus gesture must be studied as an art built upon a foundation of nature, seen here as simultaneously individual and as a product of a geo-humoral environment, moulding 'the undigested motions of Nature' into a form 'fit for the intention of rhetoric'.[26]

Exercise and mindful practice is absolutely vital if one is to 'manage the art skillfully'. Bulwer recommends 'exercitatione' or deliberate practice: 'Use Exercise ... Bend and wrest your arm and hands to the right, to the left, and to every part, that having made them obedient unto you, upon a sudden and the least signification of the mind, you may shew the glittering orbs of heaven, and the gaping jawes of earth.'[27] Bulwer emphasizes above all extended practice and observation until the scholar 'by diligent study hath attained to an exquisite experience in the properties of the fingers, and what the natural motions of the *Hand* are wont to be'.[28] The scholar should ensure his hands are nimble by employing a range of motions: sometimes placing 'your arguments upon your fingers; sometimes lifting up your hands', practising such actions as threatening, abominating, rejecting. The result of such training is a fluid, mindful practice so that the student 'may be ready for all variety of speech'. The point is not simple replication but an act of skilful recreation when the moment calls for it.

Bulwer's practice is remarkably akin to the training that athletes undergo. He advocates long practice of particular patterns of movement – preferably with a Censor 'who shall inform truly and skilfully of all our gestures', or failing a coach, practising 'in a great looking-glass' in order to ensure that one's gestures are so sedimented in the body that they can be produced at precisely the right time, seemingly effortlessly or 'upon the sudden'.[29] This deliberate mindful practice helps the orator to bring pre-noetic movements, normally buried 'behind the scenes of awareness' in Shaun Gallagher's phrase, into full conscious awareness.[30] Or as Sheets-Johnstone might put it, the rhetorician seeking expertise in the art of gesture must learn to hear and to build upon his or her own distinctive 'kinaesthetic melodies'.[31]

Gesture is a particularly powerful form of kinaesthetic melody, as it is linked intimately and mostly unconsciously to speech, and, more broadly, thought itself. Researchers in gesture have shown that spoken language is inherently multi-modal; moving the hands is not merely an incidental add-on to speech, but instead an activation of an inherently connected system. So tightly bound is the hand to speech that in a recent article Kim Sterelny has argued that elaborated manual skill and gesture co-evolved as twin precursors to language, which, he argues, arises later as a powerful mechanism for taking human activity 'off-line'.[32] As David McNeil, Susan Goldin-Meadow and other researchers in gesture have shown, 'gesture affects thinking by grounding it in action'.[33] Hands help speakers to manage attention and memory; gesturing helps to 'facilitate the link between the words a speaker utters and the world that those words map onto'.[34] The philosopher Andy Clark has drawn upon this research to claim that gesture is not simply an aid to thought; rather it is constitutive of it:

> The wrong image here is that of a central reasoning engine that merely uses gesture to clothe or materialize preformed ideas. Instead, gesture and overt or covert speech emerge as interacting parts of a distributed cognitive engine, participating in cognitively potent self-stimulating loops whose activity is as much an *aspect* of our thinking as its result.[35]

Pouw et al. hypothesize that gestures work by providing mnemonic and attentional externalization and, hence, stability: 'gestures are not only a way to externalize speech and thought content, but also allow for temporal cognitive stability that might be more reliable than internal means of temporal cognitive extension (e.g. consciously attending to a thought to keep in mind) ... gestures fulfill a cognitive function because they are bodily.'[36]

Moreover, research has shown that gestures 'primarily emerge in intersubjective contexts'.[37] Such contexts do not require actor and audience to be co-present. The early modern actor seeking to 'grace' his part in private study imagines an intersubjective context. Thus the production of gesture both boot-straps thought for the actor himself and helps him to make that thought present to the (future) audience. Even though preparation of the part took place putatively through 'private study', this practice is in fact embedded, embodied and extended; it is a complex cognitive intersubjective act that imaginatively constitutes an audience.

The contemporary researchers on gesture mentioned here take as the object of their study not gestures consciously produced, but instead the apparently spontaneous co-production of gesture in the course of natural speech. The formal study of gesture, such as that advocated by Quintilian or Bulwer, is beyond their remit. But there are two points to be made here: the first is that theoreticians of gesture such as Bulwer made many of the discoveries of contemporary researchers on gesture in the wild, so to speak, and the second is that lifting a powerful natural system from pre-noetic to conscious awareness precisely exemplifies the way that training shapes the body, or experience gets under the skin. The conjunction of 'nature, art, and exercise' recommended by Bulwer – the wresting of the hands this way and that in anticipation of the moment at which they will be needed – exemplifies how training generates mindful practice. As Tim Ingold suggests, 'hands are not instruments operated remotely from a command and control centre located in the cerebrum'.[38] Instead, they are deeply implicated one in another: intelligence is not located in the brain, in the hand, in the body or in the tool, but in the 'technical act, the gesture, in which they are brought together'.[39]

If early modern writers viewed the art of action and gesture as a powerful and dangerous force, today these are more likely to be viewed as an outmoded, stagey and artificial endeavour. As I have argued elsewhere,[40] in Shakespearean scholarship there is a persistent denigration of gesture as a mere formal device. To take just one example, in his entry on the boy players in the *Oxford Companion to Shakespeare*, Gabriel Egan remarks, 'The mere fact that boys played great tragic roles such as Cleopatra, Desdemona, Hermione, and Lady Macbeth, indicates that a degree of unrealistic formalism (symbolic gestures and convention) must have been used.'[41] Gesture here is arrayed with symbolism, lack of realism, and convention, perhaps akin to crib notes for inexperienced young actors. Here and elsewhere gesture is dismissed as inevitably reductive; in his *Action and Eloquence*, David M. Bevington notes that Bulwer's treatise 'testifies both to the continued popularity of this classificatory line of thought about gesture long after Shakespeare's time, and to the ultimate absurdity of quasi-scientific precision dealing with a phenomenon of potentially infinite nuance'.[42]

It is true that the vocabulary in which Bulwer describes gesture – 'artificial', 'formal', 'regulated accessories' – has decidedly negative connotations in contemporary theatrical discourse. The connotations of the word 'artificial' (*OED* definitions 8, 9 and 10) that emphasize skill in construction or performance are obsolete. Whilst the basic opposition in all definitions of the word is the distinction between that which naturally occurs and that which is 'produced by or resulting from human skill or design' (2b), the definition of 'artificial' as a term of praise meant to emphasize skill, technique and expertise has fallen completely out of usage, and its primary connotations today are deceit and pretence: 'not natural or genuine in appearance or manners, affected', 'contrived ... for deception'. We might see a similar trajectory in the word 'theatrical', which begins as a simple descriptive adjective but gradually becomes laden with connotations of pretence and hamminess. Similarly, Bulwer's claim to take 'natural' gestures and force them into formal strictures seems contrived or old-fashioned, especially in an environment that prizes the natural. It is perhaps for these reasons that Bulwer's work – and the role of gesture in the theatre in general – is almost always dismissed as an old-fashioned, formal, artificial practice. Actors often disavow such formalities. The early film actor Paul Muni's account of preparing for a role is representative – he figures gesture as a mindless copy/paste of emotion to body movement:

> I never think, in reading a script ... that I will use such and such a gesture here, or that this is the point at which effect number twenty-two should be pulled out of the hat. If I were consciously to do certain things to attain certain effects, I'd become self-conscious and lose the ability to create a spontaneous impression.[43]

Such oppositions between creativity and craft underpin a wide range of discourses in contemporary acting theory and can still be seen in debates about actors trained in the 'Method' and those trained in 'technique'. In 1960, Sherman Ewing complained that young devotees of Stanislavski 'refused to make meaningful movements of hands or bodies on stage (that was considered "ham") and ... could not be heard'.[44] Cedric Hardwick's complaints about 'the moribund craft of acting' similarly acknowledge that although 'there is no longer any necessity for the excessive gesturing of yesterday when stages were poorly lit and acoustics bad ... since it has given up adequate gesture as being too theatric, acting has tended to become more and more inarticulate'.[45] As Rick Kemp has suggested, many contemporary acting training methods, such as Strasberg's, 'avoid conscious use of the body for fear that this will be somehow inauthentic'.[46]

Of all elements of acting that might be considered 'technique', gesture is likely to be seen as the most outmoded. Contemporary acting training programmes require coursework in voice, dance and movement to train actors with a high degree of technical facilities and flexibility (rada.ac.uk), but the idea of a technical class in gesture might seem outmoded. The vein of technical voice work used in the UK – as exemplified by Cicely Berry's well-known *The Actor and the Text* – emphasize training 'breath' and 'verbal muscularity' to make the language 'active and interesting' and to help the audience not only 'hear the words but realize them fully'.[47] But self-conscious training of the art of gesture would seem to fall between the two stools of 'voice' and 'movement' work.[48] Kemp notes that while all trained actors are keenly aware of the importance of non-verbal communication, 'the paradoxical situation that obtains in most theatre training programmes is that there is no systematic organization of the elements that communicate non-verbal meaning, or even a comprehensive vocabulary'.[49] Similarly, John Lutterbie notes that 'most training programmes offer classes in voice and movement, assuming the latter includes the techniques intrinsic to gesturing. However, imaging studies show that gesture uses the areas of the brain associated with language more than those linked to movement.'[50] Because gesture is sometimes considered to be a non-naturalistic device, or is subsumed into movement, and neglected in 'voice', this potentially powerful tool has to some extent been overlooked in contemporary discussions of the craft of acting, just as gestural arts have tended to be denigrated in theatre history.[51]

If we return to our early modern player, we can imagine gesture as a form of kinesic intelligence. Through his study the skilled actor prepares to animate his part. He has at his command his embodied experience, a lifetime of training that might include long practice at conning Latin verses whilst at school; the training of breath and body, and social coordination and intelligence gleaned from learning to sing in a choir school; or training on an instrument such as a lute; the experience of attending on stage, perhaps long before any lines have been spoken; the part, the cognitive artefact from which he works, on which is inscribed the lines of the playwright, as mediated by the organizing activity of the playhouse scribe who has written out the part; training in rhythmic, intelligent, socially coordinated practices such as fencing and dance; and an apprenticeship in 'action', knowledge of how to 'grace' a part, gleaned both from observation and experience, as well as direct instruction from a master. Thus the actor in conning his part is making something, albeit in invisible relationship with the writer. He is deeply embedded in a *techné*, engaging in the 'rhythmicity and mnemonic character of technical activity'.[52] These are forms of action that, Ingold notes, are at the heart of skilled human activity. The movement of the hand in this case is exactly analogous to the movement of a tool. For a skilled practitioner, repetitions are not merely mechanical; rather, 'they are set up through the continual sensory attunement of the practitioner's movements to the inherent rhythmicity of those components of the environment with which he or she is engaged'.[53] The language of the part has a rhythm, whether the overtly regular rhythm of iambic pentameter or the more idiosyncratic rhythms of prose.

The actual gestures used by Shakespeare's players of course

are lost, long gone, vanished. What did Burbage do with his arm when he demonstrated sawing the air 'thus'?[54] Karim-Cooper notes that we must be attentive to the *variety* of gestural modes used on the early modern stage:

> [G]estures were fundamentally varied: sometimes iconic, sometimes natural or drawn from everyday life; sometimes subtle, other times transgressively passionate ... . Actors would have 'sawed' the air if *suiting the action to the word* required it, even if it is simply to provoke laughter from the audience or to perform a dumb show. There are a number of factors that determine the performance of gestures: the type of theatre or performance space, the lighting conditions within that environment, the generic context (though this is not always fixed), the costumes the actors are wearing (restrictive in some cases), the passion beneath the gesture and the skill of the actor. All of these variables suggest there is more than one way of performing and interpreting gesture in the theatres of Shakespeare's time.[55]

The way that gesture is inscribed into the text is often readily apparent; there are numerous examples in Shakespeare of embedded directions to the actor such as 'cease wringing of your hands'. Sometimes the language and the reactions of other characters alert us to the links between the prosody of the language and the prosody or 'kinesthetic melody' of the body. In Act 1 of *The Winter's Tale*, for instance, Leontes' language becomes increasingly incoherent and fragmented as the conviction steals over him that his wife is 'slippery'. He becomes increasingly distracted from his conversation with Mamillius:

> – Can thy dam? – may't be? –
> Affection? thy intention stabs the centre: ... then 'tis very credent
> Thou may'st co-join with something; and thou dost,

(And that beyond commission) and I find it,
(And that to the infection of my brains
And hard'ning of my brows). (1.2, 136–7; 142–6)[56]

This passage is one of the densest and most annotated in
Shakespeare; editors vie to punctuate and parse it in a way
that makes at least a modicum of sense for the reader. While a
lucid paraphrase may be elusive, the mangled syntax and the
use of brackets are faint traces on the page of the increasingly
perturbed and twitchy movements of the hands and body
exhibited by Leontes. Polixenes and Hermione immediately
note that he 'something seems unsettled', as though 'he held
a brow of much distraction'. Although he briefly recovers
himself, Leontes has allowed his body to betray his thoughts.
Advice to control one's gestures was commonplace in the
period precisely for this reason; the conduct book *Youth's
Behaviour* enjoins against such failures to control gesture: 'In
thy walkings alone, express no passion in thy gesture, lest by
that means thou shouldest turn thy brest into Christal, and
let others read thy mind at a distance.'[57] Similarly, Prospero's
sudden 'start' during the wedding masque occasioned by the
recollection of the 'foul conspiracy' of Caliban is remarked
upon:

FERDINAND
   This is strange. Your father's in some passion
   That works him strongly.
MIRANDA   Never till this day
   Saw I him touched with anger so distempered! (4.1.143–5)

Prospero retires to walk a 'turn or two / to still my beating
mind' (162–3), to regain control. Of course, while characters
such as Leontes and Prospero allow their emotions to
overcome them, the actor personating them does not, instead
using his skill and training to manage the dangerous business
of passion-work.

Reading for skill: *Troilus and Cressida*

Karim-Cooper's argument about the variety of gestural codes in play on the early modern stage is especially helpful in uncovering the kinesic intelligence Shakespeare expected from his actors, especially the command they had over diverse vocabularies of gesture. We can see this range of gestural engagement at work in one of Shakespeare's most puzzling plays, *Troilus and Cressida*.

One of the ongoing debates about the Greek Council scene (1.3) in *Troilus* is whether or not it should be seen as part of the satire; in particular, how is the audience meant to perceive the opening speeches of Agamemnon and Nestor? Heather James argues that 'Nestor and Agamemnon are obsessed to the point of incoherence with the dignity and rhetoric they are accorded in epic and chronicle traditions ... their language is hyperbolic, horribly stuffed with epithets and similes.'[58] In his Cambridge edition of the play, Anthony Dawson notes that 'Agamemnon and Nestor's speeches are full of windy rhetoric and circumlocution, with simple ideas weighed down by abstraction and tortured expression ... . Many performances have, all too easily, delighted in mocking the rhetorical pretentions of the various Greek speakers, even including Ulysses.'[59] Certainly it is hard to imagine contemporary actors delivering these speeches straight, as the obvious rhetorical structure and imagery is a hard sell to modern audiences.

Gesture disposes language into space, and the speeches in the scene show the actor's command over a range of gestural vocabularies. Agamemnon's and Nestor's gestures are constructed around a simple trajectory: apparent contraries are temporarily united and then blown apart. Both speeches work upon a series of apparent antitheses, which in turn call for a simple yet powerful series of gestures: on the one hand, and on the other hand. As Bulwer states, 'If both *hands* by turns behave themselves with equal art, they fitly move to set off any matter that goes by way of *antithesis* or *opposition.*' The bilateral nature of the human form affords binary thinking.[60]

Like most binaries, these two 'hands' are not equal. Throughout the book, Bulwer inveighs against the use of the left hand except under special circumstances: 'For the truth is, the left hand wants that agility, excellence, force and grace in point of action, being made contrary and unhappy by its situation: whereupon 'tis called *sinistra* in Latin .... The best way (therefore) that it can be employed, is in attendance on the *right*.' Thus when two ideas are under comparison, the better is held in the right, the worse in the left.

This simple trope informs much of Agamemnon's speech. The Greek commander argues that their setbacks are 'indeed nought else / But the protractive trials of great Jove' (19–20) in an effort to test their mettle in adversity. In 'fortunes love', he says:

> The bold and coward
> The wise and fool, the artist and unread,
> The hard and soft, seem all affined and kin. (1.3.24–5)

Here, the bold, the wise and the artist are arrayed on the right hand; cowards, fools and the 'unread' on the left. The two groups are momentarily 'affined and kin' – perhaps physically brought together in joined hands – but soon parted:

> But in the wind and tempest of her frown,
> Distinction, with a broad and powerful fan,
> Puffing at all, winnows the light away,
> And what hath mass or matter by itself
> Lies rich in virtue and unmingled. (1.3.26–30)

Those of 'light' quality are winnowed away, and the weighty and solid remain behind, secure in the hand of the speaker. Bulwer and other advisors on oratory inveigh against direct miming; there should be no one-to-one imitation of word and action; thus miming the 'puffing' of Distinction's 'broad and powerful fan' would be a solecism. But the joined hands, now parted, with the 'rich and virtue' remaining in the right, bring the elaborate metaphor before the audience by disposing thought in space. As Smithson and Nicoladis suggest, 'when people gesture they may be sustaining the activation of imagistic representations'.[61]

Nestor's speech follows a similar trajectory, as he seeks to 'apply' Agamemnon's words through an extended analogy that juxtaposes the 'shallow bauble boats' who remain alongside those of 'nobler bulk' so long as the sea is smooth. But when 'ruffian Boreas', his version of the 'broad and powerful fan', unsettles the sea, 'the saucy boat' is 'either to harbor fled / Or made a toast for Neptune' (1.3.31–45). The exact allegory may differ, but the gestural dynamics are nearly identical; both speeches oppose strength and weakness; the two 'hands' may be temporarily allied, but soon are disposed according to their true qualities. Skilful use of gesture in the course of these speeches renders the central metaphors visible.

Ulysses extravagantly praises both leaders for their speeches: Agammenon's speech should be held up 'high in brass', and Nestor has 'Knit all the Greekish ears to his experienced tongue' (1.3.67–8). His references to their high status (Agammenon's 'place and sway') and advanced years (Nestor's 'stretched-out life') place their orations, however skilfully produced, as perhaps somewhat dated, dependent upon the relatively hoary trope of antithesis. This scheme certainly affords satirical treatment, such as that meted out by Buckingham in *The Rehearsal*, when he sends up the 'one hand / other hand' trope by employing feet rather than hands in the 'combat betwixt Love and Honour'. Volscius laments:

My Legs, the Emblem of my various thought,
Shew to what sad distraction I am brought.
Sometimes, with stubborn Honour, like this Boot,
My Mind is guarded, and resolv'd: to do't:
Sometimes again, that very mind, by Love
Disarmed, like this other Leg does prove.[62]

Unable to resolve the conflict, Volscius '*goes out hopping with one Boot on, and the other off*'.[63]

In contrast, Ulysses' famous speech on degree uses a rhetorical and gestural schema based upon the figure *gradatio* rather than upon antithesis. An enormous amount of ink has been spilled about this speech, with scholars disagreeing on whether it is to be taken as normative or satirical, and whether the play endorses or questions the view of degree that Ulysses espouses. Anthony Dawson notes that the rhetorical/gestural schema and the logic of the speech are mismatched: 'the image of climbing a ladder to get to the top ... undermines his central point that degree and high place are fixed and immutable'.[64] Would such mismatches be apparent to an audience, especially one attentive to the gestive creation of the *gradatio* figure? Although clearly 'rhetorical ironies'[65] are apparent here, it is possible that a skilfully designed gestural 'ladder' might draw attention not to the logical inconsistencies of the argument but instead to the sleight of hand by which gestural coherence masks logical incoherence.

Ulysses' next speech employs an entirely different gestural dynamic. Ulysses' account of Achilles and Patroclus scoffing at their leaders is a *tour de force* of imitation, demonstrating the 'subversive communicability of Achilles' local theater'.[66] Here Ulysses no longer uses gesture to express rhetorical tropes in spatial form; rather, he describes how Patroclus 'pageants' the Greek commanders with 'ridiculous and awkward action' (149) for Achilles' entertainment. While this moment has been rightly understood as an example of a sustained critique of the 'pathological disunity of political structure and spirit, a contagious emulation of disorder',[67] it is equally a stunning display of the gestural skill that animates the actor. As Henrich Plett has pointed out, Ulysses here employs what Henry Peacham terms 'mimesis' in *The Garden of Eloquence*:

> Mimesis is an imitation of speech whereby the Orator counterfaiteth not onely what one said, but also his utterance, pronunciation and gesture, imitating everything

as it was, which is alwaies well performed, and naturally represented in an apt and skilfull actor. The perfect Orator by this figure both causeth great attention, and also bringeth much delight to the hearers, for whether he imitateth a wise man, or a foole, a man learned or unlearned, insolent or modest, merrie or sorrowful, bold or fearfull, eloquent or rude, he reteineth the hearer in a diligent attention, and that for a threefold utilitie, in the imitated gesture a pleasure to the eie, in the voice a delight to the eare, and in the sense, a proft to the wit and understanding.[68]

Oratorical treatises such as that of Quintilian differentiate the proper orator from the mere mime, suggesting that direct imitation of actions – for example, blowing like a fan – is beneath the dignity of the rhetorician and should be left to the province of the actor, those 'expert counterfeiters of mens manners'. Peacham goes on to caution that whilst such counterfeiting 'causeth great attention' and 'bringeth much delight', it is, when abused or 'blemished by excesse or defect', associated with 'flattering gesters and common parasites, who for the pleasure of those whom they flatter, do both depraue and deride other mens sayings and doings'.[69]

Yet Ulysses is not simply imitating the foibles and turns of speech and gesture of the Greeks; he is imitating Patroclus's imitation of them. Putatively disapproving of the antics of Achilles and Patroclus, Ulysses recounts the action of the 'slanderer' who 'pageants us'. In a dizzying array of levels, the actor playing Ulysses plays Patroclus playing Agamemnon for the amusement of Achilles; Agamemnon in turn is likened to a 'strutting player, whose conceit / Lies in his hamstring, and doth think it rich / To hear the wooden dialogue and sound / Twixt his stretched footing and the scaffoldage' (1.3.153–6). To portray the pageant, Ulysses must simultaneously imitate the slanderous parodies and disavow their aptness. Patroclus's mimicking of Agamemnon is 'to-be-pitied' and 'o'er-wrested'; his imitation of Nestor's 'hems' and strokes of his beard is only as 'near as the extremest ends Of Parallels, as like as Vulcan and his wife' (1.3.167–8). Through this clever frame, Ulysses achieves a pitiless and minute rendering of the foibles of the Greek leaders: Agamemnon's voice like a 'chime a-mending', the fumbling of Nestor and the faint defects of age. This level of mimesis is mediated through an equally critical imitation of Patroclus and Achilles, who appear more like 'drawing room dandies rather than ancient epic warriors'.[70] In this brief scene, Shakespeare asks his actors to command highly divergent gestural repertoires, from selecting gestures to express traditional rhetorical schemas in the opening speeches to the extraordinarily animate performance of Ulysses.

Walking

> The hardest thing for an actor to do on stage, though he had been doing it all his life, is to walk. (Stanislavski)[71]

For most human beings, walking is among our first accomplishments, the end-point of pulling ourselves upright, of 'cruising' along furniture, of holding on to our parents' hands while they painfully stoop over to guide us. Walking is equated with simplicity; only a true half-wit is unable to walk and chew gum at the same time. Yet Stanislavski singles out this simple action as the 'hardest thing for an actor to do on stage'. Perhaps it is difficult because of its very ordinariness: 'he has been doing it all his life'. The very familiarity of walking buries the act in habit, below conscious awareness. The actions that are sedimented so thoroughly in the body are the most difficult to pluck out and make fresh for the stage. As John Lutterbie notes, 'For the actor, it is necessary to recognize that ways of behaving in everyday life are incommensurate with the demands of the stage.'[72] Just as dialogue that is simply transcribed speech seldom works on the stage or the page, neither can actors simply transfer their 'daily body techniques'[73] to the stage successfully. If this point is accurate for contemporary actors, who work within a skill ecology much less suffused with patterns of deference and hierarchy, it must have been even more pertinent for the actor within the social world of early modern England, in which minutiae of gesture and movement were keenly scrutinized.

So skilled walking is much more complex than it might appear at first blush. An actor who moves across the stage must fluidly combine speech, gesture – the animation of that speech – and the walk itself. Walking must transport him across the stage whilst conveying the social demeanour of his character, which in turn demands a distinctive rhythm. This rhythm might be the stately gait of the nobility, the mirroring yet subordinate walk of his courtiers, the glide of the female aristocrat or the staccato running rhythm of the servant.[74] It is difficult to coordinate all these elements at once.

This complexity is perhaps the reason that many young actors appear on the stage in what I have described as 'scaffolded' roles – as pages or junior servants, either with no lines or with a carefully prepared cue. The act of walking on the stage demanded all of the cognitive resources available to the novice actors. Such 'attending roles' may have been more common than we think. For example, in *Romeo and Juliet* when Mercutio is stabbed he demands, 'Where is my page? Go villain, fetch a surgeon' (3.1.95). Were it not for this command, this character would have been entirely invisible. Attendants were ubiquitous in everyday life among the upper classes in early modern England and were vital measures of rank and importance, as is made painfully clear by King Lear's devastation at being stripped of his knights. Young actors working as silent attendants were practising the vital skill of stage presence and movement long before they had the added demands of speaking roles.

The difficulty experienced by novice or amateur actors attempting to integrate dialogue and movement is satirized in the Cambridge University play *Return from Parnassus*. One of a series of plays about the vicissitudes of young graduates in finding employment, *Return from Parnassus* features young men considering seeking employment through acting. The characters 'Burbage' and 'Kemp' assess the acting abilities of the amateur actors. One of the jokes centres upon the students' inability to talk and walk at the same time:

> The slaues [scholars at Cambridge] are somewhat proud; and besides, it is a good sport in a part, to see them neuer speake in their walk, but at the end of the stage, just as though, in walking with a fellow, we should neuer speake but at a stile, a gate, or a ditch, where a man can go no further. (4.3.1796–801)[75]

This observation is a pretty accurate and acute assessment of amateur acting, and it probably takes a rather skilled eye to notice it. So while walking and talking may not seem to be an especially difficult feat, it is a marker of difference between the skill of the professional and even a talented amateur. Walking, especially in concert with another actor, involves falling into a rhythm with him, whether mirroring or contrapuntal. In everyday life, achieving this rhythm might present few challenges, as it scaffolds upon a natural tendency to coordinate or synchronize with others. Yet if we add the additional cognitive demands of acting – remembering lines, 'gracing' them with action and maintaining the meta-cognitive skills of appraisal and situation awareness necessary in any high-stakes time-pressured activity – it is easy to see why amateur actors prefer to walk across the stage, stop and then speak. Walking and speaking is not a mere mechanical act, but involves constant and subtle attunement among actors and space.

Moreover, walking is a highly situated and specific skill. Renaissance England inherited an ecology of skill from disparate traditions, one of which was the classical tradition. Rhetorical manuals such as those discussed in the previous section instructed the speaker in the use of decorous and graceful gesture; equally, an emphasis upon movements of the entire body was part of that inheritance. In Timothy O'Sullivan's recent book on *Walking in Roman Culture*, he notes that 'walking, for the Romans, was a marker of identity.

There is a constant emphasis on the performative quality of Roman walking, and a constant assumption of an audience to appreciate ... something about that individual's identity ... . Roman walking, in other words, was not only a way of moving through space but also a performance of identity.'[76] Attitudes towards walking and gait reflected a tension in ways of imagining the relationship between bodily comportment and identity: 'The gait was on the one hand an irreducible, visible feature of individual identity, yet on the other hand, in a society where the performance of social identity was so important, was also treated as a technique of the body susceptible to instruction and manipulation.'[77]

Like gesture, the kinaesthetic melody of walking is often outside of focal awareness, or pre-noetic. Normally proprioception is unconsciously monitored in a 'system of sensory-motor processes that constantly regulate posture and movement ... without reflective awareness or the necessity of perceptual monitoring'.[78] But those whose bodies have been made mindful through long and demanding training regimes, such as dancers, obtain a kind of 'postural musicality', in Hubert Godard's term: 'A person's kinesic style manifests itself at this specific level of a corporeal organization of meaning.'[79]

So one manifestation of the kinesic intelligence of the actor is gait, and, more generally, posture and carriage of the body. Gait is uniquely identifiable as a personal signature and is notably difficult to disguise. Kerri Johnson and Maggie Shiffrar write:

Human bodies in motion, for example, are among the most frequently occurring dynamic stimuli in our inherently social environments. Typical observers, from a young age, spontaneously direct their attention toward bodies in motion ... . Bodies can be readily perceived at physical distances and visual vantages that preclude face perception. Moreover, body motions convey meaningful psychological information such as social categories, emotional states, intentions, and underlying dispositions. Thus, there are several reasons to believe that visual analyses of body postures and body motion serve as a first-pass filter for a vast array of social judgments from the routine (e.g. categorizing men and women) to the grave (e.g. discerning threat).[80]

The attunement of human beings to gait has been confirmed by the work of Michael Richardson and Lucy Johnston, who show that 'human gait is a signature of personal identity and that it is a marker of identity to which the perceptual system is highly attuned'.[81]

Gesture and gait profoundly shape our perceptions of others, but often in implicit ways, so that most people are highly competent at recognizing others from gait and gesture but relatively poor at putting such fleeting impressions into words. Whilst we are readily able to identify others from their gait, the exact mechanisms by which such identifications are made are usually tacit rather than explicit. For example, Gunns et al. found that certain styles of walking were readily identifiable as showing vulnerability to attack, but untrained subjects were unable to articulate the precise components of the gaits of, say, a confident or vulnerable way of walking. The experiments also recruited 'expert subjects' to assess vulnerability: convicted violent criminals.[82] Skilled in discerning who made a likely victim, these subjects attended less to external factors such as clothing and were 'much more likely to consciously attend to a target's gait in making their vulnerability judgments'.[83] Like the skilled dancer who is especially attentive to movement, the 'skilled' criminal is attuned to and articulate about bodily signals that might be only implicitly perceived by others.

In contrast, our own gaits are virtually invisible to us, outside our focal awareness. Our gait and gestures – our little personal signatures or kinaesthetic melodies – are rarely brought to our conscious awareness unless someone brings them to our attention. This point was noted by Montaigne:

I want to say this first, that it is not unbecoming to have characteristics and propensities so much our own and so incorporated into us that we have no way of sensing and recognizing them. And of such natural inclinations the body is likely to retain a certain bent, without our knowledge or consent.[84]

Similarly, in *How Societies Remember*, Connerton suggests that 'the impressions created by physical conformation and bodily carriage are those manifestations of the person least susceptible to willed modification, and it is for this reason that they are held to signify the habitual "nature" of the person'.[85] These views are apparently borne out by research that asks subjects to attempt to alter their gaits. Gunns et al. found that their subjects were very poor at disguising their gaits, and their attempts were readily discovered by untrained observers.[86] In a related study, Johnston et al. attempted to train subjects on a more consistent basis to alter their gait. Such attempts were in the first instance successful, but the effect was relatively weak and transient. As is typical of such studies, the subjects were convenience samples drawn from psychology classes – that is, they were typically white, middle-class undergraduate students, the group which comprises the basis of a large number of psychological studies.[87] Such subjects are likely kinesically naïve, which may explain why the effects of training in gait were transient. For those untrained in movement, the body quickly settles back into its natural grooves, made smooth not only by one's inherited muscular-skeletal-nervous system, but also by a lifetime of somatic habits and disposition.

However, those who have been trained in physical disciplines are different. Expertise is above all about bringing the tacit into focal awareness and thereby shaping it, a long and arduous process that explains why true experts in movement – dancers, gymnasts and martial artists for example – must train so long and begin so early. The expertise in movement may also explain why such fashioned bodies excited what Marcel Mauss in his 'Techniques of the Body' described as 'prestigious imitation'.[88] In *Henry VI Part II*, Hotspur is described as spurring just such desires:

LADY PERCY   He was indeed the glass
   Wherein the noble youth did dress themselves.
   He had no legs that practis'd not his gait;
   And speaking thick, which nature made his blemish,
   Became the accents of the valiant;
   For those who could speak low and tardily
   Would turn their own perfection to abuse
   To seem like him. So that in speech, in gait,
   In diet, in affections of delight,
   In military rules, humours of blood,
   He was the mark and glass, copy and book,
   That fashion'd others. (4.3.21–32)

Gait was seen as a natural outpouring of the animal spirits; in a quasi-physical-medical model, movement was thought of as expression of these spirits as they surged through the body and out into the environment.

Thus skilled movement, gait and gesture were keenly sought after and contested markers of breeding, elegance and class: on the one hand, graceful bearing and gait was seen as a natural attribute of aristocratic descent; on the other, treatises such as *The Book of the Courtier* and its numerous imitators aimed to train and instruct aspiring courtiers 'to imbue with grace, his movements, his gestures, his way of doing things, and in short, his every action'.[89] Conduct treatises typically provided minute prescriptions for ways of carrying the body. Anna Bryson argues that sixteenth- and seventeenth-century conduct books exemplify 'a new way of seeing', a term she appropriates from Norbert Elias. Bryson notes a 'marked additional preoccupation with the full-scale dramatization of social identity'.[90] This concern with the 'precise impression' made by any social act is, Bryson argues, particularly well exemplified by James Cleland's exhaustive advice about the correct way of walking for the young gentlemen:

Hippomachus knew the good wrestlers only by their going through the street, as *Lysippus* carued a Lyon, seeing but one foot; so many men seeing you passe by them, wil conceiue presently a good or bad opinion of you. Wherefore yee must take very good heed vnto your feete, and consider with what grace and countenance yee walke, that yee go not softly, tripping like a wanton maide, nor yet striding with great long paces, like those Rhodomonts and Kings in Stage Plaies. Walke man-like with graue ciuil pace, as becommeth one of your birth and age. Away with all affectation, either in hanging downe your head, as *Alexander* did, or stooping for greater comlines, or bending your body backward. Many are so monstrous in their manner of going, that they must needes either bee nodding with their head, shaking of their shoulders, playing with their hands, or capering at euery step with their feete, rouling from side to side, like a Turkey Cocke. As they goe through the streets, yee shall not see them goe forward one step, without looking downe to the rose vpon their shooes, or lifting vp their hand to set out their band, as if it were in print; or setting vp the brimme of their hat, or doing some such apish toy: whereof I councel you to beware, if you would not be mocked with them.[91]

This passage conveys the wide range of ways of carrying the body available to the young gentleman. Cleland first notes the ways that habitual motions are sedimented into the body by repeating an anecdote from Plutarch's *Lives* about the wrestling-master Hippomachus, who claimed he could recognize his pupils from a distance by the way they moved their bodies when carrying meat from the abattoir.[92] Two things are apparent here: the way that the trained body takes on a particular disposition, and the way that 'skilled viewing', in this the expert eye of the wrestling master, can distinguish the skilled from the unskilled. The gentleman is to 'walke man-like with graue ciuil pace', avoiding womanish steps on the one hand and striding like 'Kings in Stage Plaies' on the other. Cleland also proscribes an entire array of 'apish toys', such as capering, constantly fiddling with one's garments or foolish movements of the body.

Cleland's catalogue of somatic solecisms calls the early modern theatre irresistibly to mind, especially the foibles of the fops and gallants that Jonson so minutely documents. This catalogue reminds us that the stage player might be asked to imitate the bearing of a wide range of social types – from the striding king to the 'tripping' woman, from the grave elder to the 'apish toys' of the many man-boys who inhabit the comedies. Players performed before audiences themselves practised in observing and judging the minutiae of their social world. This ability requires specialist knowledge of one's own body, its habitual ways of being and the forms it naturally holds. The skilled actor's ability of body must encompass that 'willed modification', that 'voluntary, deliberate transformation' that converts his body to another, whilst simultaneously retaining traces of the actor beneath.

Reading for skill: *All's Well That Ends Well* and *Cymbeline*

In this section I consider kinesic skill on Shakespeare's stage through readings of *All's Well That Ends Well* and *Cymbeline*, focusing on two moments that have generated interpretive controversy: the 'choosing scene' in *All's Well That Ends Well*, and Imogen's mistaking of Cloten for Posthumus in *Cymbeline*. In general, editorial attention naturally tends to focus upon textual cruxes rather than elements of skill that underpin the performance. Attending to the moving body – especially closer attention to bearing, walking, gesture and animation – may shed light on scenes that have puzzled editors and commentators.

All's Well That Ends Well

Osric, Oswald and the unnamed lord spurned by Hotspur notwithstanding, Shakespeare is generally less concerned with portraying the minutiae of courtly life than a playwright such as Jonson. An exception to this general rule is *All's Well That Ends Well*, a play which can be said to interrogate courtly codes of conduct, gesture and bearing. In particular, the play shows careful attention to movement and carriage. Set at the French court, *All's Well* is minutely concerned with status, hinging as it does upon the vast social gulf between Bertram, the ward of the King of France, and Helena, the 'poor physician's daughter' brought up by Bertram's mother. Bertram, an 'unseasoned courtier', is the son of a man who is praised as an ideal of the type. His dead father is described as showing no pride or contempt, affable to those below him and speaking only when the 'true minute' bade him: 'Such a man / might be a copy to these younger times' (1.2.46).[93] But Bertram chooses as a mentor the braggart Parolles, and the other young Lords seem similar to the new generation that old Rossillion disparages:

> younger spirits, whose apprehensive senses
> All but new things disdain; whose judgments are
> Mere fathers of their garments; whose constancies
> Expire before their fashions. (1.2.59–62)

The preoccupation with courtly behaviour is also signalled in 2.1, when the Lords take leave of the King to fight in the Florentine war. Chafing at being left behind with 'no sword worn / but one to dance with', Bertram exchanges some compliments with the young men as they depart: 'I grow to you, and our parting is a tortur'd body' (37). Parolles tells him that his leave-taking has lacked courtly grace:

> Use a more spacious ceremony to the noble lords; you have restrain'd yourself within the list of too cold an adieu. Be more expressive to them, for they wear themselves in the

cap of time; there do muster true gait, eat, speak, and move, under the influence of the most receiv'd star; and though the devil lead the measure, such are to be followed. After them, and take a more dilated farewell. (2.1.49–56)

Bertram rushes off to follow Parolles's advice, although the exact nature of the 'spacious ceremony' for leave-taking is consigned to off-stage space.

The vacuity of courtly conduct is also underscored in an otherwise gratuitous scene between the Clown and the Countess, inserted between the scene in which Helena cures the King and in which she is invited to choose among the young bachelors. The Clown first enumerates courtly courtesies: 'he that cannot make a leg, put off's cap, kiss his hand, and say nothing, has neither leg, hands, lips, nor cap; and indeed such a fellow, to say precisely, were not for the court' (2.2.9–11). The Clown also performs 'saying nothing', promising the Countess that he has 'an answer that will serve all men ... ask me if I am a courtier, it shall do you no harm to learn' (13, 35):

> COUNTESS I pray you, sir, are you a courtier?
> CLOWN O Lord, sir! There's a simple putting off. More, more, a hundred of them.
> COUNTESS Sir, I am a poor friend of yours that loves you.
> CLOWN O Lord, sir! Thick, thick; spare not me.
> COUNTESS I think, sir, you can eat none of this homely meat.
> CLOWN O Lord, sir! Nay, put me to't, I warrant you. (2.2.39–47)

The Countess and the Clown play the game together, showing the emptiness of courtly language by ringing changes on the empty phrase 'Oh Lord, sir'. The actor playing the Clown no doubt imitates the action and bearing of the young men taking leave in 2.1 with the elaborate and meaningless compliments to one another: 'O my sweet lord ... Sweet Monsieur

Parolles' (23, 38). The phrase 'O Lord, sir' incidentally alludes to Jonson's send-ups of courtier pretentions in such plays as *Every Man in his Humour*, where the catch-phrase is associated with the empty-headed and pretentious young men about town.

This backdrop is necessary to fully understand the choosing scene in 2.3, which has long puzzled editors of the play. Here the court is on full display when the King orders the 'youthful parcel of noble bachelors' to accept Helen's 'frank election' of her choice from among them. The young men are arrayed before her:

> KING   Fair maid, send forth thine eye. This youthful parcel
> Of noble bachelors stands at my bestowing,
> O'er whom both sovereign power and father's voice
> I have to use. Thy frank election make;
> Thou hast power to choose, and they none to forsake ...
>   Peruse them well
> Not one of them but had a noble father. (2.3.53–64)

Helena speaks to each lord in turn and their replies are apparently favourable:

> HELENA   Sir will you hear my suit?
> 1 LORD   And grant it
> HELENA   Thanks, sir, all the rest is mute.
> ...
> HELENA   [*to Second Lord*]   The honour, sir, that flames
>   in your fair eyes
>   Before I speak, too threat'ningly replies.
>   Love make your fortunes twenty times above
>   Her that so wishes, and her humble love!
> 2 LORD   No better, if you please. (2.3.76–84)

As Helena moves from Lord to Lord, however, Lafew comments upon the action, becoming increasingly irate at the young men's lack of response to her. After the second Lord replies, he says, 'Do they all deny her? And they were sons of mine, I'd have them whipp'd, or I would send them to th'Turk to make eunuchs of' (86). His response to the third Lord, who says nothing, is 'These boys are boys of ice; They'll none have her. Sure they are bastards to the English; the French ne'er got them' (94–5).

From Samuel Johnson on, textual editors have suggested that Lafew misreads the scene. The Norton edition suggests that 'either Lafeu, standing apart, misunderstands what is happening, or (less probably) the lords' polite replies are belied by their evident relief when Helen rejects them'.[94] The Cambridge edition goes so far as to print C. Walter Hodges' drawing of a staging configuration that shows Lafew's line of sight blocked by the pillars at the Globe. As the editor (Fraser) remarks, 'This would be particularly helpful for the scene in which Helena, working up to her choice of Bertram, rejects the other young lords while Lafew, evidently at some distance from the action, thinks they are rejecting her.'[95]

Here editors clearly privilege the words of the courtiers over their actions. If the text indicates a disjunction between the two, in this view the words must be correct, even if it means positing that Shakespeare wrote the scene expecting that pillars would block Lafew's sight-lines, which is absurd. As the Clown has amply demonstrated in the previous scene, words mean very little to courtiers. The formal courteous replies of the first, second and fourth young Lords (the third remains silent) stand in marked contrast to the florid compliments they paid to other young men in the leave-taking scene. Moreover, the scene actually reveals Helena's acute reading of non-verbal communication. Her nerve almost fails her when she first confronts the line of young aristocrats and she attempts to abandon the choice: 'Please it your majesty, I have done already' (69). The King intervenes: 'Make choice, and see, / Who shuns thy love shuns all his love in me' (74). These lines read like an admonition to the young men to feign more enthusiasm; it is perhaps their rigid disdain that causes Helena to pause. She reads the second

Lord's 'honour' that 'flames' in his eye and notes the third Lord's reluctance:

> Be not afraid that I your hand should take;
> I'll never do you wrong, for your own sake.
> Blessing upon your vows, and in your bed
> Find fairer fortune if you ever wed. (2.3.90–3)

The cues for action – or rather for stillness, for these are 'boys of ice' – are, I argue, very clearly made, and they all accord with Lafew's reading of the scene. Shakespeare relies on the kinesic intelligence of the young actors, as cued by Lafew's aside, to show the audience that Bertram's disdain is shared by the rest of the young lords, although they are better able to conceal it than he through the studied divorce of word and action. The actors move between the animation of the courtiers in the homo-social banter whilst they are amongst themselves and the icy stillness they show whilst on display in the court. The failure of editors to recognize the gestural dynamics of the scene shows that bodies, especially bodies in motion, tend to disappear in textual commentary; words are always privileged over skilful bodies.

Cymbeline

Cymbeline is another play that hinges upon the kinesic intelligence of actors in motion; it particularly foregrounds the relationship between movement, gesture, spirits and the passions. The idea that the movements of the body are the corporeal register of the passions was articulated eloquently by Thomas Wright in *The Passions of the Mind in General*:

> The passion in the persuader resembleth the wind a trumpeter bloweth in at one end of the trumpet, and in what manner it proceedeth from him, so it issueth forth at the other end, and cometh to our eares, even so the passion

proceedeth from the heart and is blowne about the bodie, face, eies, hands, voice, and so by gestures passeth into our eyes and by sounds into our ears.[96]

Shakespeare plays upon this idea in his description of the 'sparks of nature', displayed by Guiderius/Polydore and Arviragus/Cadwal, the 'stolen' sons of Cymbeline, raised in the woods by Belarius. Like Perdita in *The Winter's Tale*, the fostered brothers display their princely origins despite themselves. Although they have no overt knowledge of their birth, the brothers apparently spontaneously embody aristocratic and martial virtues in response to Belarius's vivid stories:

> When on my three-foot stool I sit, and tell
> The war-like feats I have done, his spirits fly out
> Into my story: say 'thus mine enemy fell,
> And thus I set my foot on's neck', even then
> The princely blood flows in his cheek, he sweats,
> Strains his young nerves, and puts himself in posture
> That acts my words. The younger brother, Cadwal,
> Once Arviragus, in as like a figure
> Strikes life into my speech, and shows much more
> His own conceiving. (3.3.90–8)

Belarius's account draws upon the idea of contagious affect that underscored the theory of 'action' of actors and orators. His oral tales of prowess infect the young princes with a desire for imitation, and the sympathy between their innate 'spirits' and the compelling accounts of war spontaneously has a physical effect on Guiderius, who 'puts himself in posture / That acts my words'. This account bears similarities to Massinger's argument that action can 'swell the veins with emulation': potent words acting upon especially powerful 'spirits' can convert language to action almost spontaneously.

The young princes are held in implicit contrast to Cloten, who is in turn opposed to Posthumus. The play is insistent

upon the differences between Posthumus and Cloten, to the
extent of surrounding Cloten with sycophantic Lords who
flatter him to his face and reveal their true opinions of their
master to the audience in a series of withering asides. Cloten is
a type almost out of a Jonson play, an inept gallant addicted to
duelling, gaming and futilely attempting to woo Imogen: 'I am
advised to give her music a-mornings, they say it will penetrate'
(2.3.12). He is also persistently referred to in humoral terms
and is both literally and figuratively hot – choleric. He is first
described as having drawn upon Posthumus:

> PISANIO My Lord your son drew upon my master
> QUEEN   Ha?
>   No harm I trust, is done?
> PISANIO   There might have been,
>   But that my master rather play'd than fought,
>   And had no help of anger: (1.2.91–3)

The choleric Cloten is an angry and thus inept fencer; as we
will see in the following chapter, fencing manuals routinely
advised that duelling in anger was a dangerous practice. In
the next scene (1.3), Cloten enters profusely sweating. The
First Lord observes, 'Sir I would advise you to shift a shirt;
the violence of action hath made you reek as a sacrifice' (1–3).
The scene continues by contrasting Cloten's foolish braggadocio with the Lords' commentary:

> CLOTEN The villain would not stand me
> 2 LORD [aside]   No, but he fled forward still, toward
>   your face. (1.3.12–14)

Similarly Cloten is described as unable to contain his oaths
whilst bowling, attacking a 'whoreson jackanapes' who objects
to his swearing: 'When a gentleman is dispos'd to swear, it is
not for any standers-by to curtail his oaths. Ha?' (2.1.10–11).
On the rare occasions when he wins at games he is 'most hot
and furious' (2.3.5). Thus Cloten is literally unable to contain

himself, as his intemperate spirits leak out and foul the air at the least opportunity. In contrast, the spirits of the two young fostered princes exhibit themselves in passionate action that is nevertheless controlled – poured into a model of military action and noble deeds – and Posthumus is described as cool and collected as he defeats Cloten.

A final clue as to Cloten's demeanour comes in 4.2, when Belarius recognizes Cloten after twenty years both by his 'lines of favour' (his face) and his manner of speaking: 'the snatches in his voice, / and burst of speaking were as his' (104–5). For an expert actor, especially in Shakespeare's time, this verbal tic would be part of a package of traits of gesture and gait. Action and accent are conjoined, so that 'snatches' and 'bursts of speaking' may well cue an equal lack of control over the body in movement – which fits well with his poor swordplay, his incontinent sweating and his swearing. His hot humours impede both speech and expert action. Hesitant and inexpert speech is linked to a general ineptness in movement.

It is in this light that we might understand Imogen's confusion of Cloten for Posthumus. One of the strangest moments in this strange play occurs when Imogen, thought dead, awakens to find herself next to the headless body of Cloten. The murdered Cloten is dressed in Posthumus's clothes, seeking revenge for Imogen's rejection of him. He is particularly fixated upon her statement that Posthumus's 'mean'st garment / That ever hath but clipp'd his body, is dearer / In my respect, than all the hairs above thee' (2.4.134–6). When Imogen recognizes Posthumus's garments on Cloten's decapitated body, she performs a kind of grim blazon:

A headless man? The garments of Posthumus?
I know the shape of's leg; this is his hand:
His foot Mercurial: his Martial thigh:
The brawns of Hercules: (4.2.308–11)

This complete mistaking of the two characters has been ascribed variously to failures on Shakespeare's part: to the close relationships between clothes and identity in the period; to Shakespeare's fine-tuned 'insights into human recognition under stress'; and to the play's recognition that Posthumus is simply the flip side of Cloten, mirroring his misogyny.[97]

These theories are plausible but incomplete. I argue that attention to kinesis and skill alerts us to a missing point. Posthumus's difference from Cloten derives from his gait, posture and other ineffable characteristics that marked the skilled body of the courtier or the actor. The two actors distinguish themselves in motion; in stillness they are indistinguishable.

Coda: Ben Jonson and movement

But it is Ben Jonson who, much more than Shakespeare, is keenly interested in the minutiae of bodily gestures and gaits. Few playwrights hold the body up to scrutiny in quite the way Jonson does. His plays are preoccupied with the rapid transformations of players' bodies and identities through costume, gait, accent and gesture. On the one hand he portrays players as witless buffoons liable to mar his dramatic poem through negligent playing; on the other hand he is utterly reliant on their kinesic intelligence, displayed in most elaborate form in the dizzying changes wrought in *The Alchemist*. Similarly, his keen interest in mannerisms and 'humours' and the protean ability of the actors to emulate characteristic modes of bodily comportment can be seen as part of Jonson's deeply ambivalent interest in transformation. Moreover, his plays ask actors to skilfully imitate the extraordinary lability of early modern London life, the insistent desire for social climbing, for instruction in how to walk, how to quarrel, how to dress, how to speak, what to buy that preoccupies so many of the characters in his comedies. Jonson's most sustained early meditation on courtly demeanour comes in *Cynthia's*

Revels, a play acted in 1600 by the Children of the Chapel and probably performed at court (and possibly, as Thomas Dekker notes, 'misliked there'). The play is in many ways an elaborate parody of *The Courtier*, or at least of the would-be courtiers who eagerly consume such treatises. An allegorical framework is interspersed with sustained demonstrations of courtly manner and gait, as well as tedious games modelled on those in *The Courtier*.[98]

The minute attention to movement and gait in the play is demonstrated by the scene in which Amorphus teaches Asotus the way to enter a room and address a lady:

> AMORPHUS 'Tis well entered sir. Stay, you come on too fast; your pace is too impetuous. Imagine this to be the palace of your pleasure, or place where your lady is pleased to be seen. First you present yourself, [*Demonstrating*]: thus, and, spying her, you fall off and walk some two turns; in which time it is to be supposed your passion hath sufficiently whited your face. Then, stifling a sigh or two and closing your lips, with a trembling boldness and bold terror you advance yourself forward. Try this much, I pray you.
>
> ASOTUS Yes, sir, pray God I can light on it. Here I come in, you say, and present myself?
>
> AMORPHUS Good.
>
> ...
>
> ASOTUS This is hard, by my faith, I'll begin it all again. (3.5.5–47)

Later, in *Cynthia's Revels*, Jonson uses the running metaphor of the bodily discipline of the fencing lesson – that essential accoutrement of the gentleman – to display the proper methods of displaying one's body at court. (A fuller description of the role of fencing in kinesic intelligence will be found in the next chapter.) As Eric Rasmussen and Matt Steggle argue in their introduction to the Folio additions for the Cambridge *Ben Jonson*, 'as the games are played out, what is revealed is a vision of courtship as a succession of learned movements, indeed as a martial art' (5.5). Rasmussen and Steggle note the way that Jonson builds expectations for the actors, as each performance tops the last, in which the competition among characters is overlaid with a dazzling display of skill on the part of the actors themselves. In addition, through the cleverly realized comments on the unfolding scene, the courtship trial also makes explicit some of the ways in which skill of all sorts is discussed and evaluated in the period.

This is a long and complex scene, needing sixteen actors. The competition is viewed by a large and boisterous on-stage audience, using the terms of art of the elaborate Master of Defence 'prizes':

> Be it known to all that profess courtship, by these presents … that we, Ulysses-Polytrops-Amorphus, master of the noble and subtle science of courtship, do give leave and license to our provost, Acolastus-Polypragmon-Asotus, to play his master's prize against all masters whatsoever in this subtle mystery, at these four, the choice and most cunning weapons of court-compliment, viz, the bare accost, the better regard; the solemn address; and the perfect close.

These four 'weapons' are then played in turn. After 'a charge is sounded', '*They act their accost severally to the lady that stands forth.*' The precise way in which the 'accost' is performed is left to the actors, but the judgements of the audience make clear that Amorphus's actions are done 'excellent well; most fashionably', whilst the comments on Asotus are decidedly tepid: 'Very good. / For a scholar, – Oh, 'tis too Dutch. / He reels too much.'

The competition takes an unexpected turn when Mercury challenges Amorphus. The audience is well versed in the nuances of each 'weapon': Amorphus performs a version of the accost which they term 'th'exalted foretop', which is deemed to be 'comely' and 'worthily studied', but deficient in critical details: 'Oh, his leg was too much produced. / And his hat was carried scurvily.' Mercury's is 'rare', 'sprightly and short', but perhaps a bit too humble: 'he does hop. He does bound too much' (5.4.131). The second bout is the 'solemn band-string', which Rasmussen and Steggle gloss as fiddling with the lace to a ruff. While it is rated as an 'excellent offer', Hedon remarks that 'Foh, that cringe was not put home', a phrase taken directly from fencing ('an incomplete or unconvincing thrust').

The preoccupation with evaluating and watching the most minute of gestures and movements of the body shows that Jonson's stagings are resolutely *animate*. They demand both the speaker and the interlocutor to engage in what almost amounts to a dance:

> but now put case she should be *passant* when you enter, as thus, you are to frame your gait thereafter ... then if she be *guardant*, here, you are to come on ... . If reguardant, then maintain your station, briske and irpe, show the supple motion of your pliant body, but, in chief, of your knee and hand, which cannot but arride her proud humour exceedingly.

Jonson demands a very different kinesic style for his actors to that of Shakespeare. Shakespeare's large-scale scenes are generally synoptic – attention is focused on the speaker, and secondary players throw attention on the main action. But Jonson's are distributed, atomistic – his comedies are distinguished by their relentless busyness; characters are in constant motion all at once. This kinesic style written for the actors in turn demands a different mode of kinesic awareness from the audience – and here we might bear in mind that Shakespeare and Jonson often wrote for the same actors and the same audience, a sign of the fluidity of kinesic intelligence of both player and audience.

3

'Skill of Weapon'

*This potential – even necessity – for collective,
self-conscious and intentional manipulation of
abilities, skills and traits suggests that the systematic
development of bodily technologies extends to primary
human capacities, such as self-defence, making humans
a technological species 'all the way down'.*[1]

Skill of weapon, like the other abilities on Gainsford's list,
is made 'plausible by practice', by long hours honing the
techniques necessary to integrate body, mind and weapon.
The necessity for and exigencies of such training are constantly
acknowledged in the literature on the art of swordplay.
Learning to use a weapon is a particularly complex form
of bodily knowledge, and a full account of embodiment
needs to take account of training, as well as the way that
the tools and artefacts themselves become absorbed into
bodies and minds of the adept. What is learned *alongside*
learning a skill? As Downey writes, 'we cannot fulfil the
promise of studies of embodiment if we assume that "bodily
knowledge" is just another form of stored information like
explicit knowledge ... . Instead, we must ask, how does
the body come to "know", and what kind of biological
changes might occur when learning a skill.'[2] In his famous
essay, Marcel Mauss defines 'techniques of the body' as the

'physio-psycho-sociological assemblages of series of actions' taken for granted within a culture, but widely variable across cultures and historical periods.[3] He argues that 'the child, the adult, imitates actions which have succeeded and which he has seen successfully performed by people in whom he has confidence and who have authority over him'.[4] Mauss saw that forms of training and shaping of the body across cultures can be seen as forms of *techné*. Such body techniques – how one moves, how one breathes, how we sleep, stretch, spit, run and swim – all become part of the fabric of skill, identity and embodied knowledge woven through a community.[5] Building upon Mauss's observations, current anthropological research into techniques of the body provides a foundation for understanding the forms of bodily knowing fostered by the martial disciplines of early modern England.

Anthropologists are particularly interested in variation and change in embodied skill-building, as well as how such skills are implicated in the larger value system held by a given community. Although mastering such skills as balancing objects on one's head, learning Venezuelan stick fighting and practising *capoeira* may seem far removed from the world of the early modern stage, anthropologists studying such practices provide valuable insights into the ways that skill is woven into the fabric of communities. Kathryn Linn Geurts's account of 'bodily knowing' in East Africa, for example, notes the high value placed on balance, particularly the ability to balance objects on one's head, that informs cultural life in villages in Ghana; one's physical skills, developed from very early on in life, are tightly linked to values such as upright conduct.[6] Such a finding recalls Georges Vigarello's argument about 'upward training' of the elite male body in early modern Europe.[7] In his essay on Venezuelan stick fighting, Michael Ryan notes that the teaching of particular bodily skills does not simply train the muscular system, but affects an entire array of physical and mental dispositions: 'Moreover, in the same fashion that students incorporate new practices into their habitual comportment, ways of belonging and identity are similarly incorporated and embodied through this disciplined training.'[8] In the course of his training as a stick fighter, Ryan discovered that 'over time these specialized physical attributes could alter my emotional and experiential relationship with my environment – a stance Heidegger referred to as the "mooding of the world"'.[9] A related perspective is offered by Downey, who has trained in the Brazilian martial art of *capoeira*. In 'Seeing with a Sideways Glance', he notes that in the course of learning the art, the novice must train his visual system; in learning to look, 'the world will appear differently than it might through another style of seeing'.[10] Thus the body 'retains experience, refines skills, and learns cultural lessons in distinctive physiological ways'.[11] In contrast to cultural anthropology, which tends to read acts of skill within the framework of the symbolic commitments of the culture, neuroanthropology instead directs attention to 'behavior, habit, built environment and training'.[12]

The idea that training has a dispositive effect would be very familiar to the writers of early modern manuals of skill. Early modern writers were highly attuned to the ways that skill training could shape not only the body but also one's entire 'emotional and experiential relationship' with the world, as Ryan notes. Indeed, the sixteenth and early seventeenth centuries saw vigorous debates about just these issues, as new forms of skill and training, linked to innovations in warfare and weaponry, sparked controversy.

As I have written elsewhere, perhaps the best example of this controversy are the disputes over the decline of the longbow and the attempts upon the part of the elite to revive interest in the art of archery.[13] The longbow was tightly linked to English national identity and narratives of martial prowess, especially against the French during the Hundred Years War, culminating in victory at the Battle of Agincourt. But the longbow was an exceptionally difficult weapon to master, requiring years of training from boyhood, and the military effectiveness of the longbow waned from the late fifteenth century on in the wake of advances in the art of warfare. Strong nativist defences of the ancient art of the longbow collided with changes in military technology and tactics that gave pride of place to munitions, gunpowder and massed pike warfare. The sixteenth century saw robust state attempts to shore up archery skills among the populace, as evidenced by proclamations ordering children to be trained in 'shooting' and communities to provide facilities for target practice. But nostalgic exhortations were not enough to produce militarily effective archers, and shooting with the longbow ultimately became a pastime rather than a legitimate military pursuit.

The example of the longbow shows that the nature of skill and identity becomes particularly pressured around weaponry. What you hold in your hand really matters; people shape tools, but tools in turn shape them. The fortunes of native English disciplines of edged weapons are in many ways similar, with older forms of swordplay competing with and ultimately giving way to new technologies and new theories of training. Early modern England saw marked shifts in the status of weapons and skill as continental technologies and training came to compete with, and to some extent supplant, the use of more traditional modes of combat. As with the discourse around the longbow, defenders of traditional weaponry intimately link modes and means of fighting with nationhood and masculinity. Like those who believed that abandoning the longbow in favour of weapons of fire would erode English manhood, George Silver (whose passionate defence of the English short sword and the native methods of 'defence' will be discussed more fully later in the chapter), argued that transferring allegiance from the native short sword to the continental rapier converted the English into 'degeneratte sonnes', who have forsaken 'our forefather's vertues with their weapons'.[14]

The result was a clash of styles and a shift in the status of traditional weaponry as young men, especially those who were or aspired to be gentlemen, became enamoured of the new Italian weaponry and the concomitant code of honour and duelling the rapier afforded. The rapier was a highly specialized weapon – long and razor sharp, it was deadlier than other weapons in one-on-one encounters. It was also more than a weapon: it was an expensive and highly coveted status symbol, an article of fashion that could be kitted out with elaborate accoutrements and that, if fashioned with enough workmanship, was considered a particularly appropriate diplomatic gift. In 1577, Sir Francis Walsingham wrote to Thomas Randolph that Elizabeth wished him to go to Scotland:

> For that the colour of your going thither is chiefly to visit the King and to convey a present to him, I pray you see if you can find any fit thing to be bought at London meet for his years and state. Some rare rapier or dagger were in my opinion the fittest present. To send him a jewel, unless it be of great price or very rare for workmanship – whereunto her majesty, I fear, will not be brought – [we]re but a scorn.
> Hampton Court.
> *Signed*: Fra. Walsyngham.[15]

The preciousness of such a gift provides insight into the stakes of the bet in *Hamlet*: Claudius wagers 'six Barbary horses' against 'six French rapiers and poniards', an indication of the relative value of the wager.

In contrast, short swords, backswords and two-handed swords were slashing weapons that required very different techniques, had a military lineage and were often wielded as part of public displays of fencing prowess. On stage, there was not so much a supplanting as a visible clash of cultures that physically played out strongly held debates about the relationship of arms and identity. The ecology of martial arts, especially swordplay, in early modern England is highly complex, and the theatre does not simply reflect that complexity but participates in it. Theatrical performance can be seen as part of a media ecology that comprises the many written treatises, both native English and translated from the Italian, that sought to train the aspiring swordsman.

There are two major strands in the debate about swordplay: a native, citizen practice using a variety of weapons and best exemplified by the Masters of Defence; and an imported continental technique that emphasized the deadly rapier. These were not mere preferences, but instead reflected opposed ways of thinking, embodiment and action. Work such as Jennifer Low's excellent *Manhood and the Duel* has demonstrated the relationship between masculinity, weaponry and conceptions of personal space as manifested in the 'upright body' of the gallant.[16] However, the drama depicted not only such deadly rapier duels among the elite, but also the figure of the 'downright' fighter, who eschews fencing by the book and instead triumphs by strength and courage. As I shall show, the figure of Edgar in *King Lear* can be read through the lens of these skill debates, as the disguises he assumes include not only action and gesture, but particular forms of martial skill, in this case manifested as triumph of the 'downright' cudgel against the foppish rapier.

The dominant native form of swordplay is represented by the prominence of the Masters of Defence, a guild-like organization of men licensed to train others in the skills of swordplay.[17] As Anglin notes, no doubt there were many informal schools of defence, but there was no formal licensing system until they were incorporated under Henry VIII. Unusually detailed records of the corporation exist,[18] documenting many of their activities between 1545 and 1590. Their organization was hierarchical in structure, consisting of scholars (beginners), free scholars, provosts, masters, governed by the four 'ancient masters'. Advancement in the ranks was determined by playing for a prize with multiple weapons against all qualified comers. Free scholars' status was tested with two weapons, provost with three, and master with four weapons. These were highly elaborate public displays of skill using diverse weapons, including staff, sword and buckler, backsword (a sword sharpened on one side only), two-handed sword, rapier and dagger, pike and longsword, amongst others. Throughout the later decades of the sixteenth century, fencing displays or 'prize fights' were a common sight in London. These contests held by the 'Masters of the Noble Science of Defence' were 'a regular popular feature of the life of London and its environs'.[19] BL Sloane MS 2530 records over 100 such contests, and these were almost certainly only a small fraction of those practised.

The civic fencing matches were both trials of skill and public entertainment. They were heavily advertised, with bills put up throughout the city, and they were preceded by elaborate ceremonial marches through the city, accompanied by drums and trumpets. The trials were held at inns in the city, including the Bel Savage (Ludgate Hill) and the Bull (Bishopsgate), as well as the Theatre and the Curtain, just north of the city.[20] As Berry notes, Sloan MS 2530 lists thirty-nine prizes played in London between 1575 and 1590, thirty-seven of which were played at one of these four venues. Playing for a prize must have involved protracted displays, as candidates for the higher ranks competed with multiple weapons against a range of opponents. For example, in 1587 at the Bel Savage Inn, James Cranydge, sponsored by Richard Tarlton, played his Master's Prize with the longsword, the backsword, the sword and dagger, and the rapier and dagger against nine masters, and was 'allowed' a master.[21] In 1583, John Devell attempted a provost's prize at the Theatre, playing two provosts and four free scholars in the longsword, the sword and buckler, and the sword and dagger. Although not admitted initially 'for his disorder', presumably his lack of skill, he was later allowed 'by the goodwills of the maysters'.[22]

Playing a prize was governed by elaborate rules and ritual, and a Master was sworn to 'without respect favor or hatred of either partye, saye speake and geve true Judgement', to show mercy should 'you happen to have the vpper hande of your enemye', not to compete with other masters, and to conduct prizes fairly.[23] Prizes functioned as public entertainment, as certification of skill and as advertisement for fencing instruction. 'Playing' was on the one hand a serious exhibition of skill, but was on the other hand not fully in earnest – that is, not entered into with the direct aim of injuring, maiming or killing. The distinction is important in one of the last examples of trial by battle in England, the contest between Master of Defence Henry Naylor and George Thorne, who represented the opponents in a civil action. The two combatants were to fight at Tothill Field in a specially erected arena, complete with stands for spectators. Thorne, a 'bygge, brode, stronge set fellowe', was to fight the 'proper slender' Naylor.[24] The two were to square off bare-headed, with exposed calves and arms, using 'bastons' or cudgels and small shields until one was defeated. After a protracted ceremonial opening, the suit was announced to have been settled (recalling the interrupted battle between Bolingbroke and Mowbray in *Richard II*). Naylor refused to give up the gauntlet, challenging Thorne to 'playe with him halfe a score blowes, to show some pastyme to the Lorde chiefe Iustice and the other there assembled', but Thorne refused, saying 'that he came to fight and would not playe'.[25]

This distinction offered here between fighting and playing is crucial to understanding the complex ecology of martial display of skill in early modern England. 'Skill of weapon' is in the first instance tied up with martial identity and masculinity. As Gregory Colón Semenza has noted, the 'gradual weakening of the traditional arguments for sport's functionality – due to the development of military technology and the relatively rapid transformation of the economy in the sixteenth century – had the effect of further blurring the lines between lawful sport and mirth'.[26] The various modes of martial arts can be seen as a continuum (or perhaps more precisely as a set of overlapping and conflicting categories), with contests that look more like performance and entertainment at one end and those that look more like war or murder at the other. But these categories overlap – for example, Castiglione emphasizes the performative nature of war when he advises his courtier to perform valiant feats of arms only in a setting in which they can be noticed and applauded. And even conflicts that look simply like interpersonal violence are often governed by clearly recognized if not always fully articulated rules and boundaries. Acts of physical domination and violence were generally governed by what Alexandra Shepard has described as 'tacit rules' and conventions governing their display, and combatants brought one another to law in large part for 'disregarding the implicit codes of conduct expected to regulate physical confrontation'.[27] Such codes are commonly observed in subcultures that valorize fighting; fights are not randomly entered into, but take place in clearly demarcated circumstances, with ritualized escalation leading to the fight itself.[28] Fighting is framed action, although these frames are subject to negotiation, violation and change – as exemplified perhaps most famously in Laertes' attack on Hamlet, in which the revenge frame transforms into a fencing frame, which is in turn transformed by Laertes' frustrated attack on Hamlet outside of the orchestrated framework of the sporting contest: 'Have at you now!'

Swordplay as art: Native and continental fencing treatises

The early modern period sees an enormous spike in how-to books and treatises of every kind, from hawking to vaulting to husbandry. These treatises of course cannot be read as though they were transparent documents; they are aspirational and often tendentious, advocating for rather than reflecting a worldview. Treatises such as Roger Ascham's beautifully written apology for archery – *Toxophilus: or the School of Shooting* – are not simple instruction books, but are also deeply felt arguments defending the ways of life underpinned by these skills. Authors of skill treatises are eager to make the point that theirs is no mere bodily act, the result of custom or simple repetition. All skills involving the body seem to be in need of some form of justification or defence – the more so if, like dance and swordplay, they carry with them apparent scriptural prohibitions or other negative associations. The authors of such treatises argue that their practice is an art, reducible to rules and principles, and not simply a result of 'nature', here understood as natural physical ability (and hence untrainable). The author of an English treatise on vaulting defends his art on these very grounds:

> Some count it an unnecessarie and dangerous exercise ... another sort ... will by no meanes have it an art, but rather the child of an accidental and undigested experience, receiving the degrees of its excellencie, from blind custome onlye and difference of bodies.[29]

The authors of treatises on skilled action legitimate themselves through reference both to authority as well as by piggybacking on other, widely accepted high-status activities. As dancing treatises buttressed their claims to be an art with allegiances to the liberal art of music, the authors of the Italian treatises on fencing translated into English relied upon mathematics, especially geometry. Skilled practice was linked to fundamental rules based upon basic mathematical principles.

In England, these principles are put under particular pressure because of the disputes between the continental and native tutors in the art of defence. These disputes spilled over into the instructional literature – in the form of George Silver's polemical treatise defending English practice – and were also played out on the stage. These debates are especially relevant because they are in many ways arguments about the nature of skill itself. Three treatises published in England between 1594 and 1599 lay the groundwork for these debates: Giacomo di Grassi, *His True Arte of Defence* (1594); Vincentio Saviolo, *His Practice* (1595); and George Silver's *Paradoxes of Defence* (1599).[30] Di Grassi's treatise was originally written in Italian in 1570, and Saviolo's manual popularized the Italian method of defence.[31] Saviolo was one of a number of foreign fencing masters in London who set up schools to teach Italian methods of fencing; they were much in demand by aspirational young gentlemen who desired training in the continental techniques, and they were equally resented by the native Masters of Defence.

The Italian treatises follow the familiar skill-discourse method: they claim to have reduced a multitude of particularities to a coherent method, grounded in science and framed as principles that can be easily held in memory. The title page of Di Grassi's treatise, published in English translation in 1594 (with woodcuts copied from the 1570 Italian edition), promises to teach by 'infallable Demonstrations, apt Figures, and perfect Rules. Skill in fence demands both "judgement and force".' Di Grassi provides some advice for acquiring the latter by increasing 'strength and agilitie of body'[32] through 'priuat practise', noting that unlike vision and hearing, strength can be 'encreased by reasonable exercise' such as practising with overweight weapons or cudgels. But most of the treatise is devoted not to specific exercises, but to the principles of judgement that must be kept 'stedfastly in memorie'.[33]

These are, simply, that a straight line is shortest; he that is nearest, hits soonest; circular movements have more force at the extremity; smaller forces can be withstood more easily than greater; and 'every motion is accomplished in tyme'.[34] Thrusts are to be favoured over cuts and slashing blows, for the simple reason that they arrive first and are 'wont to kill'. The mathematical groundings of the science are illustrated by geometrical woodcuts (executed very clumsily in the English edition). Courage and skill are not opposed qualities, but are rather intertwined. So-called instinctual responses of the trained swordsman are 'no other thing then the knowledge of the rules before laide downe: which knowledge, because it is naturally graffed in the mynde, is something the rather holpen and qualified by Arte, and maketh a man so assured and bolde, that he dares to enter on any great daunger'.[35]

The case for fencing as an art is made even more vociferously by Vincentio Saviolo in 1595. Dedicated to the Earl of Essex, this treatise justifies the art of rapier and dagger through its affiliation with the military arts. Learning 'time and measure' will allow the reader to 'open [his] spirites in the knowledge of the secrets of arms'.[36] Saviolo argues that 'perfect knowledge' of the rapier and dagger is more valuable for 'the Militarie profession' than the traditionally recommended practices of hunting, hawking and wrestling, which train only strength. In contrast, a man 'hauing the perfect knowledge and practice of this arte, although but small of stature and weake of strength, may with a little remouing of his foot, a sodain turning of his hand, a slight declining of his bodie, subdue and ouercome the fierce brauing pride of tall and strong bodies'.[37]

Saviolo's treatise is organized as a dialogue between 'V' and 'L' and begins with a discussion of the 'slight account' in which swordsmanship is held, a state of affairs 'V' attributes to the false belief that fencing demands only 'great strength and brauing courage'.[38] To 'L's' suggestion that 'nature is she which worketh and performeth all, and not art', 'V' replies that although 'nature may doo very much to frame a man apt and fit for this exercise', art is essential: '[F]or as a man hath voice and can sing by nature, but shall neuer doo it with time and measure of musicke vnlesse he haue learned the arte … . So much more should a man learne how to manage and vse his body, his hand, and his foote, and to know how to defend himselfe from his enemy.'[39] All arts – from rhetoric to carpentry to sailing – require 'reason and skill'.

These claims to elevate rapier fighting to an art based on scientific principles are vigorously contested by George Silver, whose *Paradoxes of Defence* is not so much an instruction manual as a sustained xenophobic diatribe against the rapier, duelling and the continental principles underpinning these practices.[40] Silver vigorously defends the native English short sword tradition and attacks the rapier method as a fraud, not an art at all. Silver's text is outright polemic against Saviolo and other foreign fencing masters, who claim to teach their students the true art of fencing. He argues that the rapier is a false and imperfect weapon: it is too long and therefore useless in battle, and it is impossible to defend effectively. In private quarrels, victory is simply a matter of chance, and no skill at all is involved. A strong nativist strain is apparent throughout as he attacks 'the apish toys' and 'strange vices and deuices of Italian, French, and Spanish Fencers'.[41] This is coupled with a defence of justification that 'ancient English weapons of true Defence', adjusted to their statures, makes men 'safe, bold, valiant, hardy, strong, and healthful', whilst the rapier makes men fearful, weak and useless in war. Saviolo and his ilk are accused of:

> Teaching men to butcher one another here at home in peace, wherewith they cannot hurt their enemies abrode in warre ... when the battels are ioyned, and come to the charge, there is no roome for them to drawe their Bird-spits, and when they haue them, what can they doe with them? can they pierce his Corslet with the point? can they vnlace his Helmet, vnbuckle his Armour, hew asunder their Pikes with a Stocata, a reuersa, a Dritta, ... or other such like tempes-tuous termes? no, these toyes are fit for children, not for men, for stragling boyes of the Campe, to murder poultrie, not for men of Honour to trie the battell with their foes.[42]

As defenders of the longbow argued that skill in this weapon inherently confers strength, masculinity and English valour, so Silver claims that the rapier is inherently emasculating, a toy for children rather than a proper weapon for warfare. The Italian terms of art that he mocks – *stocata, reversa, dritta* – were widely adopted by young gentlemen eager to demonstrate their skill. Here the foreign terms underscore the uselessness of the rapier in the hands of 'men of Honour'.

Silver argues that claims to teach rapier fighting as an art are a mere sham, and that young men who pay the exorbitant fees charged by foreign masters are simply being cozened. Rapier instruction promotes 'Italianated, weake, fantasticall, and most diuellish and imperfect fights'[43] that end only in disaster: even the best students 'do neuer fight, but they are most commonly sore hurt, or one or both of them slaine'.[44]

The outcomes of encounters are dependent entirely upon luck: 'None vndertake the combat, be his cause neuer so good, his cuning neuer so great, his strength and agilitie neuer so great, but his vertue was tied to fortune … [they are taught] to bring their liues to an end by Art.'[45]

If the art of fencing is simply a sham, it follows that unskilled fighters may well have an advantage over the falsely trained fencer. Silver argues that a 'down right fellow, that neuer came in schoole' can, using his natural courage, strength and ability:

> put one of these imperfect schollers greatly to his shifts. Besides there are now in these dayes no gripes, closes, wrestlings, striking with the hilts, daggers or bucklers, vsed in Fence-schooles. Our ploughmen by nature wil do all these things with great strength & agility: but the Schooleman is altogether vnacquainted with these things. He being fast tyed to such school-play as he hath learned, hath lost thereby the benefite of nature, and the plowman is now by nature without art a farre better man then he.[46]

Overly coached and distracted by strange terminology, the fighter is undermined by the art itself, which places too great a demand on memory and is full of vain terms that do not animate the body but simply confuse the mind. 'Troubled in his wits' by the arcane terminology, the man schooled in 'false fights' will be defeated by the 'unskillful' man who 'standeth free in his valour with strength and agilitie of bodie'.[47] Silver attempts to make his case by noting the unwillingness of the foreign fencing instructors to fight publicly, noting that they failed to answer his challenge to fight with numerous weapons at the Bel Savage.

The Italians refused to 'play' both at the Bel Savage and with a Master of Defence who, Silver writes, requested Saviolo to come 'to my schoole, and play with me'.[48] Vincentio refuses – 'Play with thee said maister *Vincentio* (verie scornefully) by God me scorne to play with thee', and the encounter ends with a street brawl.[49] These encounters have a certain theatricality about them, and indeed the drama uses the clash between the foreign fighter and the downright Englishman on a number of occasions. But they also show a clash of fight frames – Silver and the Master of Defence challenge the Italian to 'play', or to display his ability in a trial of skill. But the Italian masters were uninterested in such play; instead, they claimed to be preparing men for the deadly serious event of a duel: public display of one's skill could only be a disadvantage in such circumstances. George Hale, in *The Private Schoole of Defence*, condemns such public prize-fights as little more than cheap theatrics: 'fights at many weapons vpon stages, are mere shadowes without substance'.[50]

Opinion is divided about the relevance of these disputes and, more largely, the question of the relationship between public prize-fighting and theatrical displays of fencing skills. Charles Edelman argues for strong homologies between these practices. At the outset of *Brawl Ridiculous*, he invites the reader to imagine that the final scene of *Hamlet* takes the form of a boxing match and that, moreover, the play is itself performed in the same arenas used for actual boxing matches; players could expect an audience avid for action and well versed in the nuances of the sport. In such a context, the audience would have had a sporting eye for the contest and would vociferously reject inept play. Hamlet and Laertes would have had to adopt correct stances, use correct footwork, maintain proper distance and show that they knew how to give – and take – a punch. Nothing less than a full-blown Masters-of-Defence-style fight would have been sufficient to satisfy such knowledgeable audiences: 'the audience would have wished to see only the most convincing of fights'.[51] In contrast, Alan Dessen marshals evidence from a number of moments of allegorically rendered stage violence to ask whether such conflicts need only to be thought of in terms of realism, or whether their performance might be 'linked to a symbolic or patterned logic relevant to the world of the play'.[52] For Dessen, such moments as Talbot fighting

Joan, or Edgar defeating Oswald, are not fully accounted for by a realistic dramaturgy, but instead may have been staged to take account of larger symbolic patterns within the play. These views are not necessarily mutually exclusive; in fact, what seems clear is that a wide variety of fighting styles and situations were called for by early modern dramatists; they engaged the skilled viewing of an audience with a sporting eye for swordplay and a knowledge of contemporary debates and tropes of combat.

But skilled viewing involves more than simply knowledge of fighting techniques, however acute such knowledge would have been in early modern London. Audiences were also skilled at watching plays; they would have been able to discern the differences between fights staged within the fiction of the plays and events such as playing a prize. Indeed Shakespeare and other dramatists employ the skill of the actors to intervene in debates about swordplay and duelling, in the process interrogating the framework of masculine codes of honour. Silver's observation that rapier fights often result in the deaths of both parties, for example, is borne out in the drama. This outcome is staged in *Friar Bacon and Friar Bungay*, when Lambert and Serlsby meet to fight with rapier and dagger over Margaret. Their sons at Oxford watch them kill one another in Bacon's magic glass, after which their own fight ends in mutual destruction. A similar outcome is staged in Christopher Marlowe's *The Jew of Malta*, when Lodowick and Mathias, duped by Barabas, slay each other in a duel, after which Barabas mordantly observes that 'now they have shew'd themselves to be tall fellowes'.[53]

Perhaps the most famous instance of such an intervention into contemporary swordplay debates is made in *Romeo and Juliet*. As Edelman, Ian Borden and Jennifer Low have noted, in *Romeo and Juliet* at least four separate schools of fighting are mentioned or displayed.[54] What is less noticed are the significant differences in the major fight scenes between the 1597 and the 1599 quartos. The provenance and the authority of the 1597 quarto has long been debated. Relegated to the category of bad quarto for many years, *An Excellent Conceited Tragedy of Romeo and Juliet* of 1597 has numerous substantive differences to the *Most Excellent and Lamentable Tragedie of Romeo and Juliet, Newly corrected, augmented, and amended*, published in 1599.[55] Lukas Erne, in his edition of Q1, claims that the two versions should be seen as independent versions, with Q1 a cut version suitable for touring. Like most so-called bad quartos, the exact origin of the text is difficult to determine, and René Weis concurs with Erne's view that it may be 'a creative combination of abridging and remembering with a view to performance'.[56]

Of particular note are the stage directions, two of which directly affect readings of the major fight scenes. While editors have tended to view explicit stage directions as valuable guides to stage practice, this is not always the case. John Jowett has convincingly argued that famous Q1 directions such as '*Paris strewes the tomb with flowers*', or '*They all but the Nurse goe forth, casting Rosemary on her and shutting the Curtens*', which have been adopted in all major editions, may have been added by Henry Chettle at the printing house.[57] As Weis notes, 'rather than being a record of performance, they may constitute the most exciting padding in the textual history of Shakespeare's plays'.[58]

The first scene of *Romeo and Juliet* depicts an unfolding and escalating spectacle of violence, albeit tinged with humour that belies tragic outcomes. Quarto 1, however, collapses much of the action and seems in general much less interested in the range and diversity of fighting styles and motives that are so marked in Q2. The initial stage direction simply reads '*Enter 2. Seruing-men of the* Capolets.' They engage in comic cross-talk that conflates masculinity, swords and violence, but the fighting styles are not specified, as they are in Q2. Once the Montague servants enter and the quarrel is begun, the conflict is concluded through the following stage direction: '*They draw, to them enters* Tybalt, *they fight, to them the Prince, old* Mountague, *and his wife, old* Capulet *and his wife, and other Citizens and part them.*' Unlike the other Q1 stage directions, this one is omitted from modern editions, as it conflates action that is otherwise carefully delineated in the second quarto and is ambiguous about who is partaking in the fight and who is acting as a peacemaker. The stage direction simply describes a generic fight that is abruptly ended by the Prince. Moreover, Benvolio's response to Montague's demand to explain the action provides no further information and implies that only servingmen were involved: 'Here were the seruants of your aduersaries, / And yours close fighting ere I did approach' (TLN 108–9). This particular stage direction, then, seems unlikely to be a reconstruction of stage action from the text by 'someone looking at the text before him', as there is no way of piecing together the fight or its participants from the dialogue alone. Rather, the stage direction seems more likely to be a somewhat confused memory of a scrum on stage involving most of the major characters.

Especially in contrast with the confusion of Q1, Q2 shows the extent to which the initial quarrels of the first scene reflect distinctive fighting styles linked to class, status and age. Quarto 2 specifies that Sampson and Gregory enter '*with swords and bucklers*'; these are the weapons described as '"clownish" … and not fit for a gentleman' by John Florio.[59] Further evidence of the fighting style of the serving men is Samson's injunction to Gregory to 'remember his swashing blow'. This term describes the slashing method used by weapons sharpened on the edge rather than thrusting weapons such as the deadly rapier.

The Q2 stage direction '*They fight*', then, clearly indicates the first stage of fighting among the servingmen, which is interrupted by Benvolio's attempt to part the men using his rapier, the weapon of the nobleman. Tybalt mistakes – or pretends to mistake – Benvolio's drawn weapon to mean that he is actually engaging in fights with the lower-class 'heartless hinds'. Drawing on a lower-class man would be a shaming engagement for a gentleman, and Tybalt and Benvolio begin a parallel fight with their rapiers. Thus the explicit '*they fight*' for the servingmen and the implicit stage direction for Tybalt cue very different styles of movement and skill. Swashing blows and buckler make a great deal of show and noise, possibly to mask the reluctance for much actual engagement and danger on the part of the 'heartless' or fearful servingmen. Rapier combat by contrast demands more space, more calculation and is much more likely to have a fatal outcome. The entrance of exasperated citizens with '*clubs or partisans*' aiming to beat both sides down both increases the chaos, divides the attention of the audience, no longer able to focus on any one combat on stage, and prepares the way for the comic turn in the action, as the elder generation becomes involved. Old Capulet calls for his longsword, an old-fashioned two-handed weapon that he is almost certainly too feeble to even hold upright, as his wife witheringly notes: 'A crutch, a crutch! Why call you for a sword!' (1.1.78). The chaos of this inter-generational, inter-class brawl is indicated by the Prince's inability to stop them – 'will they not hear?' (1.1.85) shows that his verbal authority is at first insufficient to stop the fight. The scene is deliberately orchestrated to call attention to the relationship between technologies (swords and bucklers, rapiers, partisans and longswords) and ways of bodily knowing. The technical precision of the actors' work is attested by Benvolio's retrospective description of the scene to Montague:

Here were the servants of your adversary
And yours, close fighting ere I did approach.
I drew to part them; in the instant came
The fiery Tybalt, with his sword prepar'd,
Which, as he breath'd defiance to my ears
He swung about his head and cut the winds,
Who nothing hurt withal, hiss'd him in scorn. (1.1.106–12)

As Joan Ozark Holmer has pointed out, the description of Tybalt is clearly indebted to the fencing treatises of the 1590s discussed above, especially Saviolo's use of Italian terminology.[60] Soens also notes that 'the cut whistling about the head suggests the Spanish school of fence', which used the upper body as the target.[61] The shaping power of the weapon and of bodily regimes of training are satirized by Benvolio's mocking of Tybalt's showiness, which is presented as style without substance.

The differences in fencing styles are used as a means of vividly drawing the characters. The young noblemen fence with dagger and rapier, using European styles that had displaced the sword–buckler techniques used by the servingman. Mercutio fences Italian style, which at this point had become appropriated as a native English style, a thrusting and fluid style in which the rapier moves between *stoccato* (low) or *imbroccatta* (high) position. The fluidity of his fencing style and his keen verbal abilities are intimately linked, demonstrating the entwining of verbal and physical wit.

In contrast, Tybalt fights by the 'book of arithmetic', as Romeo kisses by the book: 'He fights as you sing prick-song, keeps time, distance and proportion, rests me his minim rest, one, two, and the third in your bosom.'[62] Silver describes the 'Spanish style' in this way: 'They stand as braue as they can with their bodies straight vpright, narrow spaced with their feet continually mouing as if they were in a dance.'[63] Mercutio's jibe about Tybalt fighting by the book recalls Silver's scorn for overtrained young men who are conned into believing that they have learned secrets for victory in the duels, when in fact they will enter into 'weake, fantasticall, and most diuellish and imperfect fights', dependent upon mere chance rather than skill.

The fight between Tybalt and Mercutio falls out in precisely this way. In the world of the play, the framework for fighting predominates: the challenges, the strutting self-display of the young men, the showing off of their skills acquired through long practice, perusing treatises and (presumably) studying under fencing masters. But in contrast to the elaborate shows of the Master of Defence, the fights are chaotic, confusing, quick and deadly, with the outcome less a result of real skill (on the part of the characters, not the actors) than of the luck of the draw – who is unlucky enough to be in the path of a razor-sharp weapon.

As at the conclusion of *Hamlet*, no one on stage has any idea what has happened after Mercutio is wounded. Rapiers were deadly because they could so easily pierce the rib cage and puncture the lung or another organ; the merest pin-prick with the 'Bird-spit', as Silver calls the rapier, could inflict a mortal wound with little outward mark. In Q2, the dialogue around the fatal injury reads:

> MERCUTIO Will you pluck your sword out of his
> pilcher by the eares?
> Make haste, lest mine be about your eares ere it be out.
> TYBALT I am for you. [Draws]
> ROMEO Gentle *Mercutio*, put thy Rapier vp.
> MERCUTIO Come sir, your Passado.
> ROMEO [Draws] Draw *Benuolio*, beate downe their
> weapons,
> Gentlemen, for shame forbeare this outrage,
> Tybalt, Mercutio, the Prince expresly hath
> Forbid this bandying in Verona streetes,
> Hold Tybalt, good Mercutio.
> PETRUCHIO   Away, Tybalt.
> MERCUTIO I am hurt.
> A plague a' both houses, I am sped,
> Is he gone and hath nothing? (3.1.79–93)

The dialogue indicates fast-paced confusing chaotic action; the participants themselves have little idea of what can have happened. Romeo at first minimizes Mercutio's injury: 'Courage, man, the hurt cannot be much.' Only when Mercutio is carried offstage does the outcome become clear.

In Q1, the fight itself is shorter, but the stage direction describing the action is so useful that it is printed in all modern editions:

MERCUTIO Come drawe your rapier out of your scabard, least mine be about your eares ere you be aware.

ROMEO Stay *Tibalt*, hould *Mercutio*: *Benuolio* beate downe their weapons.

Tibalt under Romeos arme thrusts Mercutio, in and flyes.

MERCUTIO Is he gone, hath hee nothing? A poxe on your houses. (TLN 1510–15)

The young men in the play imagine swordplay to be a matter of skill and honour, but here it is merely a matter of chance. In Susan Snyder's memorable phrase, *Romeo and Juliet* 'becomes, rather than is, tragic'.[64] Nowhere is this point clearer than in these two scenes, which so closely resemble each other: a challenge is issued, the fight is engaged and escalates, peace-making is attempted but is misinterpreted. The shift from comedy to tragedy hinges literally upon a razor point.

Jonson: Staging ineptitude

The gallant's preoccupation with the technical language and the bodily dispositions inculcated by fashionable pretensions engendered by the continental fencing traditions are explored in a comic vein in Jonson by the same company that engaged their tragic implications in *Romeo and Juliet*. Performing ineptitude requires as much, if not more, kinesic intelligence than performing skilful action. In *The Court Jester*, Danny Kaye plays a hapless minstrel who is mistaken for a court jester-cum-trained assassin. The highlight of the film is the fencing match between Kaye and Boris Karloff, in which Kaye oscillates between the persona of comic inept fighter paralysed with fear and the expert fencer. The pleasure of the viewer is in watching the sheer variety of physical actions, showing the skill of the actor across bodily registers.

Jonson in particular takes delight in asking his actors to contort their bodies in attempts to ape the fashionable comportment of the gallant. Indeed, some of our best evidence about fencing practices comes from his work. Jonson was himself a skilled swordsman. He bragged to William Drummond that he had slain a Spanish soldier in single combat whilst serving as a soldier in the Low Countries: 'In his service in the Low Countries he had, in the face of both the camps, killed an enemy and taken *opima spolia* from him.'[65] More notoriously, he pled benefit of clergy and was branded on the thumb for manslaughter for killing fellow actor Gabriel Spencer in a duel; the jury concluded that he had:

> made an assault with force and arms etc. against and upon a certain Gabriel Spencer, when he was in God's and the said Lady the Queen's peace, at Shoreditch in the aforesaid county of Middlesex, in the fields there, and with a certain sword of iron and steel called a Rapier, of the price of three shillings, which he then and there had in his right hand and held drawn, feloniously and wilfully struck and beat the same Gabriel, then and there with the aforesaid sword giving to the same Gabriel Spencer, in and upon the same Gabriel's right side, a mortal wound, of the depth of six inches and of the breadth of one inch, of which mortal wound the same Gabriel Spencer then and there died instantly in the aforesaid Fields at Shoreditch aforesaid in the aforesaid County of Middlesex.[66]

Jonson's early comedies extensively feature fencing, as the young gallants and gulls seek to master the codes of honour and fashion upon which the plays hinge. The rapier is if nothing else a form of conspicuous consumption; equally important to these young men is mastering the terminology and the bodily disciplines that will distinguish them in London. Hence the plays contain elaborate descriptions of duels, some of which only injure the elaborate clothing worn by the young men, are peppered with Italian fencing terms and feature hilarious fencing lessons in which gallants attempt to tutor one another in the art of defence. The 'humours' or dispositions and traits of these young gentlemen are externalized in the weapons that they covet. As with much skill discourse, we glimpse the mechanics of teaching and learning skill in parody and polemic.

Both *The Case is Altered* (1597) and *Every Man in his Humour* (1598, rev. 1616) have parodic scenes of fencing instruction. *The Case is Altered* was written for the Children of the Blackfriars, so its physical comedy may well have been inflected with the mismatch between the children's size and physique and the adult activities they parody. In 2.7, Onion proposes 'some exercise or other', and cudgels are fetched so that the young men can 'play a prize'.[67] The language is larded with the terms of art taken from manuals on rapier fencing: 'I have the phrases, man, and the anagrams, and the epitaphs fitting the mystery of the noble science' (2.7.7–8). Rather than rapiers, however, they 'play' with the decidedly downmarket weapon of the cudgel. Cudgels were widely used in fencing instruction, particularly instruction in the slashing techniques of the short sword, as taught by the Master of Defence. The inexperienced and timorous Martino reluctantly agrees to fight Onion: 'Will you not hurt me, fellow Onion?' Onion attempts to instruct Martino in the nuances of striking and defending:

Ha, well played! Fall over to my leg now; so, to your guard again. Excellent! To my head now. Make home your blow; spare me not, make it home. Good! Good again! (2.7.80–2)

The instruction is too good, or Onion underestimates Martino, because the dialogue indicates that he catches a good thump on the head: 'Godso, Onion hath caught a bruise.' The remainder of the scene is an attempted re-hash and analysis of the fight, again put in the terms of art. Juniper attempts an instant replay:

JUNIPER Why I'll give you demonstration how it came.
    Thou open'st the dagger to falsify over with the back

sword trick, and he interrupted before he could fall to the close.

ONION No, no I know best how it was, better than any man here. I felt his play presently, for look you, I gathered upon his thus, thus – do you see? – For the double lock, and took it single on the head (2.7.96–101).

Jonson here plays with the mismatch between the physical humour: Martino simply whacks Onion on the side of the head, oblivious to the neat fencing tricks Onion is keen to show; in the aftermath, Juniper attempts to paper over the outcome with technical language – Onion was feinting (falsifying) with the dagger to set up a backhand attack. Ultimately Onion's store of fencing terms is exhausted, and he resorts to a physical re-enactment – 'thus, thus, do you see?' Jonson stages comically one of the truisms often repeated in fencing manuals; it can be more dangerous to fight against an 'unskilled' (or untrained) fencer than a skilled one, because the unskilful man does not react as expected. It is for this reason that Onion says that 'I had rather play with one that had skill by half.' As Jennifer Low notes, 'fencers are engaged in a partner relation not unlike that of paired dancers';[68] if one of the partners does not know how to play, the match cannot go on. Of course the joke here is also Onion's braggadocio at having been defeated by a mere amateur.

This scene is reprised in *Every Man in his Humour*, staged by the Lord Chamberlain's Men in 1598, in which Shakespeare himself performed. Unlike *The Case is Altered*, the play is included in the 1616 Folio. In revising the play, Jonson moves the setting from Italy to London, renaming his characters in the process. He retained the fencing instruction scene between Bobadilla (Bobadill F) and Matheo (Matthew F) (1.3 Q; 1.5 F). As in *The Case is Altered*, the scene shows the close link between fencing and playgoing. The scene presents a cluster of traits associated with the young man around town, as satirized by Dekker in the *Gull's Hornbook*; Bobadill has just arisen at 6.30 in the evening; Matthew has drunk his health the night before, brings a copy of Hieronimo (*The Spanish Tragedy*) with him and has written a few sonnet lines for good measure. From here the conversation moves to clothing and fashion. Matthew compliments Bobadill on how well his boot 'becomes' his leg, a conversation which leads to Matthew's account of a dispute with Master Wellbred [Prospero in Q] about the beauty of a 'hanger', defined by the *OED* (definition 4b) as 'a loop or strap on a sword-belt from which the sword was hung; often richly ornamented': 'This the day I happened to enter into some discourse of a hanger, which, I assure you, both for fashion and workmanship was most peremptory-beautiful [Q has merely 'beautiful'] and gentleman-like; yet he condemned and cried it down for the most pied and ridiculous that ever he saw' (1.5.67–72).

What follows is a fencing lesson which satirizes the pretentious and fashionable discourse and claims of fencing masters and manuals. Matthew entreats Bobadill to instruct him in the 'mystery' and 'science' of swordplay: 'I have it spoken of divers that you have very rare and un-in-one-breath-utterable skill' (F 96–7). The two practice with bedstaves – rods used in the place of cudgels – and the scene depends upon the physical comedy of Matthew's attempts to force his body into the absurd positions that will mark him as accomplished in continental rapier-play:

> Twine your body more about, that you may fall to a more sweet, comely gentleman-like guard. So, indifferent. Hollow your body more, sir, thus. Now stand fast o'your left leg. Note your distance; keep your due proportion of time. Oh, you disorder your point most irregularly. (F 111–15)

Despite his disgust with Matthew's failure to 'manage [his] weapon with any facility or grace', and his 'dearth of judgement', he promises that he will 'learn you, by the true judgement of the eye, hand, and foot, to control any enemy's point i'the world'. Should your adversary confront you with a pistol, 'there nothing, by this hand; you should, by the same rule, control his bullet in a line, except it were hail-shot, and spread' (132–6). The ludicrous bragging satirizes the claims of fencing masters to 'privately' tutor young men in secret wards or lines of defence. In 4.7, when Matthew's confidence in the 'excellent trick' he has learned is brought to the test, Bobadill claims that he has singlehandedly defeated the entire company of Master of Defence: 'I have driven them after me the whole length of a street in open view of all our gallants, pitying to hurt them' (4.7.36–8). Like all braggart soldiers, Bobadill proves himself a coward at the end, claiming that he cannot draw against Downright because he had a 'warrant of the peace served on me even now as I came along' (4.7.97–8). Knowell says, 'Go, get you to a surgeon. "Slid, an these be your tricks, your *passadas* and your *montantos*, I'll none of them"' (115).

Fencing scenes for Jonson serve several functions. They are a highly effective means of skewering social pretensions, particularly the 'humour' of the would-be gallant to display his masculinity – and his fashion sense – through skill in weaponry. While parodying the aspiring gentlemen, these scenes also showcase the actors themselves. Inset instructional scenes are invitations to physical virtuosity, asking the actors to employ physical comedy in coordinated movements of demonstration and imitation, all conducted in deadly earnest. Moreover, fencing scenes show the agonistic nature of Jonson's comedy, the extent to which it is played out in essentially competitive terms. Adam Zucker's brilliant discussion of the role of wit in the early modern drama emphasizes verbal wit, but playwrights such as Jonson saw verbal and physical wit as essentially linked – just as inarticulacy and ineptitude are joined together.

Reading through the lens of skill:
Tom Strowd and Edgar

The triumph of the untutored downright man with a cudgel or baton is a fairly common trope on the stage. An example is the concluding scene of John Day and Henry Chettle's *The Blind Beggar of Bethnall Greene* (Admiral's Men, 1600), featuring what the title page describes as the 'merry humour of Tom Strowd the Norfolk yeoman'.[69] Tom is portrayed as a naïve countryman cozened and corrupted by city gallants. Towards the end of the play, he converts to the virtuous side, siding with the disguised aristocrat Mowbray (now impersonating the serving-man brother of the 'Blind Beggar'), his daughter Bess and Captain Westford against the villains Sir Robert Westford, Young Playnsley, Frank Canbee and Jack Hadland. Entering with drums at separate doors, the opposing parties arrange a trial by combat. Under orders from the King, who hopes to limit the mayhem by allowing free choice of weapon, Sir Robert chooses sword and target against the disguised Mowbray, calculating that servingmen are 'unskilful' in that weapon. Playnford, noting that Captain Westford has been in Spain and is thus 'practiced in the desperate fight of single rapier', first chooses that weapon, but that choice is rejected by the King as 'too desperate' and they settle on the less dangerous backsword. Tom by contrast refuses sword-and-buckler and asks instead for an ashen gibbet: 'Weapon me no weapons, I can play at wasters as well as another man; but all's one for that, give me but an ashen Gibbet in my hand, and I do not dry-bang them both, I'll be bound to eat hay with a horse, so will I.'[70] Once he is furnished with his cudgel, he challenges Frank and Jack simultaneously. The stage direction is typically terse: '*Alarum. They fight, and Momford's side wins.*' This encounter must have been dramatic, with three fights conducted simultaneously. Tom's fight with the cudgel against the two swordsmen seems to have been at the centre of the action, as the King speaks to Tom first once it is concluded, asking him his name, calling him a lusty fellow and noting that 'we have too few such subjects in our Land'.

The spectacle of the downright countryman with a staff defeating two swordsmen may seem far-fetched. However, the quarterstaff could be a highly efficient weapon in the hands of a trained fighter. Cheap and convenient, a staff was a down-market weapon that could be surprisingly effective against swords. Indeed, George Silver argued that the staff, 'by reason of its nimbleness and length', could have the advantage 'against two sword and dagger men, or two Rapiers, poniards, and gaunlets'.[71] The length and lightness of the staff gives the 'staff-man' the advantage of distance: 'If he fight well, the staffe-man neuer striketh but at the head, and thrusteth presently vnder at the body; and if a blow be first made a thrust followeth; and if a thrust be first made a blow followeth.'[72] Rapiers in particular were quite heavy and cumbersome; their advantage was length, so a lighter longer weapon, even blunted, could easily gain the advantage over that weapon. In a stage fight the length and lightness of the weapon, which was managed by both hands, may certainly have stolen the show, the more so since the two armed opponents would have been made to look foolish by the speed and agility of the skilled 'staff-man'. The triumph of the plain-spoken country underdog with his staff had perennial appeal. Henslowe clearly attempted to capitalize on this popularity by commissioning two sequels to *The Blind Beggar*, now lost. Tom Strowde seems to have been the main draw: the second sequel is called the *Third Part of Tom Strowde*.[73]

It is in this context that we might take a fresh look at Edgar in *King Lear*. We tend to think of Edgar as part of the 'subplot', his adventures with his father happening in parallel with the main plot. But he is featured heavily on the quarto title page: 'with the unfortunate life of Edgar, sonne and heire to the Earle of Gloucester, and his sullen and assumed humor of Tom of Bedlam', suggesting that 'when the play was first staged Edgar was seen as a much more prominent role than Edmund'.[74] Today Edgar is probably better considered a puzzle or a problem than a drawing card; Foakes notes that 'Edmund offers a more satisfying part for a modern actor than the role of Edgar'; modern productions often cast Edmund as 'suavely intelligent' in contrast to the 'bumbling, even stupid' Edgar.[75] Modern actors looking for a through-line for their character are apt to be stymied by Edgar, whose bewildering array of disguises and accents, as well as his cryptic rationales for his actions, resist easy explanation.

The reference to Edgar's 'sullen and assumed humours' indicates that, as in many early modern plays, it was his *variety* that appealed to playgoers. Particularly popular, I argue, would have been his defeat of Oswald in 4.5, a scene that has attracted only limited attention.[76] Oswald has already distinguished himself by his lack of fighting ability in 2.2. After insulting him thoroughly, Kent challenges Oswald:

> KENT Draw, you rascal … . Draw, you rogue, or I'll so carbonado your shanks! – draw, you rascal, come your ways.
> OSWALD Help, ho! Murder, help!
> KENT Strike, you slave. Stand, rogue, stand, you neat slave, strike! [*Beats him*].
> OSWALD Help, ho! Murder, murder! (2.2.34–8)

While no explicit stage directions are provided, Kent's repetition of 'draw', 'stand', 'strike', interspersed with Oswald's frantic calls for help, clearly indicates a comic scene, in which Kent, weapon drawn, pursues the terrified Oswald across the stage, to the point that he is 'scarce in breath' (51). When asked for his account, Oswald begins, 'This ancient ruffian, sir, whose life I have spared at suit of his grey beard' (2.2.61–2), rekindling Kent's wrath 'that such a slave as this should wear a sword, / Who wears no honesty' (2.2.70–1).

This view of Oswald as a sycophantic social climber wearing a weapon above his station informs our view of him in 4.6, when he discovers Gloucester, 'the proclaimed prize'. Edgar is by now in another disguise, dressed in the clothing the Old Man apparently brought to him (as promised in 4.1.52). Afraid to draw his sword to fight Kent, Oswald does not hesitate to wield it to threaten the old blind Gloucester: 'the sword is out / That must destroy thee' (4.6.225). When Edgar intercedes, he says:

> Wherefore, bold peasant,
> Dar'st thou support a published traitor? Hence,
> Lest that th'infection of his fortune take
> Like hold on thee. Let go his arm. (4.6.227–30)

It is only at this point that Edgar assumes his countryman accent, 'another verbal disguise, as a West Country yokel, using what for dramatists of the period was the more or less standard dialect'.[77] This dialect, coupled with his dress, sharpens the distinction between the upstart courtier and the downright fellow. The fighting methods further underline the contrast, when Edgar says 'I'se try whether your costard or my baton be the harder. Chi'll be plain with you' (4.6.237–8). Edgar here reveals himself as a 'staff-man' like Tom Strowd. Part of his peasant disguise might well have been a staff; as James Cockborn notes in his research on early modern violence, 'Travellers in the sixteenth and early seventeenth centuries routinely carried ... swords, daggers and knives, but also pikestaffs or cudgels.'[78] The quarto stage direction reads 'They fight', but attention to the skill of the actors, the nuances of status in pitting staff against rapier and affordances of the two weapons indicate that the fight between Oswald and Edgar may well have been staged as a *tour de force* almost as satisfying to the audience as the elaborately formal challenge between Edmund and Edgar later in the play. Edgar's lines 'I'll pick your teeth, zir. Come, no matter vor your foins' (4.6.240–1) signal the contempt of the skilled fighter for the flourishes of the showy yet inept fencer (in this, Edgar recalls Mercutio's contempt for Tybalt's fancy Spanish ways). The *OED* defines 'foins' as thrusts with a pointed weapon. If Edgar has skill with a staff, such thrusts would indeed have been of 'no matter' to him. Armed with a light and long weapon, and matched against an opponent who probably chose his rapier for its fashionable rather than its fighting qualities, Edgar can easily best Oswald. It is simply a matter of staying out of the distance of the thrust and employing Silver's recommended combination of blows to the head and thrusts to the body. The staff, handled nimbly, can easily make a rapier look cumbersome and heavy, since its principal advantage of length is neutered. The relative mobility and strength afforded by the staff makes the defeat of Oswald reasonably easy, although exactly how the death-blow is given is not entirely clear. As Foakes suggests, some productions have Edgar disarm Oswald and thrust him with his own rapier or dagger, which has the advantage of providing more plausible cover for Oswald's five-line death speech and could incidentally show Edgar's skill with rapier as well as staff. But the staff could easily have been a lethal weapon in itself.

Edgar's fighting skills are of course further demonstrated by the trial by combat in Act 5, in which the fighting takes place in what Edelman describes as a 'neo-medieval' register. Edgar is in armour and thus disguised again, although Edmund can detect his status nevertheless: 'thy outside looks so fair and warlike / And that thy tongue some say of breeding breathes' (5.3.140–1). After the fight, Albany tells him that 'thy very gait did prophesy / A royal nobleness' (5.3.173–4). Similar to the Oswald encounter, the stage direction reads only '*They Fight.*' As Foakes suggests, 'This bare direction does not mean that the fight is perfunctory; there is a stage tradition of making it a strenuous and extended encounter between two strong adversaries, Edgar winning with difficulty.'[79] Edgar is fighting here in a completely different idiom than his fight with Oswald; if the combatants are armed, they are likely fighting with longswords, possibly with short swords and daggers.[80] Heavy and cumbersome, a longsword is used two-handed and demands a completely different kinetic style than the light and nimble quarterstaff.

These two fights help us see how physical the role of Edgar

is. Yet not merely physical: it demands an extraordinarily high level of kinesic intelligence to animate the array of characters Edgar must embody. When he awkwardly draws his rapier at Edmund's hurried request, when he confronts Oswald with his staff, when he defeats Edmund at a formal trial by combat, each of these moments demands an entirely different kinesic style, a style again completely removed from the demands of playing poor, mad Tom. Reading Edgar through the lens of skill helps us to recapture the reasons that he receives such high billing on the Quarto title page.

'Skill of weapon' is much more complex than may first appear. Although Edelman is no doubt right that audiences had a sophisticated sporting eye for good fencing, this is a relatively narrow lens through which to view early modern stage combat. In the early modern period, weapons are viewed as extensions of the self, and whether or not characters show 'ready aptnesse' with a sword or cudgel reveals how their 'belonging and identity are ... incorporated and embodied through this disciplined training', in Ryan's words.[81] Spectators would have been adept at judging what counted as a good fight, to be sure, but equally they could read the character through the command (or lack thereof) of the weapon, the more so when a character such as Edgar is fluent in multiple styles. More importantly, perhaps, fencing trained mindful bodies, demanding cunning, vigilance, timing, command of space, memory, anticipation and coordination. When Simon Jewell incurred a debt of nine pounds to fencing masters, he was not simply investing in self-defence or techniques to impress the punters; he was also learning a way of being in the world – as well as a way of being on stage in concert with others. Like dancing, the subject of the next chapter, fencing on stage involved exquisite coordination with one or more fellow actors, and the stakes of an error were much higher. Swordplay on stage involved embodying passion whilst staying in control: carefully timed coordination and mutual modulation of movement whilst maintaining multiple levels of consciousness. Staged combat involves representing one set of intentions to an audience whilst simultaneously communicating an entirely different set to one's stage partner(s). The art of fighting, then, and the long regimes of training that underpin it, becomes in itself a mode of rehearsal and preparation for the fast-moving, high-stakes, mindfully embodied practice of making theatre, especially in the time-pressured environment in which early modern actors performed.

4

The Art of Dance

What are the forms of writing that will allow us to
hold the moving body? The moving body is always
fading from our eyes. Historical bodies and bodies
moving on stage fascinate us because they fade.

PEGGY PHELAN[1]

Dance, the first of the qualities in Gainsford's list of the accomplishments of the player, is closely linked to 'actiuitie, musicke' and 'song'. Its connection to 'actiuitie', or feats of physical skill similar to gymnastics and tumbling, reminds us of the highly virtuosic nature of dance in this period. Linked to the divine, built upon frameworks of antithesis, contrast, rhythm and harmony and demanding extraordinary dedication and continual practice, in the early modern period dance laid claim to the pinnacle of human achievement. No skill in the period was as sought-after, as visible and as freighted with moral, social and ethical significance. These qualities placed peculiar demands upon the early modern player, the more so as the dances functioned both within the fiction of the playworld and as an act of dance *qua* dance.[2]

Dance also laid claim to be the most mindful of skills, both producing and revealing the kinesic intelligence of the dancer. In manuals and conduct books, dance functioned as both an inherent marker of status and a means of aspiring to that status.[3] The authors of treatises on dance, as with the writers of other manuals of skilled action, use a range of strategies to legitimate their practice. These include long lists of allusions to ancient classical approval of dance, scriptural citations, the healthfulness of dance as a means of moderate and wholesome exercise, and the connection of dance to the liberal arts by way of music. As Jennifer Nevile notes in *The Eloquent Body*:

> The dance practice of the elite section of *quattrocento* Italian society had an intellectual and philosophical framework: it was not just a set of physical skills. The dance masters were fully aware that for dance to be included (through its association with music) in the liberal arts, it had to be understood both on a physical level and at an intellectual level.[4]

Nevile uses the term 'corporeal eloquence' to describe the combination of natural ability and the trained body that was so prized by authors of dance treatises in the humanist tradition. Far more than simply knowing steps was necessary: the eloquent dancer 'had to possess a thorough understanding of the interaction between the music and the dance, the ability to adapt the patterns of each dance to the space available, the wit and invention to subtly vary each step so that it was not performed the same way several times in a row, a knowledge of movements of the body which accompanied many of the steps, an awareness of the phrasing of each step, and the agility and "bodily quickness" to carry them out'.[5] The kinesic intelligence honed by training in dance was tightly linked to that fostered through the mastery of gesture, horsemanship and fencing, a kind of conduit of mindful movement encompassing mind, body and environment.

In one of the earliest Italian dance manuals, written in 1468, the master Guglielmo Ebreo labours to differentiate true 'spiritual' dancing from its misuse at the hands of 'vile and rude mechanicals who often, with corrupt souls and treacherous minds, turn it from a liberal art and virtuous science into something adulterous and ignoble'.[6] Guglielmo claims dance as a liberal art through its kinship with music, which in turn links it to the 'movement of the soul':

> This virtue of the dance is simply an outward manifestation of the movements of the soul, which must accord with the measured and perfect consonances of that harmony which, through our hearing, moves down with delight to our intellect and our affections.[7]

Such views were commonplace in early modern theories of dance and reach back to antiquity, including Plato's discussion of the 'figures of the [heavenly bodies] circling as in dance'[8] and Lucian's aetiology of dance as having 'come into being contemporaneously with the primal origin of the universe ... the concord of the heavenly spheres, the interlacing of the errant planets with the fixed stars, their rhythmic agreement and timed harmony, are proofs that the Dance was primordial'.[9] These views are given English expression by Sir Thomas Elyot in *The Boke of the Governour* and Sir John Davies's poem *Orchestra*, as well as in Ben Jonson's masques. As Nevile notes, Elyot's prolonged defence of dance is integral to his humanist project: dance is crucial to the 'civilising educational program of the humanists ... knowledge of and skill in dance became a sign of education and intellectual ability'.[10] Dance is not simply an accomplishment like any other; instead, 'the orderly and structured movements of courtly dancing facilitate self-control and virtuous thoughts in young men and women'.[11] Anne Daye argues that 'the moral value of dancing in the Renaissance was inseparable from the discipline of technique'.[12] As Kate Van Orden suggests in the context of early modern France, dance is linked to other mindful, rhythmic, ordered practices such as the martial arts; she notes that the labour needed to master such practices shows that 'understanding how rhythm was believed to affect the body and its passions makes possible a more pointed analysis of dance as a moral practice relevant to the civilizing process'.[13]

Like treatises on gesture, dance manuals distinguish between dancing by nature and dancing by art. Spontaneous dancing can result from the inevitable and natural synchrony that results from human beings moving together in time.[14] But Guglielmo argues that the true artist of dance displays a 'keen intelligence' as a 'clear sign of good practice and of adroitness and of unconstrained mastery of his body and his foot'. This mastery can be tested through a variety of increasingly different exercises, including attempts to draw the dancer out of time, which the experienced dancer counters by remaining 'so alert and adroit that he never allows himself to go or to be drawn out of time in any way'.[15]

Dancing is above all a mindful practice. The discipline needed to master the steps and to coordinate body, mind and the social world successfully, as must be done by the artful dancer, involves a fusion of on-line and off-line thinking. Guglielmo defines a 'perfect memory' for a dancer as 'collecting one's thoughts and paying careful attention to the measured and concordant music so that if it should in any way change, either slowing or quickening, whoever has begun to dance need not be scorned for his lack of forethought or want of memory'.[16] This view of memory is fluid and intelligent. The novice dancer may betray the effort of remembering, counting under his breath; in contrast, the skilled dancer does not learn by rote, as a hedge priest mumbles Latin prayers, but possesses an active intelligence, perhaps akin to the vigilance that Gainsford ascribes to players, that enables her to modulate movements and adapt to changing conditions. The sort of situation awareness – what Christensen, Sutton and McIlwain describe as a 'mesh' of automatic and mindful knowledge – allows skilled dancers to subtly and on the fly adjust their memorized movements to changing circumstances such as new musicians or an inexpert partner. Domenico Pietropaolo compares this capacity to the rhetorical concept of '"fluency of rehandling" … the ability to treat the same point extempore from a variety of perspectives by making quick and clever use of arguments and turns of phrase'.[17]

Mastering dance, then, involved a highly prized and difficult to achieve combination of control, synchrony, discipline, variety and improvisation, which demanded on-the-fly intelligence. As Julia Sutton notes, 'two closely related principles – improvisation and variation – pervade all the dance manuals of the period, including Caroso's'.[18] The would-be dancer was first to learn basic step patterns and then, building upon this foundation, learn 'as many variants upon them as he can, and use them at appropriate moments when and how he chooses'.[19] The principle of chunking helps to explain how 'skilled amateur dancers can remember long series of dance variations, provided they consist of familiar steps and patterns'.[20] Building upon simple familiar patterns allows long complex dances to be remembered, and particularly experienced amateur dancers would also have the physical and mental foundations – reserves of skill and thought – necessary to carry out impressive improvisations as well.

Improvisation was valued across the arts in Renaissance Europe, in disciplines including rhetoric, theatre, musical performance and song, and dance. While today improvisation classes eschew any sort of pre-planned performances and rely entirely upon unscripted response (although clearly one can discern conventions and patterns within the genre), improvisation in the medieval and the early modern period involved mastering and building upon highly patterned foundations: 'improvisation in this period would be inconceivable without rigid constraints'.[21] As Pietropaolo notes, 'improvisation took chiefly the form of imaginative embellishment and variation within the horizon of expectations that surrounded each dance as determined by the style, music, and tradition'.[22] Anne Daye suggests that 'the Renaissance dancer was not only expected to have a high level of skill but also an ability to invent his or her own sequences of steps'. Achieving this level of expertise demanded 'a sound intellectual grasp of the structure of each dance and its music in order to construct their own variations.

They also needed a large repertoire of steps.'[23] Improvisation took place, then, within an ecology of attention and training, for it took a skilled audience to appreciate the nuances of any such act, recognizing the baseline performance and its imaginative and idiosyncratic embellishments. Thus improvisation is an embodied form of wit, linking 'vigilancy' and embodied skills such as dance and 'activitie'.[24]

Much recent research on elite dance has drawn attention to the exacting demands of dancing at this level of skill. Ravelhofer has documented the enormous amount of labour and practice it took to attain such expertise. To master the intricate steps and patterns, and to learn new fashionable dances such as one might perform at a masque, required countless hours of practice. For the *Masque of Oberon*, dancing masters were paid for 'peyns [pains] bestowed almost 6, weekes continually'[25] and both Charles I and Henrietta Maria practised for five hours a day. Nevile similarly discusses the long practice periods undertaken by amateur aristocratic dancers who wished to showcase their skill on the occasions of weddings or other events. Mastering and performing new dances was seen as a means of acquiring 'honour and fame', as the dance master Fillipus Bussus wrote to the prospective bride of Lorenzo de'Medici.[26] These are extreme cases, as the masque and other elaborate court performances were forms of conspicuous consumption not just of costume and scenery but also of time.

The early modern court gentleman or lady could not dance as if no one was looking; looking indeed was built into the dance form. The distinction between social and theatrical dancing is a blurry one indeed in this period; Julia Sutton argues that in Caroso's manual 'the importance given to the onlookers' opinion of the dancers' style and bearing tend to support a theory that one couple at a time was expected to dance before the others at a ball, thus incorporating a theatrical element into a ballroom situation'.[27] The pitiless social, evaluative gaze is inherent to courtly dance, accounting for the extraordinary hours of practice put into the form. Nevile shows that dancing was not simply an occasional event; rather, the skilled dancer was seen to literally incorporate the dignity and virtue of his or her class:

> The rules and postural codes of courtly dance were part of the mechanisms by which the court made itself appear superior and inaccessible to the rest of society. The courtiers believed that their superiority should be demonstrated to the rest of society by the different way in which they moved, walked, danced, and even stood in repose. Their carriage and demeanour when on the dance floor did not change once they finished dancing; it remained with them, as it was their normal posture. Dancing taught people control over their bodies and over all their actions, both when dancing and in day-to-day interactions with their colleagues and superiors.[28]

Poor dancing could uniquely single one out for ridicule, as Castiglione notes in *The Courtier* when 'Messer Pierpaolo' is skewered for betraying the labour behind his performance: 'Who is there among you who doesn't laugh when our Pierpaolo dances in that way of his, with those little jumps and with his legs stretched on tiptoe, keeping his head motionless, as if he were made of wood, and all so laboured that he seems to be counting every step?'[29] In an economy of performance in which *sprezzatura* is valued above all, the worst sin is to betray one's effort; counting out steps is the surest sign that the practice is not yet sedimented into the body. Castiglione contrasts Pierpaolo's laboured steps with the company at Urbino who display 'that graceful and nonchalant spontaneity (as it is often called) because of which they seem to be paying little, if any, attention to the way they speak or laugh or hold themselves, so that those who are watching them imagine that they couldn't and wouldn't ever know how to make a mistake'.[30]

Left behind the scenes in Castiglione's account is the precise means of acquiring those skills, the endless hours of training

and shaping of the body needed to produce the trained
body. While we think of the *sprezzatura*, or the 'art to cover
art', as simply a façade or cover (and it can be), true *sprezzatura* can only be gained by practice so that the act looks
fluid, natural and easy. Dance seems to have been viewed
as a virtually flawless window through which breeding and
elegance could be descried. Elegance in dancing necessitated
finding a middle way between graceful display and unnecessary showiness. Castiglione warns that too much virtuosity
might compromise one's 'dignitie', and 'that swiftnesse of
feete and doubled footings [are] unseemley for a gentleman'.[31]
Similarly Montaigne suggests that showiness simply covers
the lack of innate grace: 'just as at our balls these men of low
condition who keep dancing schools, not being able to imitate
the bearing and fitness of our nobility, seek to recommend
themselves by perilous leaps and other strange mountebanks
antics'. For Montaigne, the most difficult feat was to exhibit
natural grace: 'And the ladies can more cheaply show off their
carriage in the dances where there are various contortions
and twistings of the body, than in certain other formal dances
where they need only walk with a natural step and display a
natural bearing and their ordinary grace.'[32] Just as it is difficult
to walk across the stage, so simple 'natural' steps such as the
pavan expose the true grace – or lack thereof – of the dancer
in a way that showier forms do not.

In Anne Daye's discussion of her reconstruction of
Renaissance amateur dancing she concludes that:

> nimble footwork, good balance, and precise musicality
> was a requisite for even the simplest ballroom dance. In
> some dances, long sequences of steps had to be memorized,
> and a command of the dancing space was essential. In
> everything, a dignified and graceful bearing had to be
> mastered.[33]

Moreover, the stakes were high, as individual dancers and
couples had to be seamlessly integrated into the overall

pattern: 'Before each dance could be performed the courtiers had to memorize its individual sequence of steps and the places where the *misura* changed, as well as its floor patterns. A lapse in memory or other error by one dancer would cause the whole structure to disintegrate.'[34] Van Orden notes the similarity between the arts of fencing and dance in this respect: 'Both arts sensitized the student to the slightest gestures of others, taught them to judge their proximity to dance partners or fencing opponents, and gave them mastery of their physical surroundings.'[35] The exquisite coordination between partners and groups demanded by these disciplines was also a critical component of the kinesic intelligence of the trained player, who perforce needed to constantly modulate his actions within the performance space and in negotiation with the other actors.

Obviously long rehearsal sessions were needed to master new dances such as those that would impress spectators at a special occasion such as a wedding or a court masque. But such dances were only the top layer of skill, the icing, so to speak. Behind these top-level, highly rehearsed skill displays was a lifetime of training. Dancers had to start young if they were to have any hope at all of acquiring the level of elegance and grace that would seem natural. Those who tried to master such skills later in life found the physical and mental demands beyond them. Such was the experience of Albrecht Dürer, who wrote, 'I set to work to learn dancing and twice went to the school. There I had to pay the master a ducat. Nobody could make me go there again. I would have to pay out all that I have earned, and at the end I still wouldn't know how to dance.'[36]

The dancers discussed so far are at the pinnacle of the art, having begun training early and possessing the financial and other resources to devote a large percentage of their time to the art. Lying between these accomplished amateurs and novices like Dürer beginning late in life were a vast number of those of somewhat more humble station, who were nevertheless eager to master basic social dancing to secure advancement or simply to avoid ridicule. In England, rival dancing masters attempted to take advantage of this large market. As Brissenden notes, a petition for monopoly in 1574 sought to establish licensed schools:

> [T]here has late been a great increase in the number of dancing-schools established; these have been conducted by persons unqualified both by their knowledge and their morals, and have been set up in suspect places, to which the most lewd persons resort. The Queen is particularly anxious to suppress those who under the pretence of good exercise entice the young to exercise lewd behavior.[37]

Schools were set up not only in London, but also in the provinces, as Christopher Marsh has documented, although we often hear of them only when they run afoul of civic authorities.[38]

What happened in such dancing schools is known only through scattered references, as the nativist rivalry that sparked George Silver's minute description of Italianate fencing schools in London – unfortunately for later generations of historians – was not replicated among dance masters. The popularity of such schools as entertainment for spectators is shown in the pamphlet *Newes from the North* (1579), which describes the reactions of 'Pierce Plowman' to contemporary London.[39] As a visitor to London from the country, Pierce is taken to see 'some pleasures of the city that were strange and noveltie to those of us from the Cuntrie', amongst which was a dancing school. The companions watch a dancer perform a galliard 'trick': 'wunderfully he leaped, flung and took on', so much so that a deaf man watching took him for a madman and tried to seize him by the arms; a fracas ensued.[40]

Parodic depictions in plays also provide some sense of what may have gone on at dancing schools. The difficulty of remembering dances – the demands on memory of the intricate patterns of court dancing – is satirized in John Marston's *The Malcontent*. A dancing master explains the 'easy' steps to the 'brawl': 'Why, 'tis but two on the left, two on the right, three doubles forward, a traverse of six round; do this twice, three singles side, galliard trick-of-twenty, coranto-pace; a figure of eight, three singles broken down, come up, meet two doubles, fall back, and then honor.'[41] In discussing this passage, Emily Winerock observes that 'the stage directions suggest that the other courtiers dance the steps as Guarino describes. Having attempted to reconstruct this dance, I can confirm the impossibility of dancing the named steps in the time allotted. However, the spastic and abbreviated results if one tries are hilarious for the audience.'[42]

Dancing instruction is often satirized in seventeenth-century plays, especially Caroline comedies about the newly fashionable West End London. As Jean Howard has shown, the dancing master figures in a number of these plays, including James Shirley's *The Ball* (Monsieur LeFriske), as well as Richard Brome's *The City Wit* (Footwell) and *The New Academy* (Lightfoot).[43] Howard argues that scenes of dancing instruction in these plays demonstrate 'the effort necessary to school bodies into proper dancing postures and serving to separate those who can attain mastery of these skills from those who cannot – in effect creating a new kind of social distinction based on the ability to conform to French standards of bodily control'.[44] Shirley targets attempts by dancing masters to mould their aristocratic clients into the upright stance that marked the French fashion. Monsieur LeFriske admonishes his student to 'aller, aller, looke up your Countenance, your *English man* spoile you, he no teach You looke up, pishaw, carry your body in the swimming fashion'.[45] As Ravelhofer notes, although these lines are parody, 'they may give us a feeling for practical issues during masque rehearsals',[46] the more so since injunctions to 'look up' are extremely common in sport and dance practice of all sorts. As novices begin to master any complex skill involving training the body in unfamiliar ways, it is almost impossible not to look at the body part(s) being trained – are the feet doing what they are supposed to? But where the eyes go, the rest of the body follows, so looking down results in a hunched, unbalanced inelegant posture, a far cry from the elegant, upright 'swimming' posture associated with expert dancing. Jean Howard's argument that comedies such as *The Ball* served to 'adumbrate new standards of mannerly conduct and bodily deportment for West End audiences' convincingly accounts for the highly focalized interest in comedy of this era in wit, grace and fashionable bodies, as inherited from Ben Jonson's acute analysis of city social climbing.[47]

It is tempting to simply unmask the discourse around courtly dance, exposing the ideological dimensions of the rhetoric around links between cosmic harmony and elite dance. This is the approach taken by Skiles Howard's influential account of dance in the period, *The Politics of Courtly Dancing in Early Modern England*, in which she relates courtly dancing 'to the material practices of writing and civility, one that regulated and socialized the activities of the nether limbs as writing transformed the signifying hand and civility re-presented the body'.[48] She traces a Foucauldian-inflected history of the dance, in which the art moves from a 'spontaneous response to sexual, seasonal, or religious impulse' to a form akin to a 'forensic oration ... classically authorized, codified, rehearsed, and devised to control response'.[49] While acknowledging that courtly dance might be 'pleasurable', Howard suggests that undergoing the discipline of dance produced Foucault's '"docile" body ... "manipulated, shaped, trained"': 'the dancer was forced to maintain a relationship of "constant coercion" with himself that inscribed a contradiction between self- and social empowerment'.[50] In this view, the body of the dancer is operated upon, fragmented 'at the level of the mechanism itself – movements, gestures, attitudes, rapidity: an infinitesimal power over the active body'.[51] Courtly dancing is linked to an Althusserian 'state apparatus', and 'the dancing body was, foremost, a signifier'.[52]

The connections among dance, gender and power are undeniably crucial to understanding this elite practice. But reducing dance to a Foucauldian inscription of power neglects the element of skill and training, the pleasures as well as the pains attendant upon shaping the body, remembering and

mastering choreography and adjusting on-the-fly in real time
to one's partner, the space and the musicians. The complexities
of such embodied and extended skills are explored in detail
by Ravelhofer, who challenges this dominant model, noting
that it has become 'critical commonplace that choreographic
codification constrains individual self-expression'.[53]

The idea that constraints are stultifying – that, in
Skiles Howard's trajectory, dance moves from a 'spontaneous response' to a coercive power imposed from above
– is widespread. Yet constraints enable creativity. The value
placed upon improvisation depends upon mastering and then
overgoing a set of codified practices: 'subversion – in the sense
of creative interpretation – is integral to formalism itself'.[54]
As Ravelhofer astutely notes, 'The human body is singularly
fond of formalisms. If they are not imposed, it will invent
them ... when an external code is imposed on a body engaged
in formalisms of its own, it invites reaction. It may provoke
resistance or creative appropriation.'[55] The view of courtly
dance as a kind of zero-sum power-game ignores the kinesic
intelligence of the dancer, who trains his body for ends that
are not entirely subsumed by others:

> Depending on the dancer's will and ability, the body
> becomes an army, orchestra, elaborate toy, or clockwork,
> whose perfectly attuned movements infuse an individual
> with a sense of control ... . The body's precise, beautiful
> motions are a bulwark against the chaos outside.[56]

Dance can provide both a measure of individual control –
'performance can work like an empowering drug'[57] – as well
as the pleasures of mastering synchronicity and temporality,
of 'keeping together in time', in the phrase of William H.
McNeill.[58] Exposing the ideological underpinnings of such
practices is important work, but the danger is the erasure of
the intelligence of the body.

Michael Kimmel's careful study of the *tango argentino*
as an 'embodied conversation' provides a potentially

illuminating analogue to the practice of courtly dance.[59] Obviously the two practices have enormous differences, as one would predict from any culturally embedded practice. However, *tango argentino* and courtly dancing hold in common the qualities of 'complexity and rigor', 'elegance, expressive quality, and creative potential'.[60] Kimmel analyses the tango through the lens of distributed cognition, noting the interplay of careful patterning and improvisation that marks expert practice: 'dancers need to be trained over years to work quickly, in proper form, whilst maintaining improvisational creativity'.[61] While not choreographed in the way that courtly dances were, *tango argentino* nevertheless 'imposes a strict form on creative expression'.[62] Motion principles are carefully defined, if not always directly articulated; however, expert dancers have a strong sense of what sort of movements are 'un-tango-like'.[63] A tango body is 'upright and in axial alignment without bending; the "outer" muscles move around a relatively fixed and strong body core; weight distribution must be clear at all times; weight falls on the forefoot … oblique steps are off-limits'.[64] So improvisation, only available to adept and experienced dancers, must take place within this embodied framework. Success in the tango depends upon 'elaborate, culturally shaped co-regulation skills as are found in dance, martial arts, sports, healing practice, horseback riding, and so on … . Expert-level co-regulation skills take years to learn.'[65]

Tango is less choreographed and more dependent upon the dyad than is courtly dancing, which does not employ a leader–follower model. But the two forms share technical rigour and an attention to bodily techniques and carriage. As Ravelhofer notes, 'In a rare consensus, early modern theorists shared the belief that the more animated and gesticulatory a performance, the more histrionic and undignified it was.'[66] Eloquence of body revealed eloquence of mind: 'Elegant movements … involved a fluidity and flexibility in the dancer's body so that her or his rising and falling throughout the length of a step was always controlled.'[67] The recommendation to

achieve bodily control in dance was a commonplace in the
advice literature:

> I will not praise those Ordinarie Dauncers, who appeare
> to be drunke in their legs ... in shaking alwaies their feet,
> singing continaullie, one-two-three: foure: & five. When
> you go to Daunce in anie Honourable companie, take
> heede that your qualitie, your Raiment, and your skil go
> al three togither: if you faile in anie of those three, you wil
> be derided. Imitate not so much the Masters Capers, as to
> haue a good grace in the carriage of your bodie; this is the
> principal, and without the which al the rest is naught.[68]

So to dance well was not simply to master a few basic steps,
as anxious Inns of Court students hoped to do in mastering
the standard 'measures' that underpinned social dance.[69] It is
to master a way of being in the world, a way of social coordination and movement through space. All of the movement
arts that actors had to master – gesture, walking, swordplay
and dance – are intimately linked to the development of a
distinctive kinesic intelligence that could on the one hand
emulate the elite and on the other hand descry a range of
postures, body types and social classes.

Reading through the lens of skill: Dancing in *A Midsummer Night's Dream* and *Much Ado About Nothing*

Dancing is mentioned or called for relatively frequently in
early modern drama. Dessen and Thomson note that the stage
direction *dance* is 'widely used' (almost 350 examples),[70] a
few shy of the 380 directions calling upon actors to fight.
Many of these are simply terse calls such as in *Romeo and
Juliet*: '*Musick playes and they dance*' (Q2 *RJ* C3r; 1.5.25).
Others call for a wide range of dancing expertise: '*Dance to*

music of Cornets and Violins' (*English Moor*, 16); '*dance a short nimble Antic to no music*' (*Landgartha*, E4v); '*dances the Spanish pavin*' (*Blurt*, 1.1.158); '*Dances Sellenger's round, or the like*' (*Court Beggar*, 262); and '*dancing a Coranto*' (*Duke's Mistress*, F4r). Still others indicate the quality of the dancing, as in '*Dances looking on his Feet*' (*Court Beggar*, 261) or '*dances vilely*' (*English Moor*, 67). Other references, sometimes in the form of parody or apology, reveal the many moments of interstitial or paratextual dances: between the acts in the indoor theatres, after the performance in the amphi-theatres. The Citizen's Wife in *Knight of the Burning Pestle* calls attention to the skill of the boy who dances: 'But look, look! Here's a youth dances. – Now good youth, do a turn of the toe' (1.1.470). The same boy 'danceth' at the end of Act 4, at which point the Wife notes that he 'capers' and asks for 'a turn of the toe, and then tumble. Cannot you tumble, youth?' (3.1.618–20). Such meta-theatrical references call attention to performances that otherwise go unremarked and undocu-mented in the playtexts. As Tiffany Stern notes:

> Though published plays often have a 'finished' appearance, they will be shown regularly to be missing some of those sections written for manifestation in the theatre but also lost there, which might extend from prologues to epilogues to songs to choruses to interim entertainments to internal masques to Arguments to playbill lures as well as other paper witnesses of the text.[71]

As with all sorts of stage action, the extant directions represent a fraction of what may have occurred on stage. The call for dancing in *Midsummer Night's Dream* at the conclusion of the wild night in the woods seemingly reveals relatively little. After removing the charm from Titania's eyes, Oberon says:

> Sound, music! Come my queen, take hands with me,
> And rock the ground whereon these sleepers be
> Now thou and I are new in amity,

And will tomorrow midnight solemnly,
Dance in Duke Theseus' house triumphantly,
And bless it to all fair prosperity. (4.1.84–6)

The directions are implied: it is not clear exactly when Oberon
and Titania dance, nor how long the dance lasts. Most likely
the dance is concluded before the line 'Now thou and I are
new in amity', since this line indicates that the dance does not
simply represent but actively brings about the reconciliation
between the couple. Brissenden reads the passage through
the lens of Elyot's assertion that dance between a man and
a women 'holding each other by the hand or the arm ...
betokeneth concord'.[72] Skiles Howard's view is much more
sceptical, and she emphasizes the coercive patriarchal nature
of the request to dance:

> [Oberon] however, has declined to dance 'patiently' in a
> round but instead offers his hand in a gesture that immedi-
> ately defines the kind of dance he has in mind – the couple
> dance, which served as an icon of gendered comportment:
> 'Come, my queen,' he orders, 'take hands with me' ...
> Oberon's invitation to 'rock the ground' effectively specifies
> a courtly dance, one that rejects the linked hands of the
> group and privileges the dexterous feet of the individual,
> which tap out intricate rhythms.[73]

While Brissenden suggests that the dance to rock the ground
is designed to 'ensure that the lovers and Bottom sleep well
and wake refreshed',[74] Howard sees it instead as a form of
masculine entitlement which symbolizes 'the subordination of
popular culture to a patriarchal elite'.[75]

How shall we find the concord of this discord? Apart from
the textual evidence that they join hands, there is no clear guide
to how the dance is performed, and contemporary productions
will rightly choose an approach in keeping with their vision
of the play. But while dancing is undeniably embedded in
multiple structures of power, viewing this moment as entirely

symbolic neglects both the skill of the dancers and the effect of the dance upon the audience. As Claire Hansen argues, 'This dance not only symbolises but also *enacts* the couple's structural reunification. Further, it does more than revert the couple to an earlier state of unity: in reuniting they are not the same but, as Oberon says, "are new" (4.1.86) versions of themselves.'[76]

Skilled dancing can introduce an alternative temporality into the playworld. Control over temporality – over the delicate balance between stillness and movement – was essential to skilled dancing. As Jennifer Nevile writes, the concept of *fantasmata* was widely discussed in dancing treatises. Fantasmata is a moment of 'cessation of movement [and] time':

[A]ll normal movement had to be suspended; that is, the movement of the dancer's legs forwards, backwards, or sideways ... . It was all these 'normal' movements that signalled the passage of time to those watching. When these movements were suspended or frozen, then time itself seemed as if it were also suspended, to be resumed when the dancer entered into the next step in a light and airy manner.[77]

As Nevile notes, the term 'fantasmata' evokes the liminal period between dream and waking: 'the fifteenth-century dancer's application of this grace had to be so subtle, so light, the moment of repose so quick as to seem almost insubstantial, almost as if it were just a dream'.[78]

At this point in the play, the stage is populated by sleepers – Hermia, Helena, Demetrius, Lysander and Bottom all lie sleeping, their stillness and regular breathing in marked contrast to the frenetic movement of the previous two acts. The audience has been hard at work following the flurry of entrances and exits of the four young lovers. As performed by skilled dancers, this moment of stillness in the play – just before the entrance of Theseus marked by the harsh noise of hunting horns – can have a profound effect upon the audience, changing the experience of temporality and working as a liminal space between states of consciousness. Such a phenomenon might be understood as a form of 'entrainment', acting to synchronize actors and audience in 'temporally coordinated actions' which, as will be discussed further in the final chapter, Robert Shaughnessy has discussed in a recent article on the context of the rebuilt Shakespeare's Globe. Shaughnessy refers to Daniël Lakens's statement that 'temporally coordinated actions are a fundamental feature of connectedness and mutual responsiveness in social interaction'.[79]

Such moments of entrainment may work both within and without the fictional framework; dances such as those at the end of *Midsummer* seem to have a sort of apotropaic function. Within the fiction the fairies form a ring: 'Hand in hand, with fairy grace, / Will we sing, and bless this place' (5.1.394–5). Grace has a complex meaning; the fairies perform gracefully, confer grace and their configuration recalls the Three Graces, which Brissenden describes as 'one of the more potent triadic images for the Renaissance ... they represented, among many ideas, the triple rhythm of generosity'.[80]

The circular formation is common to many kinds of dances, especially country dances, and is closely related to charms and to the supernatural. The circular dance of the witches in *Macbeth* is perhaps the best-known example of the use of music and dance by supernatural forces:

The Weird Sisters, hand in hand,
Posters of the sea and land,
Thus do go about, about;
Thrice to thine, and thrice to mine,
And thrice again, to make up nine
Peace! – the charm's wound up! (1.3.32–7)

The 'charm' is efficacious within the fiction, since it apparently seems to summon Macbeth and Banquo; performatively, as Lin suggests, a moment such as this is 'clearly experienced as powerfully *affective* in its ability to move theatregoers, physiologically and emotionally. It was thus also crucially *effective*.'[81] For these reasons, dancing in Shakespeare is not ornamentation or decoration, but is absolutely crucial to the embodied experience of the playgoer, as mediated by the skilled action of the player.

As a crucial mode of kinesic intelligence, dancing is also at the heart of the coordination characteristic of early modern playing. These are modes of what I would call kinesic habits of mind that result from training in disciplines such as dance and fencing, especially apparent in the interplay between coordination and antagonism that so often marks Shakespeare's drama. Such an interplay is pervasive in *Much Ado About Nothing* which, as numerous critics have noted, is deeply engaged with one of the best-known skill treatises of the early modern period: Castiglione's *Book of the Courtier*. Phillip Collington argues that *Much Ado* does not simply reflect Castiglione's text but instead offers a 'skeptical examination of the source's courtier-ideal',[82] a point also made by Stephen Greenblatt's discussion of *sprezzatura* in the play: it 'is pervasively concerned with social performance that seems at once spontaneous and calculated'.[83] *Much Ado* foregrounds the subject matter and the skills of courtiership and courtship: fashion, fence, dance, song and wit. These skills mingle and intersect in the play and are apparent not only at the level of theme and subject matter, but also in the interstices of the action, in the kinesic encounters of the actors.

The tight connections that Van Orden describes between highly mindful practices such as fencing and dance underpin these encounters. Famously Leonato describes the relationship between Beatrice and Benedick as 'a merry war ... they never meet but there's a skirmish of wit between them' (1.1.59–60). This is not as metaphorical as it might sound. The repartee between Beatrice and Benedick is a reworking of earlier battles of wits such as that between Petruchio and Katherine, and Richard and Lady Anne. These moments have in common an antagonistic relationship between a male and female character, a pattern of repetition and countering and a struggle to gain the upper hand. Lady Anne attempts to defeat Richard's language by ringing changes on it: 'Divine perfection of a woman ... diffused infection of a man'; 'Fairer than tongue can name thee ... fouler than heart can think thee.' Like a skilled fencer, however, Richard is leading Anne into his trap, using a series of feints and counterattacks to lure her in a discourse of his own making. Richard explicitly acknowledges the fencing frame when he attempts to alter the tempo and topic of their confrontation: 'But, gentle Lady Anne, / To leave this keen encounter of our wits / And fall something into a slower method' (1.2.118–20). The training in mastery of space, distance and tempo that fencing and dancing instil here functions as an embodied substratum of kinesic knowledge that informs the encounter between the two characters.[84]

The 'keen encounter' in *Much Ado* is a more equal battle of wits than the easy domination of Richard over Anne. Their sparring in the first scene, like that between Richard and Anne, is marked by repetition and play upon each other's language:

> BENEDICK Well, you are a rare parrot-teacher.
> BEATRICE A bird of my tongue is better than a beast of yours.
> BENEDICK I would my horse had the speed of your tongue, and so good a continuer. But keep your way, a God's name, I have done.
> BEATRICE You always end with a jade's trick, I know you of old. (1.132–9)

The 'battle' is conducted along the same lines as that in *Richard III* and *Taming*, but the skirmish ends inconclusively, with the two opponents apparently pausing to 'breathe' after their bout.

Beatrice and Benedick 'fight' their next bout in the dance, again showing the close kinship of these skilled practices. Dance is both a central theme and a central activity in the play: 'wooing, wedding and repenting is as a Scotch jig, a measure, and a cinque-pace' (2.1.65–6), Beatrice warns Hero.

Don John's alienation from the other characters is manifested both in his parsimony of speech and his lack of 'measure', or his deliberate refusal to fall in step with society. Dance as embodied wit – as an interplay of coordination and antagonism – is revealed most fully in the dance scene at the end of Act 2, Scene 1. Brissenden argues convincingly that the 'scene is structured so that the dialogue fits the movements of a dance … a pavan is the obvious choice for the dance Shakespeare had in mind, for in that elegant perambulation the couples can be side by side with hands linked at arm's length and the steps involve turns back and forth, retreats and advances, so that it is ideal for highlighting dramatic conversation'.[85] As discussed above, the pavan is a deceptively simply dance: slow and stately, it was said to reveal true grace of movement more than showier dances such as the coranto. The pace of the dance allows each pair to be showcased in turn, in an almost cinematic fashion. The male dancers are vizarded, but as might be predicted from the discussion on gait and gesture in Chapter 2, many are identifiable by some characteristic tic or movement. Ursula recognizes Anthony 'by the waggling of your head' (2.1.100), and Borachio identifies Claudio from his 'bearing' (2.1.142). As Brissenden notes, the first set of dancers follow a clear pattern of 'groups of essentially four exchanges of line per partner and a concluding sentence'.[86] This patterning and rhythmic exchange is disrupted at the entrance of the final couple. Beatrice views the dance as a continuation of the fencing match; her two long passages of prose insults cause Benedick to lose concentration and timing, as he implies when he complains of his treatment: 'huddling jest upon jest with such impossible conveyance upon me that I stood like a man at a mark with a whole army shooting at me. She speaks poniards and every word stabs' (2.1.218–20). Taken off-guard, Benedick stands 'like a man at a mark', unable to move and hence 'losing' the dance. These kinesic markers would alert an audience skilled in judging the grace or lack thereof of dancers; for the actors, the battle of wit and the dance scenes signal shifts in timing and movement, alerting them to the subtle dance between antagonism and synchrony inherent in the form.

The role of music in the play is also crucial. The singing is offloaded to a peripheral character, Balthazar, who, Collington argues, may well be a sly allusion to Baldassare Castiglione himself.[87] Like the song just before Bassanio's choice in *Merchant of Venice*, this musical interlude comes at a crucial time. Before the song Benedick bemoans the fact that 'sheeps' guts should hale souls out of men's bodies' (2.3.55–6), and afterwards he berates the incompetence of the singer, in opposition to the judgements of the other listeners. But it is this song, I argue, that primes him to believe that Beatrice may love him, and, more importantly, that he may love her. The skill of the singer hangs in the air, pulling his soul from him, demonstrating the power of music even as he disavows it.

In *Much Ado*, then, Shakespeare uses the lens of skill display – and especially the play's preoccupation with performative social skills – to interrogate love and its configurations within the play. Moments of conflict, stasis, movement and listening are profound non-linguistic modes of representing plot and theme. Skill is often torn between competition and cooperation, antagonism and synchrony, rivalry and concord. As such it is the perfect vehicle for thinking the social world, and Shakespeare writes this world in full awareness of the mindful bodies of the actors who will people it.

5

The Skills behind the Skills: Variety and Overtopping

Thus far I have been discussing what might be called the more visible of the qualities ascribed to the actor. Dancing, music, agility, fencing: these are skills that are presented to the audience. Others can perhaps be characterized as the 'skills behind the skills', qualities of concentration and attention that underpin expert performance but are seldom themselves on explicit display. Attributes such as 'memory, vigilancy, and pregnancy of wit' are perhaps more behind the scenes. Feats of memory only occasionally become visible on the stage, as, for example, Surly's recitation of alchemical terms that 'would burst a man to name', a line that, as Lois Potter notes, 'practically invite[s] the audience to applaud him for getting through the speech at all'.[1] Only amateur actors, as they are represented in *Midsummer Night's Dream* or *Love's Labours Lost*, betray the effort involved to remember their lines.[2] 'Vigilancy' is perhaps one of the more unexpected skills listed in *The Rich Cabinet*. It might be otherwise described as a quality of alertness and attentiveness: that is, the ability to cope with the unexpected, the flexible mindfulness that comes only from long practice and experience. As McIlwain and Sutton note:

Mindful coping includes the flexible roaming of attentiveness, as it shifts, on the fly, to the level of chunking required for smooth coping. The mind is required even in the most seemingly automated skill if that skill entails accommodating action to changing situational contingencies. This, we suggest, is keeping mind involved in body.[3]

Ralph Richardson's comparison to controlling four horses, quoted in the introduction, captures the levels of attentiveness needed for expert 'vigilancy', for monitoring and adjusting in real time. If accounts of the relative boisterousness of early modern audiences are at all true, the ability to perform whilst monitoring and appraising audience reaction, all the while adjusting on the fly, must have been a valuable quality indeed.[4]

'Pregnancy of wit' could be such a behind-the-scenes skill, or it could equally have been a highly presentational quality, especially as exhibited by the clowns. In *An Apology for Actors*, Heywood observes that actors should have, at minimum, a good tongue or a good wit:

Actors should be men picked out personable, according to the parts they present; they should be rather scholars, that though they cannot speak well, know how to speak, or else to have that volubility that they can speak well, though they understand not what, and so both imperfections may by instructions be helped and amended: but where a good tongue and a good conceit both fail, there can never be good actor.[5]

If 'pregnancy of wit' refers to the extemporaneous abilities of the actor, the players most known for yoking a good tongue and a good conceit were the clowns. Clowns of course were also associated with physical prowess: clowning of highly skilled and virtuosic sets of performances by men trained in physical and verbal gymnastics. William Kemp's athleticism in leaping over a ditch earned him a reward from the Earl of Leicester; his marathon Morris dancing from London to Norwich attracted huge attention and incited numerous amateurs to attempt to match his pace and skill of dance.[6] But theatre historians often describe clowns and playwrights in agonistic terms. Hamlet's advice to the players is sometimes seen as reflecting Shakespeare's own views, the aggrieved playwright's complaint about the clown interfering with the 'necessary questions' of the play. In this view, the comic energy of the clown is gradually contained by the writer, as exemplified by Hamlet's advice to the players to control the extemporizing of the fool: 'let those that play your clowns speak no more than is set down for them – for there be of them that will themselves laugh, to set on some quantity of barren spectators to laugh too' (3.2.39–42). In a teleological view of the theatrical history, the clown is gradually brought within the purview of the dramatic fiction, except for those at citizens' theatres such as the Red Bull, which retain an unsophisticated taste for broad comedy.[7] What Lois Potter describes as the 'suggestion that often gets repeated as fact', that Will Kemp was expelled from the company for too much improvisation, has proved remarkably durable; this narrative is one of the hinges of James Shapiro's *1599*, for example.[8] A recent essay sketches a fundamentally antagonistic relationship between playwright and clown: 'As fledgling playwright, Shakespeare depended on the clown to make popular a role, yet as a shareholding member of a large theatre company, he needed to keep the clown in check.'[9] Leaving aside the fact that Kemp himself was a sharer, this narrative of intra-company rivalry neglects the reality that 'the relation between comic improviser and writer has always been close'.[10] Thus, as Potter notes, the apparent condemnation of the Clown's improvisation in *Hamlet* may well have been as much a shared joke with the audience as a 'public rebuke of a famous and popular comedian'.[11]

Far from falling out of favour, clowns were consistently popular throughout our period. Perhaps a reason for the persistence of the narrative of clown–playwright rivalry is a failure to account for the pleasures of skill. In *Clowning and Authorship in Early Modern Theatre*, Richard Preiss provocatively argues that:

> From the Romantics onward, every theory of the clown has taken at face value his status as a character, seeking to reconcile his meaning with that of the overarching aesthetic structure in which we find him, 'the play'. This is an understandable assumption: playbooks are what we have, and plays, along with everything in them, have meanings.[12]

A text-based approach to the theatre results in relegating the clown, 'a stage figure whom Elizabethan and Jacobean audiences would have associated far more intimately with the organizing agency of the theatrical event', to a 'minor species of dramatic character, his theatrical role coterminous with his fictional one'.[13]

Early modern playgoers may well have had different evaluative categories, and reading plays through the lens of skill may yield new interpretive possibilities. For instance, Thomas Middleton's and William Rowley's *The Changeling* is read today for its extraordinary portrayal of female desire and treachery, and the comic subplot generally garners little attention. As Lois Potter puts it, *The Changeling* is one of 'perhaps ten non-Shakespearean plays that are frequently edited, have performance histories, and are thus beginning to acquire something of the aura (made up of multiple page and stage interpretations) that makes Shakespeare's plays seem so complex'.[14] Its present status is something of a twentieth-century phenomenon. Samuel Pepys saw it in 1661 and notes that 'it takes exceedingly', and it was performed at court in 1668.[15] However, it sunk from sight until the mid-twentieth century, when some well-known productions also spurred renewed critical interest in the play. *The Changeling* was revived in 1961 by Tony Richardson, followed by two 1978 productions: Peter Gill's at the Riverside, and Terry Hands's Royal Shakespeare Company production at the Aldwych.

As Roberta Barker and David Nicol have noted, the critical reaction to this revival focused almost entirely upon the daring psychological portrait of the leading characters DeFlores and Beatrice-Joanna; they argue that 'what passes for a "straight" interpretation of a classic playtext is often the one that most closely reproduces a particular culture's established assumptions about it'.[16] Critical interest in turn has primarily been focused upon the DeFlores/Beatrice-Joanna plot, the contemporary resonances of the play that make it 'disturbingly familiar' and the play's 'febrile, oppressive atmosphere' as manifested in its relentless exploration of interior states and places.[17] Modern productions and scholars attend primarily to the main plot, with Rowley's madhouse subplot cut, ignored or relegated to a thematic echoing of the madness of the main plot.

Yet focus on the apparently prescient psychological dimension of the play, however valuable, may well distort the reasons for its appeal in its own time. Contemporary audiences apparently highly valued the antic subplot of fools and madmen. Antonio, the titular changeling of the play, was especially popular, as evidenced by numerous references in the period.[18] As N. W. Bawcutt notes, Robert Brome's prologue to Thomas Goffe's play *The Careless Shepherdess* stages a pre-play conversation among a countryman (Landlord), a citizen (Thrift), an Inns of Court man (Spark) and a courtier (Spruce). Spruce challenges Landlord to answer the question 'What part you think essential to a play?'[19] The answer, of course, is 'The Fool':

> LANDLORD Why I would have the Fool in every Act,
>   Be't Comedy or Tragedy, I 'ave laugh'd
>   Untill I cry'd again, to see what Faces
>   The Rogue will make: O it does me good
>   To see him hold out's Chin hang down his hands,
>   And twirle his Bawble. There is nere a part
>   About him but breaks jests. I heard a fellow once
>   On this stage cry *Doodle, Doodle Dooe*

> Beyond compare; I'de give the other shilling
> To see him act the Changling once again.

The citizen enthusiastically agrees:

> THRIFT And so would I, his part has all the wit,
>   For none speaks Craps and Quibbles besides him:
>   I'd rather see him leap, laugh, or cry,
>   Then hear the gravest Speech in all the *Play*,
>   I never saw Rheade peeping through the Curtain,
>   But ravishing joy enter'd my heart.[20]

While the part of Antonio might seem silly, inert or even distasteful to contemporary readers, the prologue tells us much about the popularity of the role, especially as performed by the company clown, Timothy Reade, who succeeded William Robbins as the clown for Queen Henrietta's Men. Thrift and Landlord recall with pleasure Reade's performances: his 'faces', his set phrases and gag lines, his physical leaps and capers, and virtuosic verbal skills in calling out 'craps' and 'quibbles' apparently commandeered most of the attention of the audience. These recollections move seamlessly across roles, plays and time. They thus work 'intertheatrically', referencing across plays not just to verbal allusions but also to repeated and familiar physical gestures of the sort that William N. West has investigated.[21] Landlord mentions the cry of 'Doodle, Doodle Dooe', which alludes to Reade's part of Buzzard in Brome's *The English Moor*. Steggle describes Buzzard's role as 'comic mayhem', and his key scene includes the stage direction *'sings and dances and spins with a Rock and spindle'*.[22] Thus Reade was remembered for outlandish physical virtuosity, expressed through gestures, dance, business with props, as well as witty by-play. Moreover, the reference to 'Rheade peeping through the Curtain' reaches all the way back to Tarlton's famous shtick, in which he peered through the curtains and caused uncontrollable laughter among the audience.[23] While this prologue is parodic, it nevertheless attests to an economy of spectatorship and skill that foregrounds the physical and witty displays of particular charismatic players.

The popularity of the part of Antonio throughout the seventeenth century is also attested to by the appearance of the figure of 'The Changeling' on the title page of *The Wits, or Sport upon Sport* (1662). The dangling arms of this figure seem to represent a favourite gestural bit described by Landlord: 'O it does me good / To see him hold out's Chin hang down his hands'. As Steggle argues, 'The changeling routines described by Landlord and Thrift are certainly not mere add-ons to the play from which they come.'[24] Verbal wit, gestural comedy, both innovative and referencing past performances, and the physical skill demanded to perform leaps and capers: these acts of skill lived in the memory of playgoers.

If Brome, the company playwright, is indeed the author of the comic prologue to Goffe's play, further light may be shed on the supposed agonistic relationship between author and comic that underpins traditional narratives of the circumscription of the clown alluded to earlier. Rivalry and jealousy between and among professional colleagues is by no means uncommon, but Brome's allusions to Reade's role in his own plays suggest that rivalries may have well been friendly rather than antagonistic – or at least friendly provocations. Comic virtuosity is a rare gift and demands highly honed physical and mental skills – ability of body, vigilancy, pregnancy of wit, all performed at high speed with the aim to 'make 'em laugh', in the words of Donald O'Connor in *Singin' in the Rain*. But it is equally a gift to write for comics, to find new and inventive uses for their talents, to integrate them into dramatic fictions while also recognizing that they may well fight themselves out at times. William Rowley, of course, who penned the comic scenes to *The Changeling*, was a comic actor in his own right, specializing also in comic writing. So rather than seeing the clown as increasingly co-opted by an author-centred drama hostile to his comic energies, we might instead see the part as both changing and evolving in response to changes in the theatrical ecology, and as functioning as a kind of theatrical palimpsest, with multiple layers of physical and verbal allusion to the clowns of the past.

Reading for skill: Edward Alleyn and *The Jew of Malta*

The clown is the most obvious example of the way that players exceeded their roles and called attention to their acts of skill. But evidence also suggests that the best-known early modern actors – including Edward Alleyn and Richard Burbage – achieved a kind of celebrity that transcended individual roles. It was not only the clown who stood out in the emergent celebrity culture of the early modern theatre. A series of tantalizing references to set competitions between players, with the outcome subject to wagering, also attests to the way that actors' skills were presented and evaluated.[25] The Henslowe-Alleyn archive at Dulwich College contains a letter to Edward Alleyn proposing that he pit himself against the actors John Bentley and William Knell, founding members of the Queen's Men, in a test of acting skill: 'I see not, how you cann eanie we[way] hurt yor credit by this action; for if you excell them, you will then be famous, if equall them; you wynne both the wager and the credit; if short of them; we must and will say Ned Allen still.' An accompanying poem reads:

> Deny me not sweete Nedd, the wagers downe
> and twice as muche, commaunde of me or myne:
> And if you wynne, I sweare the half is thyne;
> and for an ouerplus, an English Crowne.
> Appoint the tyme, and stint it as you pleas,
> Your labor's gain; and that will proue it ease.[26]

Similarly, Thomas Dekker refers to the practice of adjudicating skill by means of competition. In *A Gull's Hornbook*,

Dekker describes 'a pair of players growing into an emulous contention of one another's worth' who decline to compete head to head: they 'refus[e]d to put themselves unto a day of hearing (as any players would have done) but stood only upon their good parts'.[27] Numerous references also exist to 'acting for a wager'; one of Dekker's mock-suggestions to the gull is to 'let any hook draw you to a fencer's supper or to players that act such a part for a wager', and the Citizen in *Knight of the Burning Pestle* proudly notes that Rafe acted in *Mucedorus* and 'should have played *Jeronimo* [of the *Spanish Tragedy*] with the shoemaker for a wager'.[28]

Richard Preiss has recently examined another instance of such a 'trial of wit': an intended challenge between William Fennor and John Taylor, arranged at the Hope Theatre in 1614, but never actually carried off. As Preiss notes:

> The centrality of gambling to the affair – both in its internal logic and peripherally, in all likelihood, among its audience – makes the 'trial of wit' in essence a verbal equivalent of the early modern prizefight, a form with which it shares circumstantial features as well. Like trials of defense, their venues tended to be playhouses – the Swan, the Fortune, the Hope – that had fallen into relative dis-use, or with predominantly lower-class patronage, or expressly designed for multipurpose, combat-oriented entertainment; like trials of defense, which mustered crowds by parading the contestants through the streets to the beat of a drum, trials of wit aggressively promoted cults of local celebrity, narratives of professional rivalry, and displays of technical mastery.[29]

Preiss argues that these trials of wit bear homologies to clowning; Richard Tarlton was famous for his improvised responses to 'themes' shouted out from the audience.[30] These references raise a number of questions – What exactly did the actors *do* to compete? How were the wagers adjudicated? Who exactly was laying money on the venture? – but the passages indicate that skill was seen as an independent quality that could be contested, enacted and evaluated.

Actors pitted their skill against each other not just in such moments as these, but also within an intergenerational framework, as younger actors took on the roles made famous by their predecessors. And as the reference to 'Ned Alleyn still' establishes, it was this actor who loomed above all others. Susan Cerasano argues that:

> the career of Edward Alleyn fashioned a new and powerful professional model, ushering in an era in which players began to perform not only for contemporary audiences but, in a sense, for posterity as well. Actors, in addition to plays, became commodities to be marketed and capitalized on by playhouse owners and theatrical companies.[31]

Her position is a welcome corrective to critics who cast doubt upon Alleyn's skill, arguing that his style was outmoded and exaggerated, in contrast to the more subtle style of Richard Burbage, the primary tragedian of Shakespeare's company.[32] This invidious distinction has become a critical commonplace; a recent critic suggests that Alleyn's 'stentorial acting style no longer appealed to the younger generation of players and the public'.[33]

Yet the evidence suggests that Alleyn held a strong appeal across generations; his influence is enormous even as late as 1633. When Christopher Marlowe's *The Jew of Malta* was revived for a performance at the Cockpit in 1633, the role of Barabas, indelibly linked with Edward Alleyn, was played by his former apprentice, Richard Perkins. Thomas Heywood's 'Prologue to the Stage' emphasizes Alleyn's ownership of the role:

> by the best of poets in that age
> The *Malta-Jew* had being, and was made;
> And he, then by the best of actors play'd,
> In *Hero and Leander*, one did gain

A lasting memory; in *Tamburlaine*,
This *Jew*, with others many, th'other wan
The attribute of peerless, being a man
Whom we may rank with (doing no one wrong)
Proteus for shapes, and Roscius for a tongue,
So could he speak, so vary.[34]

Interestingly, Marlowe is memorialized through his non-dramatic verse – the wildly popular *Hero and Leander* – whilst Alleyn is remembered though his personation of Marlowe's roles, a hint of the different categories that organized theatrical experience in the early modern period. So overpowering is the memory of Alleyn, long absent from the stage even before his death seven years earlier, that Perkins, in reinhabiting the role, is said to disclaim any explicit rivalry with his powerful predecessor and former master:

          Nor is 't hate
To merit in him who doth personate
Our Jew this day, nor is it his ambition
To exceed, or equal, being of condition
More modest; this is all that he intends
(And that, too, at the urgence of some friends):
To prove his best, and if none here gainsay it,
The part he hath studied, and intends to play it.[35]

The epilogue likewise simultaneously invokes and disavows the language of rivalry:

In graving, with Pygmalion to contend,
Or painting, with Appelles, doubtless the end
Must be disgrace; our actor did not so:
He only aim'd to go, but not outgo.
Nor think that this day any prize was play'd;
Here were no bets at all, no wagers laid;
All the ambition that his mind doth swell
Is but to hear from you (by me) 'twas well.[36]

Especially viewed in the light of other references to trials of wit and playing for a wager, this paratextual material frames acting as a trial of skill, an attempt to overgo a rival. Putatively of course the agonistic nature of playing is disavowed; far from establishing that Alleyn's style looked dated and outmoded, however, the prologue and epilogue playfully reinforce the powerful hold he had over the drama decades after his heyday. As Lucy Munro notes, 'memories of Alleyn's performances had a peculiar effect: they both enabled his successors and, it seems, put pressure on them to match up to those memories'.[37] This material also invites us to re-examine the nature of his performances to see what was valued in them; as in the example of *The Changeling*, contemporaries may have prized very different qualities than are privileged today.

The Jew of Malta has often puzzled its commentators, who complain that the play 'degenerates into farce' and that 'Barabas has at the beginning of the play a humanity and dignity he soon loses'.[38] In the early twentieth century, the apparent inconsistencies in Barabas's character prompted some critics to conclude that the text was deficient and that the 1633 quarto 'presents the tragedy in a form sadly corrupted and altered from that in which it left the hands of Marlowe'.[39] Early critics were happy to ascribe the soaring language and the quick wit of the Barabas of the first two acts to Marlowe, but were less content with the gleeful nun-murderer and the comic lute instructor as the playwright's invention. In a recent survey of critical responses to the play, Robert Logan notes 'the difficulties encountered in attempting to characterize the genre of the play', as well as the 'problems one faces in arriving at a coherent understanding of the character of Barabas, including the differences in his portrayal in the first two and last three acts of the play'.[40] Logan also notes the 'diversity of tones' that characterize the play and suggests that 'Marlowe's shifts from realistic to non-realistic characterizations and episodes' can be seen as deliberate attempts 'to overturn his spectator's conventional and moral and dramaturgical

expectations', concluding that 'if the playwright creates
inconsistencies, ambivalences, and ambiguities along the way,
so much the better, for they act as dramaturgical devices that
can only help to keep an audience engaged'.[41]

Logan acutely identifies elements that seem tonally
dissonant, especially to a modern audience. In the first two
acts, Barabas speaks in heightened blank verse that belies
some of the comic potential of his stereotypical regard for
the '*heaps of gold before him*', as the stage direction of 1.1
reads. The first two acts highlight Barabas's 'pregnancy of
wit', as he quickly deduces the trajectories of his various
argosies and berates his fellow Jews for their base submission.
In the third act he seems to enter the register of what T. S.
Eliot famously termed savage farce, as his thirst for revenge
and pride in his villainy become ever more excessive. Lines
such as 'how sweet the bells ring now the nuns are dead'
and acts such as propping up dead friars seem more like
attempts to overgo other stage villains than anything that
looks to modern critics like consistent characterization.
When Barabas enters '*with a lute, disguised*' (4.4.27) as a
French musician with a comic accent – 'Must tuna my lute
for sound, twang twang' – it is hard not to read this as 'lame
role-playing'.[42]

I argue, however, that reading this play through the lens
of skill offers a different perspective than the essentially
author-oriented reading that emphasizes the deficiencies
of the play. Indeed, the prologue presents the play as a
collaborative act between the 'best of poets' and the 'best
of actors'. And as Roslyn L. Knutson reminds us, *The
Jew of Malta* should also be read within the 'networks of
commercial competition within the repertory'.[43] The play
was produced within the context of the revenge tragedy, as
devised by Kyd in *The Spanish Tragedy*, with a 'villainous
revenger', thus distinguishing the protagonist from Kyd's
work and linking him with the Vice tradition, the emergent
theme of the 'criminal passion' and the popular subgenre of
the 'foreign history play'.[44] If viewed through the prism of

the repertory, what looks like generic instability to modern readers may well be canny appraisals of the early modern playgoing market.

If Marlowe was writing within the context of a particular moment in the repertory, he was also writing for the best-known leading actor of his time: Edward Alleyn. Indeed, the play is in many ways a showcase for Alleyn's skills. Best known of these, of course, was Alleyn's height, stride and vocal command – as Cerasano notes, Alleyn 'was distinguished by his unusual height and his thundering voice'.[45] Both Cerasano and Munro quote an epigram by Edward Guilpin recalling a performance of Alleyn in a now-lost play about Cutlack the Dane:

> *Clodius* me thinks looks passing big of late,
> With *Dunstons* browes and *Allens Cutlacks* gate [gait]:
> What humours have possest him so, I wonder,
> His eyes are lightning, and his words are thunder:[46]

The first two acts of the play provide ample scope for displaying such qualities. Barabas is efficient, intelligent, energetic, commanding the stage as he disposes the merchants who enter reporting on his ships: 'Go tell 'em the Jew of Malta sent thee, man / Tush, who amongst 'em knows not Barabas?' (1.1.66–7). The opening scenes alternate soaring blank verse in the mould of Tamburlaine and Faustus with restless and commanding action.

Later in the play, Barabas becomes a semi-comic revenger, seemingly intent on overgoing all other stage revengers in his villainy. While traditional character-based criticism may find it challenging to account for this shift, a skill-based reading alerts us to Alleyn's formidable comic skills. The mastery of the comic aside is shown in the deft scenes in which Barabas explains the plot to Abigail in full view of the Maltese officials. But Alleyn's comic abilities are perhaps best displayed in the lute scene, in which Barabas spies upon Ithamore: 'I will in some disguise go see the slave / And how the villain revels with my gold' (4.3.65–6). As Andrew Gurr and Peter Hyland have pointed out, the Admiral's Men had something of a specialty in disguise plays. Disguise is a particular form of skill display, in which actors juggle personae, revealing an underlying identity to the audience whilst concealing it, however implausibly, from the other characters in the play.[47] As the lute instructor, Alleyn adopts a stage-French accent, tuning his lute in a bid for delay long enough to entice Pilia-Borza to smell the poisoned 'posy in his hat there' (4.4.32). It is not always remarked that Alleyn/Barabas is apparently a highly skilled lute player. Pilia-Borza remarks that 'he fingers very well … how swift he runs' (47–9). The short scene makes tremendous demands upon the actor: he must juggle identities by negotiating asides to the audience and comic interactions with Ithamore and Pilia-Borza; keep both the sinister and the comic elements of the characters in play; and skilfully play the lute.

Another aspect of the play that has caused critical controversy is the ending: critics puzzle over why Barabas 'foolishly makes a bargain with Ferneze for money rather than power'.[48] However, the most salient feature of the last act is Barabas's extraordinary energy. In 5.1, he is carried in 'as dead', and Ferneze orders, 'For the Jew's body, throw that o'er the walls / To be a prey for vultures and wild beasts' (5.1.58–9). The text is silent on the stage business here, but the most likely action is that Barabas is flung to the edge of the stage. Leaving aside the strength that it would have taken to heave a man the size of Alleyn, this seemingly inert action displays skill in itself, for it is no easy task to remain convincingly 'dead' whilst being tossed about the stage. The rapid change from dead body to irrepressibly alive, energetic and scheming revenger is yet another marker of the brilliant variety of turns Alleyn is asked to perform.

The conclusion of the play emphasizes above all Alleyn's physicality and agility. In the final scene he enters *with a hammer above, very busy* (5.5.sd). As he directed the merchants in the first scene, in the final scene he directs the carpenters in a complex mechanical contraption of cords, cranes and pulleys designed to rig a 'dainty gallery, the floor whereof, this cable being cut, / Doth fall asunder, so that it doth sink / Into a deep pit past recovery' (5.5.33–6). Barabas's spectacular fall into this very pit to conclude the play may be a moral comeuppance, but it is also a *tour de force* of physical theatre, however it was originally played. It reminds us that Alleyn was praised above all for his protean nature, his skill in *variety*.

Reading through the lens of skill: *Hamlet*

At one point in her masterful biography *The Life of William Shakespeare*, Lois Potter makes the speculative but extremely intriguing suggestion that Shakespeare may have reworked an old version of *Hamlet*, probably by Thomas Kyd, to provide Richard Burbage with an acting vehicle that would stand up against the revival of *The Spanish Tragedy* performed by Alleyn upon his return to the stage in 1600. Potter writes, 'Above all, perhaps, Hamlet is a composite of everything that Burbage did best, which is why he is everything that an actor wants to play and everything that an audience wants an actor to be.'[49] In this reading, the apparent inconsistencies of Hamlet's character are at least partly explained if we imagine the part as purposely written as a vehicle for the display of actorly skill, a *tour de force* of variety that could be set against Alleyn's Hieronomo and Barabas.

Potter's insight confirms numerous critical observations about the changing reception of *Hamlet* over time. As Margreta de Grazia has established, the conception of Hamlet as a character hamstrung by over-intellectual analysis is very much a modern phenomenon. In the seventeenth century, Hamlet seems to have been associated more closely with frenetic movement and an antic disposition. De Grazia argues that 'several allusions suggest that Hamlet's lunatic racing – the physical counterpart to his "wild and whirling words"

– might well have been what pleased all ... . In the early decades of its performance, Hamlet's signature action may have been not paralysing thought but frenzied motion.'[50] De Grazia and others have convincingly linked these character-istics of Hamlet to early modern clowning. David Wiles argues that 'Burbage united within Hamlet the figures of clown and tragic hero', and Robert Weimann has written on the 'double-dealing poetics that, simultaneously, informed Hamlet's antic clowning and his own advice against it'.[51]

These observations illuminate the links between Barabas and Hamlet, however superficially different the characters may seem: the oscillation between melancholic and antic dispositions as a means of showcasing the variety and range of skills – the sheer kinesic intelligence – of the actor. From this perspective, *Hamlet* is a play preoccupied with skill, skill display and trials of wit and ability.

We can find many such moments in the play, some of which are instances of what René Girard has called 'mimetic rivalry'.[52] The preoccupation with skill is perhaps first exemplified in the visit of the players, which is couched throughout in the language of rivalry and emulation. In Q1 and Q2 the visit is preceded by an analysis of the dispute between the children's companies and the adult actors, who are not 'in the same estimation' as once they were because of competition from 'an eyrie of children ... now the fashion'.[53] Hamlet's reaction to the company visit and the speech of the First Player is a confused mixture of fandom and jealousy, as he attempts to make sense of the ability of the player's skill to convey emotion – 'his whole function suiting / with forms to his conceit'.[54] During *The Mousetrap*, Hamlet behaves more as 'jig-maker' in competition with the players than as a spectator or a disinterested observer. After the performance, alone with Horatio, he breaks into song and demands applause from Horatio for his performance: 'Would not, this, sir, and a forest of feathers, if the rest of my fortunes turn Turk with me, with provincial roses on my razed shoes, get me a fellowship in a cry of players, sir?' (3.2.267–70).

The gravedigger scene is also marked by rivalry and competition, beginning with a brief trial of wit between the two clowns over the riddle 'What is he that builds stronger than either the mason, the shipwright or the carpenter?' (5.1.37–8). Although the second clown's guess – 'The gallows-maker, for that outlives a thousand tenants' (39–40) – is met with grudging approval, he is asked to try harder: 'to't again, come' (45). The gravedigger celebrates his victory by sending his companion out for a 'stoup of liquor' (56), which sets the stage for the struggle between him and Hamlet for comic priority. Earlier Hamlet has excelled in the 'witty literalism' of the clown, as in his wilful misunderstanding of Polonius's questions: 'What do you read, my lord? ... what is the matter, my lord?' (2.2.188, 190).[55] In the graveyard, the situation is reversed: for the first time in the play, Hamlet becomes the straight man, feeding prompts to the gravedigger, who adroitly avoids answering the question directly: 'How absolute the knave is! We must speak by the card or equivocation will undo us' (5.1.129–30).

It is against this background hum of skill, competition and rivalry that we can view the final contest between Hamlet and Laertes. The conclusion to the play is propelled through a kind of cascade of jealousy and envy fomented by Claudius, dreamt up to eliminate Hamlet and appease Laertes' thirst for revenge, while disguising the death so that 'even his mother shall uncharge the practice / And call it accident' (4.7.65–6). The exchange between Laertes and Claudius in 4.7, and Hamlet and Osric in 5.2, revolves around skill, rivalry and envy. Claudius calculates that Hamlet's envy of Laertes' reputation as a fencer will be enough to convince him to accept the challenge. Indeed, the confrontation between Laertes and Claudius goes out of its way to introduce skill as an independent topic, and at some length. Having finally placated Laertes, the King attempts to enlist him in the plot:

You have been talked of since your travel much,
And that in Hamlet's hearing, for a quality
Wherein they say you shine. Your sum of parts

Did not together pluck such envy from him
As did that one, and that in my regard
Of the unworthiest siege. (4.7.69–74)

Before telling Laertes which of his qualities Hamlet envies, Claudius indulges in what seems like a strange digression: an account of a visit to the Danish court of the Norman visitor Lamord (F):

> Two months since
> Here was a gentleman of Normandy –
> I have seen myself, and served against, the French
> And they can well on horseback, but this gallant
> Had witchcraft in't; he grew unto his seat
> And to such wondrous doing brought his horse
> As had he been incorpsed and demi-natured
> With the brave beast.
> ...
> LAERTES A Norman, was't?
> KING A Norman.
> LAERTES Upon my life, Lamord! (4.7.80–9)

It is safe to say that this exchange, which occurs both in the Folio and in Q2, almost never makes it onto the stage, so apparently extraneous to the plot it seems. In the note to the Arden edition, Thompson and Taylor write that 'Editors have suggested topical references – understandably perhaps, because the matter of the Norman and his horsemanship seems rather tangential to the real skill in question, that of fencing.'[56] If it is a topical reference, it is a somewhat obscure one; what it does do, however, is foreground skill as a category. Horsemanship of course is not generally a skill on display in the early modern theatre, but in conduct books and treatises it is strongly linked to other courtly skills, especially dancing and fencing. In Hoby's translation of *The Courtier*, the way a rider settles in the saddle is a key sign of *sprezzatura*: 'Marke what an yll grace a man at armes hath, when he enforceth himselfe to goe so bolt upright setled in saddle (as we use to say after the Venetian phrase) in comparison of an other that appeareth not to mind it, and sitteth on horseback so nimbly and close as though he were on fote.'[57] Given that horsemanship and fencing were seen as intimately related, the opinion of the preternaturally skilled Lamord, so adept that he seems almost grafted to his horse, may indeed be relevant to the question of Laertes' skill in fencing. Claudius continues:

> He made confession of you
> And gave you such a masterly report
> For art and exercise in your defence,
> And for your rapier most especial
> That he [Hamlet] cried out 'twould be a sight indeed
> If one could match you. Th'escrimers of their nation
> He swore had neither motion, guard nor eye
> If you opposed them. Sir, this report of his
> Did Hamlet so envenom with envy
> That he could nothing do but wish and beg
> Your sudden coming o'er to play with you. (4.7.93–103)

There is an extraordinary amount of emphasis upon Hamlet's keen desire to best Laertes at fencing, so much so that Claudius calculates that Hamlet will gladly participate in the match, especially if spurred on by courtly gossip and the lure of the wager: 'We'll put on those shall place your excellence / And set a double varnish on the fame / The Frenchmen gave you' (4.7.129–31).

When, in Act 5, Osric delivers the challenge, Hamlet tells Horatio that he has 'been in continual practice' since Laertes left for France, adding that he will 'win at the odds' (5.2.188–9). This might seem rather surprising information; Laertes departs for France after the second scene of the play, and we might perhaps think that Hamlet has been too occupied with other matters – feigning madness, murdering Polonius, tormenting Ophelia, seeing ghosts, fighting pirates – to have had enough time to keep up with his fencing. Indeed, he has told Rosencrantz and Guildenstern in 2.2 that he has 'forgone all custom of exercises' (2.2.262–3).

The fencing match is so well known that it is easy to forget how strange a conclusion it is to the play. By 5.2, when Osric invites him to the challenge, Hamlet knows the King has already employed intermediaries to kill him, and in the scene just before he has engaged in a fierce struggle with Laertes in Ophelia's grave. Yet he accepts the match, despite his misgivings. Commentators have generally seen Hamlet's acceptance of the match as a form of fatalism, of Hamlet's acceptance of providence despite his sensation of foreboding. And certainly there is textual warrant for such reading. But this view privileges the philosophical Hamlet over the physical Hamlet and implicitly ignores the evidence for Hamlet's preoccupation with skill and mastery, as well as the strong elements of jealousy, rivalry and emulation that spur his actions.

An emphasis upon skill as an independent category sheds light on a number of existing questions and problems in the drama. The categories through which we view plays are often too firmly tied to the printed page. Language present on the page can render the bodies that speak such language invisible, and the skill of the actor is often glimpsed only in the interstices of language. Gaps and inconsistencies are stitched together as attempts, successful or otherwise, to convey character. But focusing upon skill helps us to see such frameworks in potential tension with the aesthetics of variety that marked early modern playing. Such an aesthetic also entails a complex admixture of rivalry and cooperation, antagonism and synchrony, display and erasure of skill. It is also, as we shall see, in tension with modern ways of conceptualizing acting.

6

Conclusions: Reconstructing Skill

Any modern production of a Shakespearean play confronts history, memory and difference. Actors and directors must grapple not only with the wide gap of time that separates modern audiences from Elizabethan spectators, but also with the weight of intervening theatrical practices that have shaped the play. And contemporary actors in particular face a narrowly construed basis for evaluating actorly skill, what Paul Menzer has called 'the thoroughly naturalized common-place – that exhibiting an inner life is the principal work of the mainstream actor'.[1] The assumption that less is more, that 'minimal effort produces maximum affect', discourages overt displays of skill, for fear of seeming hammy or of trying too hard.[2] The perfect pause, the moment of silence and hesitation, attracts praise, not, as in previous centuries, perfect elocution or adept bearing of the body. Skill must be concealed or implicit rather than displayed in some unseemly, overly external or demonstrative fashion.

Early modern plays were written for certain kinds of mindful bodies, bodies trained in disciplines such as fencing, dance and gesture. As I have argued, such disciplines fostered kinesic intelligence that underpinned not only those particular practices but also ways of being in the world, such that even so simple a motion as stretching out a hand reveals a 'ready aptness' for action. But contemporary actors work within different ecologies of skill, and are embedded in very different institutional practices. For this reason, actors cannot simply replicate early modern skillsets.

Merely adopting or modifying some aspects of early modern practice is not in itself sufficient to produce new forms of skill. Kevin Ewert, in his combatively titled 'The Thrust Stage Is Not Some Direct Link to Shakespeare', challenges the Royal Shakespeare Company's rhetoric of replication. In their public relations material about a new thrust stage in the Royal Shakespeare's Theatre, the RSC claimed that the stage would 'transform the relationship between artists and audiences' and make the theatrical experience more 'collaborative'.[3] Ewert objects that 'architecture is not destiny in a collaborative event'; physical closeness to an audience does not guarantee a transformed experience, in part because of 'the supposed necessity of "setting" the blocking and working out the timing of all onstage (inter)action in accordance with where the lights are, when the sound cues come, what the video projections are doing, and how the scene changes run'.[4]

Of course it is correct that changing one element in a distributed cognitive ecology does not magically transform all others – new practices take time to bed in, new skills take time to master and, in any case, even a so-called original practices company cannot simply replicate the past, nor do they claim to do so. The case of original practices productions offers a particularly rewarding arena for studying distributed cognitive ecologies within the framework of skill. All original practices companies are necessarily selective about which practices they choose to engage in – including, amongst others, reconstructed stages in shared light (Shakespeare's Globe, the American Shakespeare Centre); illumination by candlelight (the Sam Wanamaker playhouse); cross-gender casting, reconstructed costuming, 'original' pronunciation (Shakespeare's Globe); and the use of rehearsal practices such as cue-scripts (the Original Shakespeare Company, the ASC Renaissance season). Other early modern practices, such as apprenticing

young boys to companies or adopting early modern reper-
tories, are less practical.[5] In all cases, collisions (sometimes
productive, sometimes less so) occur between contemporary
practices, assumptions and habits and the past practices that
are invoked or imitated.

The area of skill offers a particularly rich terrain for the
exploration of such emergent practices. Attempts to reconstruct skilled practices of the past – whether skill of weapon,
dance or gesture – are productive examples of such collisions
in action. As we have seen, stage combat has very different
resonances for early modern players and for contemporary
actors. Handling weapons was not merely a useful adjunct to
playing, but was essential to everyday life for young men in
early modern England. These practices honed a very particular
kind of kinesic intelligence, bringing everyday habits of
movement ('nature') to conscious awareness ('art'). Of course,
modern acting training also aims at inculcating such forms of
intelligence. All modern acting training includes some forms
of tuition in movement, along with more specialized courses
such as various levels of stage combat and dance. The RADA
manual explains the 'purposes of movement training' in this
way:

> [Movement training] develops ways of expressing thought
> and imagination, allowing actors to create characters from
> the inside-out or outside-in, and helps them to manifest
> the inner workings of the mind through the body. The end
> result should be that the actor gains the control of their
> body in order to use it exactly in the way that they want to.
> Actors need to have at their disposal an instrument which,
> at all times, expresses their dramatic intention.[6]

Breaking down old habits of movement and gaining 'intention'
and 'control' over the body is a declared goal of these
practices. But of course drama schools are working with
modern bodies, trained in particular ways of being in the
world. As has already been considered, even so simple an

act as walking is profoundly conditioned by environment, clothing, gait and social structures. Moving whilst wearing a sword would have been second nature to Shakespeare's actors, but is highly awkward at first for modern actors unused to the changes in personal space, movement and hand placement that a sword demands. And audiences themselves are strongly conditioned to certain ways of walking, standing, slouching, moving, gesturing. So when a modern actor attempts to inhabit a new form of skill ecology, there is an inevitable lack of fit between the body he or she brings to the enterprise and the bodies for whom such plays were originally written. Patterns of movement and ways of holding the body that are second nature to one generation seem strained and stilted to another.

In the case of swordplay, modern productions of Shakespearean plays must grapple with multiple considerations. As we have seen, Shakespeare's fights were performed by actors likely to have a high degree of skill of weapon before audiences who had a sophisticated sporting eye for the encounter. The amount of rehearsal that early modern actors engaged in is still an open question. Fight scenes could certainly have had an 'elastic' quality to them: like gags, they might go on longer if the audience was clearly enjoying the spectacle. Unlike dances, fights have particular outcomes, and Shakespeare's fights in particular are sometimes followed by detailed descriptions of the precise movements and styles of the fighters, as in Benvolio's admittedly interested account of the deadly encounter in Act 3. Actors would have relied upon their training in the 'skill of weapon', possibly building upon informal fencing practice or 'play'; particular demands in the script (for example Benvolio's description of Tybalt's sword swinging 'about his head', 1.1.13); and tacit conventions of movement and style that may well have been honed over long years of association in the company. Thus the ecology of skill in this case might be thought of as lateral, as well as extended and embedded in existing codes of training, discipline, expertise and masculine honour.

In contrast, modern stage fighting is highly orchestrated and professionalized. Fight choreography and fight direction has increasingly become a specialized activity, overseen by professional organizations such as the Society of American Fight Directors (SAFD), Fight Directors Canada (FDC) or the British Academy of Stage and Screen Combat. In addition, smaller salon-style organizations such as the Toronto-based Rapier Wit or Rc-Annie in England train numerous stage combatants and aspiring fight directors. These organizations are far from monolithic and in fact often have opposing ideas of what constitutes a good fight, how to guarantee safety, and the relative importance of 'authenticity' in staging early modern-style fights.

Fight directors must balance the absolute need for safety (both on the part of performers and the audience) with orchestrating exciting fights that give the illusion of danger. Moreover, they work with actors who have a very wide range of training and background in fighting; pitting a highly skilled stage combatant against someone much less experienced can make the task of balancing safety and excitement particularly difficult. Actors trained in martial arts, including fencing, can have difficulty 'unlearning' grooved movements. Electric foil fencing, for instance, trains small movements that are difficult to see with the naked eye; fencers are taught never to telegraph their intentions, just as boxers must not telegraph a punch. But in stage combat it is essential that the fighting partners know what the other is about to do; they must be able to convey intentions to one another without revealing them to the audience. On Shakespeare's stage, the sharers must have known each other's physical styles through long close association, but stable companies are very much the exception rather than the rule today.

In 2013 I interviewed a number of actors and fight directors involved in a curiously hybrid form of original practices theatre: Tim Carroll's *Romeo and Juliet* at the Canadian Stratford festival. Carroll came to Stratford from Shakespeare's Globe, where he had been Associate Director from 1999 to 2005, and produced the play in the Festival Theatre, the largest theatre at Stratford.

The Festival Theatre has a thrust stage, with audiences seated on three sides, and Carroll refurbished the existing stage to invoke Shakespeare's Globe. More controversial was his decision to keep the house lights up (they were slightly dimmed but the audience was entirely visible) and to eschew lighting design except for a barely perceptible change of light to mimic the passing of the day. The audience thus was in a fully indoor space, in raked seating, yet in lighting conditions meant to evoke the shared lighting of Shakespeare's Globe.

The reviews were disappointing, indicating a profound clash of sensibilities. Reviewers reserved their ire for the lighting effects:

> [T]he whole principle just seems screechingly false. Why do we have to have a series of almost invisible lighting cues to simulate the way the sun would have changed under a real sky? Why are the lights left on in the audience, destroying any sense of real intimacy and encouraging the cast to treat the whole thing like one giant stand-up routine?[7]

Another reviewer wrote:

> When I heard the production of Romeo and Juliet [*sic*] would be utilizing 'original practices', as in methods utilized by the original Elizabethan companies who first performed it, I pictured soft lighting, disjointed music plucked on obscure instruments, red handkerchiefs used to simulate flowing blood, and staid emoting. I hoped they'd draw the line at an all-male cast.[8]

This peculiar view of what original practices might be was followed by a condemnation of the lack of intimacy and complaints about the oddity of recreating daylight in a large indoor theatre.

Among other things, this experiment shows that a major component in any theatrical ecology is audience expectation and experience. The reviews indicate that the joins between the Festival Theatre environment and the conventions of original practices were perhaps just too visible for the reviewers. The mismatch between audience expectations and knowledge was also evident. As Penelope Woods has shown, audiences come to Shakespeare's Globe with a set of expectations: they know they will stand (if groundlings); they know that the theatre is open to the air; and they know to expect actor-audience inter-action.[9] Indeed directors increasingly build out the stage to get closer to the audience, and it is an established convention for actors to deliver particular lines to individual audience members, sometimes for comic effect. In contrast, Stratford audiences expect professional lighting rigs and they expect to sit in the dark. Carroll attempted to alert the audience to a new regime through a comic prologue that suddenly segued into the opening line of the play (in this production 'do you bite your thumb at me'). On the day I attended, quite late into the run, some members of the audience in the front rows were visibly uncomfortable at being addressed by the actors. Unlike groundlings at the Globe, who have the cheapest tickets and pay with their time and feet for the privilege of being close to the stage, the Canadian audience who had paid top dollar for seats close to the stage seemed to resent being drawn into the action.

A particularly interesting feature of this experiment in reconstructed staging was its use of stage combat. Staging fights on the thrust stage at the Festival Theatre is always challenging – there are numerous levels, difficult angles and multiple sightlines, which make it almost impossible to hide the action from the audience. The thrust stage makes the illusion of violence very difficult to conceal. As fight coach Brad Ruby observed:

Proscenium theatre is always way much easier – simply if you and I are in a fight and the audience is behind you I

> can throw a punch and miss you by that far and they can't
> see that, which is what film does; they just put the camera
> behind the person, add a sound effect and they miss by
> miles and you can't see it. But on the thrust stage, it's much,
> much more challenging to hide it, because there's always
> somebody who can see it. So you either have to distract the
> audience by having a loud noise somewhere or else you just
> keep trying to hide it.[10]

Shared lighting exacerbates the technical difficulties of combat
on the thrust stage, since lighting effects cannot be used to
mask the actors. The choreography of the opening fight in
the 2013 *Romeo and Juliet* fell back on what is perhaps the
oldest and most reliable method: misdirection. The scene is
written to take full advantage of the difficulties of attending to
fast movement on stage, and the complexity gradually builds
so that the entrance of exasperated citizens with '*clubs or
partisans*' aiming to beat both sides down divides the attention
of the audience, which is no longer able to focus on any one
combat on stage, and prepares the way for the comic turn in
the action, as the elder generation becomes involved.

Of course, the more chaotic a fight scene appears on stage,
the more controlled it must be in rehearsal and execution. The
actors and fight directors I spoke with at Stratford described
the technical precision they sought in designing and rehearsing
fights:

> We're very, very specific in our technical aspect of what we
> do: there's precision and a discipline that we bring that is
> rarely found anywhere else. We're very specific about our
> targets and we work on a three [point] safety system for
> every single move. The concept of rehearsing is for every
> second of stage combat you see on stage that's one hour of
> rehearsal.[11]

The 'Stratford' system relies on actions being both out of
distance and off-line, with the targets about six inches wide

of the shoulder and the hip. This approach is considered to provide a double level of safety, since if distance is breached the target will still go outside the body. Fight scenes are minutely planned and rehearsed; they are worked out in the first instance in negotiation between the director and the fight choreographer to ensure that the 'fights tell the story'. The process of rehearsal takes place separately from other forms of rehearsal, and the combat is painstakingly broken down into minute units of movement, rehearsed at half-speed and finally integrated into the production. The practice of 'fight calls' ensures that the fights do not change from night to night, and that the actors are physically and mentally prepared for each night's performance. Fight calls are part of a pre-show technical run-through that ensures continuity and safety: actors run through a truncated version of each fight under the supervision of a fight captain, usually one of the experienced actors in the show.

Even such a brief glance at modern stage combat indicates the collisions between original practices, conceived in such a hybrid form as this, and working with the embodied skills of contemporary actors. The ecology of skill might be thought of here as vertical. The elements include the kinesic intelligence of the individual actors, who may have different levels of training and may not have worked together before; the set and overall look and style of the production, especially the use or eschewing of lighting effects; the 'house style' of the organization; the time available for design and rehearsal of effects; audience expectations and knowledge (including what might be called the 'Game of Thrones effect', as audiences accustomed to large-scale quasi-medieval combat on television and film bring this form of skilled viewing into the theatre); and balancing safety and believability in a modern environment. Thus thinking – including thinking with the body or kinesic intelligence – is very differently distributed in the cognitive ecology of the 'reconstructed' stage.

However, stage combat is an emerging and changing discipline, pursued by actors and non-actors alike for its own sake, not only to prepare for a production or to garner credentials for a résumé. The Toronto-based Rapier Wit, for example, describes its constituency as 'stage combat fans who pursue our passion because it's fun and challenging and so much more than it seems'.[12] The director, Daniel Levinson, has been teaching stage combat since 1991. Rapier Wit has a similar range of classes to those on offer at most drama schools, including rapier, quarterstaff, small sword, sword and buckler, cape and rapier, as well as training in unarmed combat. Unlike the traditional school model, however, Rapier Wit also works as a salon; students attend open nights, during which they try out new weapons and techniques. Rather than training for certain parts, these actor-combatants, under the eye of instructors, learn to improvise and to gain embodied knowledge of partner-work, which is essential for skilled fighting. It is completely distinct from the discipline of electric fencing, straddling the line between sport and art. Building on a foundation of embodied experience and increasing expertise in training, this is a form of combat that is developing into an emergent practice of its own, with significant overlaps with historical fencing schools such as *schola gladitoria* in London. It remains to be seen what effect such modes of expertise and training will have on stage productions, or indeed whether these forms will become shows in their own right.

Dance on reconstructed stages

Because dance tends not to affect plot in as direct a way as a fight does, it is much easier to omit from modern productions. Dance leaves an affect gap rather than a plot gap. With limited time to produce these Shakespearean plays, and the complications of managing the verse, costumes, sets and the absolute need for specialized training in fight choreography, dance can be seen as a desirable but ultimately expendable extra. After all, modern productions have other means of manipulating affect and bridging emotional states in the plays, lighting effects being the most obvious.

The unfamiliarity of early modern dance presents challenges for actors and audience alike. Spectators may have a technical vocabulary for skilled viewing of classical ballet or ballroom dancing, but the stateliness of the pavan or the trickiness of the galliard may be beyond them. And while actors will surely have movement training and may well have trained in historical dance, dance choreographers, like fight choreographers, will normally have a cast with very unequal training and expertise in dance. While some of the basic steps may be simple, as we saw in Chapter 4, these are precisely the techniques that can be most difficult to perform with style and grace and for an untutored audience to appreciate. The more difficult 'tricks', such as those which early modern men devoted enormous time and attention to mastering, are a very particular and situated form of expertise that develops within specific skill ecologies and cannot easily be replicated or imitated.

Scholarship on early modern historical dance has always had strong research-in-practice elements, and dance research has been intimately tied to dance reconstruction. Embodied experience in dance pedagogy and practice is a virtual necessity to tease out the kinetic underpinnings of the textual accounts that remain to us. Individual researchers such as Ingrid Brainard, Julia Sutton, Anne Daye and Jennifer Nevile, as well as collaborative projects like the Shakespeare and Dance Project coordinated by Linda McJanet, Emily Winerock and Amy Rodgers, have contributed enormously to our understanding of the complexities of early modern dance.[13]

There is always tension between historical recovery work such as this and the exigencies of producing a play, whether in an original practices setting or not. The choreographer Ken Pierce recalls a director protesting, 'I don't do archaeology!'[14] Pierce identifies three approaches to historical dance in modern productions: an archaeological approach 'that aims for historical accuracy within the imagined timeframe of the play itself'; an 'unconstrained approach' that seeks 'to convey the essential story and meaning of the play in a staging adapted to contemporary tastes and circumstances'; and a 'historically informed' approach that 'attempts to recapture … both the essence of the piece and its performance details as they might have been presented to earlier audiences'.[15] Many original practices companies choose a melding of these approaches – for example the American Shakespeare Center introduces actor-led songs and improvised dances that seek to connect the play's story to contemporary musical knowledge and associations of its audience.[16]

Perhaps the best example of an 'emergent original practice' is the jig performed at the end of plays in Shakespeare's Globe.[17] These dances are 'historically informed', but they are certainly not archaeological. There is certainly evidence of the practice of dancing at the end of early modern plays. Scattered references to accounts of extra-fictional dancing include the apology at the end of *Henry IV, Part II*:

> Here I commit my body to your mercies. Bate me some, and I will pay you some, and, as most debtors do, promise you infinitely: and so I kneel down before you – but, indeed, to pray for the Queen.
>
> If my tongue cannot entreat you to acquit me, will you command me to use my legs? And yet that were but light payment, to dance out of your debt. But a good conscience will make any possible satisfaction, and so would I.
>
> (*Henry IV, Part II*, Epilogue, 13–22)

The epilogue ends by differentiating Falstaff from Oldcastle in response to objections from Oldcastle's family: 'Oldcastle died martyr, and this is not the man' (*Epi*. 32). This disclaimer was no doubt the reason for the epilogue in the first place, and may have been a 'temporary' epilogue,[18] which stayed attached to the play in the publication of the 1600 quarto.[19] Although perhaps only an unintended consequence of the disclaimer, the epilogue nevertheless gives us a sense of what might happen at the end of the play, possibly the promise of a jig: 'the final (if feigned) draining away of the players' vigor, their complete employment in the service of the audience. Perhaps it demonstrated, or seemed to demonstrate, a kind of real labour on the part of the actors, who were regularly mocked because their only work was play.'[20]

Exactly what constituted a jig is hard to determine, as references to jigs could mean 'a piece of music, a vigorous dance or singing a ballad', or in the case of professional theatre, all three: 'a musical sung-drama sometimes featuring dance'.[21] The 'robustly physical gestures and comic business'[22] that constituted a jig seems to have been primarily the domain of the clown-as-celebrity, and much contemporary scholarship on its significance sees the jig, like the clown, as a counterbalance to the waxing influence of author-centred drama. But other evidence of post-play entertainment seems to point towards a rather different kind of dance. Thomas Platter recorded his pleasure at watching the dance in a visit to London in 1599:

Den 21 Septembris [1599] nach dem Imbissessen, etwan umb zwey uhren, bin ich mitt meiner geselschaft über dz wasser gefahren, haben in dem streüwinen Dachhaus die Tragedy vom ersten Keyser Julio Caesare mitt ohngefahr 15 personen sehen gar artlich argieren; zu endt dur Comedien dantzeten sie ihrem gebrauch nach gar überausz zierlich, ye zwen in mannes undt 2 in weiber kleideren angethan, wunderbahrlich mitt einanderen.[23]

Clegg and Skeaping translate the note in this way:

On 21 September at about two o'clock I crossed over the water with my party, and in the thatched building saw the tragedy of the first Emperor Julius Caesar, very well performed by around 15 people. At the end of the play, as is customary, they danced quite elegantly with two people dressed as men and two as women.[24]

They suggest that Platter may have seen 'elegant dancing' but failed to hear bawdy jokes, which is possible of course, except that the word 'elegant' scarcely seems to describe the sort of 'robustly physical gestures' that characterized the jig.

Claire van Kampen, in her essay on the evolution of musical practice at Shakespeare's Globe, wrestles with precisely this question. She notes that Platter's description seems at odds with other accounts of the jig, nor does it provide a useful model for modern reconstructed theatres:

> If the music was instrumentally complex, and the dance therefore perhaps more than a jig and caper (would Platter have referred to a jig and caper as 'exceeding fine'?) then this would not seem to be having to battle against audience applause, as our current jigs have to. The notion of a 'curtain call' is too ingrained in modern audiences to cope with the idea of appreciatively but silently watching four actors dance a pavane at the end of a long play.[25]

Van Kampen astutely observes that whatever reconstructed practices are imported into the Globe, these must still intersect with audience expectation, desire and experience. After three hours of standing or of sitting on hard seats, the audience at the Globe is primed for movement, ready not just to applaud decorously, as they might in a proscenium theatre, but to engage in and with the action. The audience cannot hear with Elizabethan ears, nor is theirs the same skilled viewing that early modern audiences experienced. Van Kampen writes that:

> Perhaps increasingly in this area we have been pulled towards the audience's honest desire to show their appreciation for the actors in a Dionysian outburst of unbridled passion that denies musical subtlety. We must conclude that rather than having failed to reproduce an 'authentic jig' we have in fact arrived at a consensus: a 'modern' Globe audience absolutely expects there to be a 'jig' at the end of a

Shakespeare play, and would consider the play 'unfinished' if it were not there.[26]

So the jig in Shakespeare's Globe is an example of an emergent ecology of skill, shaped by audiences, actors, musicians and choreographers. In a long piece in the *Guardian* on Globe choreographer Sian Williams, Veronica Horwell writes that 'Williams doesn't create her jigs as a re-creation of a formal dance of the period. Her ideas are always more of an action replay of the play, all the important themes restated in motion.'[27] Williams works within the physical structure of the Globe, and, importantly, with the actors themselves, who have an uneven experience in dancing:

> Globe actors are the most mismatched chorus line ever – short, tall, wide, narrow, chaps with three left feet, and Jamie Parker, who can carry a Broadway musical, no problem. Most are apprehensive and Williams lets them develop things to build confidence and overcome their fears.

Horwell suggests that the actors are 'sharing ... the play experience with the audience, especially the Globe's crowd of groundlings who have stood still throughout'. 'The jigs have rhythm, rhythm first,' [notes Williams,] and as to the audience clapping along, 'you try and stop them.'

Anyone who has been to the Globe knows exactly what Williams means. Clapping to the beat of the dancing actors is one of the most powerful forms of synchronized experience. Robert Shaughnessy has argued that such moments are characteristic of the Globe experience. Observing that the 'Globe's jigs have attracted less attention than they should', Shaughnessy discusses the jig as a means of 'audience entrainment'.[28] Actors and audience are engaged in constant affective negotiation. The conditions of playing that afford entrainment demand particular kinds of skills on the part of the actors, who are both energized and unnerved by the audience response; in turn, the audience's response crosses the line from skilled viewing into embodied participation in the event.

The intersection between early modern skills and those employed by actors on reconstructed stages is complex. They are not simply replications of early modern practice, although reconstructive work such as that undertaken by historians of martial arts and dance can reveal much about the constraints and capacities of material objects, the way bodies move in space and in concert with one another, and the effect of physical space and the environment. Within a distributed cognitive ecology of skill, movements and actions can never be mere reproductions, yet the fusion of early modern skill and modern bodies is nevertheless a creative and productive collision of practices.

We still do not know precisely what was in Simon Jewell's box, the exact nature of the precious 'playing things' Robert Nicholls inherited from him. Lying inert in the box, these objects would have been as useless as Hamlet's pipe was to Guildenstern. Taken in hand with 'ready aptness', however, these objects are rendered animate; in turn they animate the player himself.

NOTES

Chapter 1: Introduction

1   Discussions of Jewell's will include Chiaki Hanabusa, 'The Will of Simon Jewell and the Queen's Men Tours in 1592', *Early Theatre* 16 (1) (2013): 11–30; Scott McMillin, 'Simon Jewell and the Queen's Men', *Review of English Studies* 27 (106) (1976): 174–7. The will is printed in E. A. J. Honigmann and Susan Brock, *Playhouse Wills 1558–1642* (Manchester: Manchester University Press, 1993), 58–60.

2   See Paul Menzer, *Anecdotal Shakespeare: A New Performance History* (London: Bloomsbury, 2015), for a description of Edwin Booth's trunk.

3   Honigmann and Brock, *Playhouse Wills*, 72–4.

4   Ibid., 73.

5   Hanabusa, 'The Will of Simon Jewell', 13.

6   Jean McIntyre, *Costumes and Scripts in the Elizabethan Theatres* (Edmonton: Alberta University Press, 1992), 83.

7   [Thomas Gainsford], *The Rich Cabinet Furnished with Varietie of Excellent Descriptions* (London: I. B. for Roger Jackson, 1616), 117v.

8   See Evelyn B. Tribble, 'Distributing Cognition in the Globe', *Shakespeare Quarterly* 56 (2) (2005): 135–55.

9   Kim Sterelny, *The Evolved Apprentice: How Evolution Made Humans Unique* (Cambridge, MA: MIT Press, 2012), xii.

10 See Evelyn B. Tribble and John Sutton, 'Cognitive Ecology as a Framework for Shakespearean Studies', *Shakespeare Studies* 39 (2011): 94–103, for a fuller account of the term.

11 Greg Downey, '"Practice Without Theory": A Neuroanthropological Perspective on Embodied Learning', *Journal of the Royal Anthropological Institute* 16 (2010): S22.

12   Barbara Ravelhofer, *The Early Stuart Masque: Dance,
     Costume, and Music* (Oxford: Oxford University Press, 2006),
     120. I take up this discussion on Foucauldian readings of dance
     in Chapter 3.

13   Pierre Bourdieu, *Outline of a Theory of Practice* (Cambridge
     and New York: Cambridge University Press, 1977), 72, 79.

14   Ibid., 94.

15   Greg Downey, 'Seeing with a "Sideways Glance": Visuomotor
     "Knowing" and the Plasticity of Perception', in *Ways of
     Knowing: New Approaches in the Anthropology of Experience
     and Learning*, ed. Mark Harris (Oxford: Berghahn Books,
     2007), 237. There is a debate in and among sociologists
     and anthropologists around the usefulness of habitus as a
     theoretical model for skill. Downey's argument that habitus is
     a 'black box' is vigorously contested by Loïc Wacquant, who
     argues instead that habitus can be seen both as a theoretical
     model and an empirical prompt to ethnographic work, such as
     his own auto-ethnographic account of becoming a boxer.

16   Greg Noble and Megan Watkins, 'So, How did Bourdieu Learn
     to Play Tennis? Habitus, Consciousness and Habituation',
     Cultural Studies 17 (3–4) (2003): 521.

17   Ibid., 524–5.

18   Ibid., 527.

19   Ibid., 528.

20   Ibid., 527.

21   Ibid.

22   Paul J. Feltovich, Michael J. Prietula and K. Anders Ericsson,
     'Studies of Expertise from Psychological Perspectives', in *The
     Cambridge Handbook of Expertise and Expert Performance*,
     ed. K. Anders Ericsson, Neil Charness, Paul J. Feltovich and
     Robert R. Hoffman (New York: Cambridge University Press,
     2006), 61.

23   Ibid.

24   Ibid., 60. Ericsson has recently argued that Gladwell radically
     oversimplifies his argument. See K. Anders Ericsson and Robert
     Pool, *Peak: Secrets from the New Science of Expertise* (New
     York: Houghton Mifflin, 2016).

25 Andrew Geeves et al., 'To Think or Not to Think: The Apparent Paradox of Expert Skill in Music Performance', *Educational Philosophy and Theory* 46 (6) (2013): 679.

26 Hubert L. Dreyfus, 'Overcoming the Myth of the Mental', *Topoi* 25 (1–2) (2006): 43.

27 Ibid., 48.

28 John Sutton et al., 'Applying Intelligence to the Reflexes: Embodied Skills and Habits Between Dreyfus and Descartes', *Journal of the British Society for Phenomenology* 42 (1) (2011): 78–103.

29 Ibid., 87.

30 Wayne Christensen, John Sutton and Doris J. F. McIlwain, 'Cognition in Skilled Action: Meshed Control and the Varieties of Skill Experience', *Mind and Language* 31 (1) (2016): 62.

31 Ibid.

32 Hal Burton, *Great Acting* (London: British Broadcasting Corporation, 1967), 71–2.

33 On fencing and timing, see Dori Coblentz, 'Killing Time in *Titus Andronicus*: Timing, Rhetoric, and the Art of Defense', *Journal for Early Modern Cultural Studies* 15 (4) (2015): 52–80. Adam Zucker's work on *The Places of Wit in Early Modern English Comedy* (Cambridge: Cambridge University Press, 2011) emphasizes the importance of wit display for the period. My work complements his in thinking of wit as an embodied and extended skill.

34 Vincento Saviolo, *His Practice* (London, 1595), C3r.

35 Ellen Spolsky, 'Elaborated Knowledge: Reading Kinesis in Pictures', *Poetics Today* 17 (2) (1996): 157–80.

36 Guillemette Bolens, *The Style of Gestures: Embodiment and Cognition in Literary Narrative* (Baltimore, MD: Johns Hopkins University Press, 2012); Shaun Gallagher, *How the Body Shapes the Mind* (Oxford: Clarendon Press, 2005), 37.

37 Quoted in Bolens, *Style of Gestures*, 22.

38 Greg Downey, 'Educating the Eyes: Biocultural Anthropology and Physical Education', *Anthropology in Action* 12 (2) (2005): 57.

39   See Lucy Munro, *Children of the Queen's Revels* (Cambridge: Cambridge University Press, 2005); Scott McMillin and Sally-Beth McLean, *The Queen's Men and their Plays* (Cambridge: Cambridge University Press, 1998); Laurence Manley and Sally-Beth McLean, *Lord Strange's Men and their Plays* (Cambridge: Cambridge University Press, 2014), as well as Siobhan Keenan, *Acting Companies and their Plays in Shakespeare's London* (London: Bloomsbury, 2014).

40   Among this rich body of work is Erika Lin, *Shakespeare and the Materiality of Performance* (New York: Palgrave, 2012); Richard Preiss, *Clowning and Authorship in Early Modern Theatre* (Cambridge: Cambridge University Press, 2014); Gina Bloom, *Voice in Motion: Staging Gender, Shaping Sound in Early Modern England* (Philadelphia: University of Pennsylvania Press, 2007); Philip Butterworth, *Magic on the Early English Stage* (Cambridge: Cambridge University Press, 2005); see also *Early Modern Theatricality*, ed. Henry S. Turner (Oxford: Oxford University Press, 2013), especially chapters on 'Games' by Gina Bloom and 'Intertheatricality' by William N. West; *Shakespeare's Theatre and the Effects of Performance*, ed. Tiffany Stern and Farah Karim-Cooper (London: Bloomsbury, 2014); and the recent collection of essays on 'Skill' in *Shakespeare Studies* 43 (2015), including essays by Richard Preiss on actors' competition, Penelope Woods on audience skill, Tom Bishop on feet and skill. Farah Karim-Cooper's *The Hand on the Shakespearean Stage* (London: Bloomsbury, 2016), which I discuss at greater length in Chapter 2, is an invaluable discussion of gesture on the historical and contemporary stage. Examples of historical work on early modern players include J. H. Astington, *Actors and Acting in Shakespeare's Time: The Art of Stage Playing* (Cambridge: Cambridge University Press, 2010); David Kathman, 'Grocers, Goldsmiths, and Drapers: Freemen and Apprentices in the Elizabethan Theater', *Shakespeare Quarterly* 55 (2004): 1–49; David Kathman, 'Players, Livery Companies, and Apprentices', in *The Oxford Handbook of Early Modern Theatre* (Oxford University Press, 2011), 413–28.

41   Alan Dessen and Leslie Thomson, *A Dictionary of Stage*

Directions in English Drama 1580–1642 (Cambridge: Cambridge University Press, 1999), 2–3.

42 Ibid., 7.

43 Ibid., 13.

44 Ibid., 37.

45 Ibid., 42, 45.

46 Ibid., 44.

47 Ibid., 55.

48 Ibid., 65.

49 Ibid., 245.

50 Ibid., 39, 92.

51 Ibid., 50.

52 Ibid.

53 Ibid., 176.

54 Ibid., 65.

55 E. K. Chambers, *The Elizabethan Stage* (Oxford: Clarendon Press, 1923), 2: 24.

56 Stephen Gosson, *Plays Confuted in Five Actions* (London, 1582), E1r. See Michael Hattaway, *Elizabethan Popular Theatre: Plays in Performance* (London: Routledge, 1982), for a discussion of the extra-dramatic elements of Elizabethan performance.

57 Chambers, *The Elizabethan Stage*, 2: 550.

58 Ben Jonson, *Bartholomew Faire*, 'The Induction', in *The Cambridge Edition of the Works of Ben Jonson*, ed. David Bevington, Martin Butler and Ian Donaldson (Cambridge: Cambridge University Press, 2012), IV: 276–82, 277.

59 Ibid., 276.

60 Ibid., 277.

61 Ibid., 281.

62 W. W. Greg, *Two Elizabethan Stage Abridgements: The Battle of Alcazar and Orlando Furioso* (Oxford: Oxford University Press, 1922); L. B. Wright, 'Variety Entertainment by Elizabethan Strolling Players', *Journal of English and Germanic Philology* 26 (3) (1927): 294–303.

63   On the relationship between sport and theatre, see Donald
     Hedrick, 'Real Entertainment: Sportification, Coercion, and
     Carceral Theater', in *Thunder at a Playhouse: Essaying
     Shakespeare and the Early Modern Stage*, ed. Peter Kanelos
     and Matt Kozusko (Selinsgrove, PA: Susquehanna University
     Press, 2010), 50–66. I discuss this point at greater length in
     Chapter 6.

64   For a discussion of 'feats of activity' on the early modern stage,
     see Butterworth, *Magic*.

65   Roger Ascham, *Toxophilus*, ed. Peter Medine (Tempe, AZ:
     ACMRS, 2002), 125.

66   Lois Potter, *The Life of William Shakespeare: A Critical
     Biography*, 2nd edn (Chichester: Wiley-Blackwell, 2012), 66.

67   Christina Grasseni, 'Skilled Vision: An Apprenticeship in
     Breeding Aesthetics', *Social Anthropology* 12 (1) (2004): 42.

68   Ibid.

69   Ibid., 43.

70   Barbara Montero, 'Practice Makes Perfect: The Effect of Dance
     Training on the Aesthetic Judge', *Phenomenology and the
     Cognitive Sciences* 11 (1) (2012): 59–68.

71   Doris McIlwain and John Sutton, 'Yoga From the Mat Up:
     How Words Alight on Bodies', *Educational Philosophy and
     Theory* 46 (6) (2014): 657.

72   Baldassarre Castiglione, *The Book of the Courtier*, trans.
     Thomas Hoby (London, 1561).

73   See Gregory M. Colón Semenza, *Sport, Politics, and Literature
     in the English Renaissance* (Cranbury, NJ: Associated
     University Press, 2005), for an excellent analysis of the
     relationship between sport and humanism in the early modern
     period.

74   Greg Downey, 'Producing Pain: Techniques and Technologies
     in No-Holds-Barred Fighting', *Social Studies of Science* 37 (2)
     (2007): 203.

75   Lin, *Materiality of Performance*, 109.

Chapter 2: The Moving Body

1   William Shakespeare, *Troilus and Cressida*, ed. David
    Bevington, *The Arden Shakespeare*, Third Series (London:
    Bloomsbury, 2015).

2   Maxine Sheets-Johnstone, 'Embodied Minds or Mindful
    Bodies? A Question of Fundamental, Inherently Inter-Related
    Aspects of Animation', *Subjectivity* 4 (4) (2011): 459.

3   Tim Ingold, *Making: Anthropology, Archaeology, Art and
    Architecture* (London: Routledge, 2013), 94.

4   Sheets-Johnstone, 'Embodied Minds', 459.

5   Ibid., 460, 459.

6   Ibid., 460.

7   For a contemporary discussion of the relationship between
    gesture and hypnosis, see Andrew Lawrence-King's work
    on historical action and baroque gesture: http://www.
    theharpconsort.com/#!historical–action/c12q3 (accessed 17
    March 2016).

8   'An Excellent Actor', in *English Professional Theatre,
    1530–1660*, ed. G. Wickham, H. Berry and W. Ingram
    (Cambridge: Cambridge University Press, 2000), 181. As
    Wickham notes, Webster, the presumed author of this
    'character', is responding to John Cocke's satirical 'Description
    of a Common Player', published in 1615.

9   Wickham et al., *English Professional Theatre*, 181.

10 For the relationship between playing and magic, see Donald
    Hedrick, 'Distracting Othello: Tragedy and the Rise of
    Magic', *PMLA* 129 (4) (2014): 649–71. The psychological
    underpinnings of the art of distraction are explored by
    Stephen L. Macknik, Susana Martinez-Conde and Sandra
    Blakeslee, *Sleights of Mind: What the Neuroscience of Magic
    Reveals About our Everyday Deceptions* (London: Macmillan,
    2010).

11 Joseph R. Roach, *The Player's Passion: Studies in the Science
    of Acting* (Ann Arbor: University of Michigan Press, 1985),
    44–5.

12 Mayne's homage to Donne is quoted by John Bulwer, *Chirologia: Or the Natural Language of the Hand and Chironomia: Or the Art of Manual Rhetoric*, ed. James W. Cleary (Carbondale and Edwardsville: Southern Illinois Press, [1644] 1972), C2v.

13 John H. Astington, 'Actors and the Body: Meta-Theatrical Rhetoric in Shakespeare', *Gesture* 6 (2) (2006): 242.

14 John H. Astington, *Actors and Acting in Shakespeare's Time: The Art of Stage Playing* (Cambridge: Cambridge University Press, 2010), 40.

15 Anthony Munday, 'Players Incline their Audience to Wickedness', in *English Professional Theatre*, ed. Wickham et al., 163. Wickham notes that Munday takes this phrase over wholesale from William Bavand's 1559 translation of Hans Eisermann's treatise *Touching the Good Order of a Commonweal*; see Wickham et al., 158.

16 Thomas Nashe, 'Pierce Penniless His Supplication to the Devil' (London, 1592), sig. H2r, in Thomas Nashe, *The Unfortunate Traveller and Other Works*, ed. J. B. Steane (Harmondsworth: Penguin, 1972), 112–13.

17 Thomas Heywood, *An Apology for Actors* (1612), C2v.

18 Philip Massinger, 'The Roman Actor' (1626), in *Drama of the English Renaissance II: The Stuart Period*, ed. Russell Fraser and Norman Rabkin (New York: Macmillan, 1976), 721.

19 Heywood, *Apology*, C2v.

20 Ibid., D1v.

21 For a discussion of the part as a cognitive artefact, see Tribble, 'Distributing Cognition', 135–55. Tiffany Stern's work on this subject includes *Rehearsal from Shakespeare to Sheridan* (Oxford: Oxford University Press, 2000); *Documents of Performance in Early Modern England* (Cambridge: Cambridge University Press, 2009); Simon Palfrey and Tiffany Stern, *Shakespeare in Parts* (Oxford: Oxford University Press, 2007).

22 For a recent thorough and sympathetic analysis of Bulwer's work, see Farah Karim-Cooper, *The Hand on the Shakespearean Stage*.

23 Robert Toft, *With Passionate Voice: Re-Creative Singing* *in Sixteenth-Century England and Italy* (Oxford: Oxford University Press, 2014), 185.

24 Bulwer, *Chironomia*, B8v.

25 Ibid., A5r.

26 Ibid., B8v.

27 Ibid., K7r.

28 Ibid., C3r–C3v.

29 Ibid., K72–K8v.

30 Shaun Gallagher, *How the Body Shapes the Mind*, 2.

31 Sheets-Johnstone, 460.

32 Kim Sterelny, 'Language, Gesture, Skill: The Co-Evolutionary Foundations of Language', *Philosophical Transactions of the Royal Society of London: B Biological Sciences* 367 (1599) (2012): 2146.

33 Susan Goldin-Meadow and Sian Beilock, 'Action's Influence on Thought: The Case of Gesture', *Perspectives on Psychological Science* 5 (6) (2010): 668.

34 Susan Goldin-Meadow, Howard Nusbaum, Spencer D. Kelly and Susan Wagner, 'Explaining Math: Gesturing Lightens the Load', *Psychological Science* 12 (6) (2001): 521.

35 Andy Clark, 'Gesture as Thought?', in *The Hand, an Organ of the Mind: What the Manual Tells the Mental*, ed. Zdravko Radman (Cambridge, MA: MIT Press, 2013), 263.

36 Wim T. Pouw, Jacqueline A. de Nooijer, Tamara van Gog, Rolf A. Zwaan and Fred Paas, 'Toward a More Embedded/Extended Perspective on the Cognitive Function of Gestures', *Frontiers in Psychology* 5 (359) (2014): 9.

37 Ibid., 12.

38 Ingold, *Making*, 112.

39 Ibid., 115.

40 See Evelyn B. Tribble, *Cognition in the Globe: Attention and Memory in Shakespeare's Theatre* (Houndmills, Basingstoke: Palgrave Macmillan, 2011), Chapter 2, for a fuller discussion of the arts of gesture in Shakespeare and Thomas Kyd.

41 Gabriel Egan, 'Elizabethan Acting', in *The Oxford Companion to Shakespeare*, ed. Michael Dobson and Stanley Wells (Oxford: Oxford University Press, 2001), 2.

42 David M. Bevington, *Action is Eloquence: Shakespeare's Language of Gesture* (Cambridge, MA: Harvard University Press, 1984), 71.

43 Morton Eustis, 'The Actor Attacks His Part: Lyn Fontanne and Alfred Lunt', in *Theatre Arts: On Acting*, ed. Laurence Senelick (London and New York: Routledge, 2008), 287–95.

44 Sherman Ewing, 'Wanted: More Stars, Less "Method"', in *Theatre Arts: On Acting*, ed. Laurence Senelick (London and New York: Routledge, 2008), 284.

45 Cedric Hardwicke, 'The Moribund Craft of Acting', *Theatre Arts: On Acting*, ed. Laurence Senelick (London and New York: Routledge, 2008), 363.

46 Rick Kemp, *Embodied Acting: What Neuroscience Tells Us About Performance* (London: Routledge, 2012), 23.

47 Cicely Berry, *The Actor and the Text* (London: Virgin Books, 2000), 22, 23.

48 Mark Evans, *Movement Training for the Modern Actor* (London and New York: Routledge, 2008).

49 Kemp, *Embodied Acting*, 37.

50 John Lutterbie, *Toward a General Theory of Acting: Cognitive Science and Performance* (New York: Palgrave Macmillan, 2011), 112.

51 An important exception to this general rule is some of the practice-based research conducted both in original practices theatres and in baroque opera and song. 'Gesture Labs' conducted at Shakespeare's Globe in London in 2010 and 2015 have shown the fluidity and variety of gestural practices in the early modern drama. See Karim-Cooper, *The Hand on the Shakespearean Stage*, and the description of Miranda Fay-Thomas's 2015 lab: https://www.kcl.ac.uk/cultural/-/Current-projects/Gesture-Lab.aspx (accessed 17 March 2016).

52 Ingold, *Making*, 115.

53 Ibid.

54 Paul Menzer, 'That Old Saw: Early Modern Acting and the
    Infinite Regress', *Shakespeare Bulletin* 22 (2) (2004): 27–44.

55 Farah Karim-Cooper, *The Hand on the Shakespearean Stage*, 78.

56 William Shakespeare, *A Winter's Tale*, ed. J. H. P. Pafford,
    in *The Arden Shakespeare Complete Works*, ed. Richard
    Proudfoot, Ann Thompson and David Scott Kastan (London:
    Arden Shakespeare, 2011), 1279–312.

57 *Youth's Behaviour: or Decencie in Conversation Amongst Men*,
    trans. Francis Hawkins (London: W. Lee, 1661), 21.

58 Heather James, *Shakespeare's Troy: Drama, Politics, and the
    Translation of the Empire* (Cambridge: Cambridge University
    Press, 1997), 98.

59 Anthony B. Dawson, ed., *Troilus and Cressida*, New
    Cambridge Shakespeare (Cambridge: Cambridge University
    Press, 2003), note to 1.3.154, 95.

60 Bulwer, *Chironomia*, 189.

61 Lisa Smithson and Elena Nicoladis, 'Lending a Hand to
    Imagery? The Impact of Visuospatial Working Memory
    Interference Upon Iconic Gesture Production in a Narrative
    Task', *Journal of Nonverbal Behavior* 38 (2) (2014): 248.

62 George Villiers, Duke of Buckingham, *The Rehearsal* (London:
    Printed for R. Bentley and S. Magnes, 1683), 33.

63 Ibid. I am indebted to Tom Bishop for this reference.

64 Dawson, ed., introduction to *Troilus and Cressida*, 45.

65 Ibid.

66 Eric S. Mallin, *Inscribing the Time: Shakespeare and the End
    of Elizabethan England* (Berkeley: University of California
    Press, 1995), 34.

67 Ibid., 29.

68 Henry Peacham, *The Garden of Eloquence* (1593): http://www.
    perseus.tufts.edu/hopper/text?doc=Perseus:text:1999.03.009
    6:part=Schemates%20Rhetorical:subpart=The%20third%20
    order:section=Amplification (accessed 17 March 2016). See
    Heinrich F. Plett, *Rhetoric and Renaissance Culture* (Berlin and
    New York: Walter de Gruyter, 2004), 272, for a full analysis of
    Shakespeare's use of this trope.

69 Peacham, *Garden of Eloquence* (1593) http://www.perseus. tufts.edu/hopper/text?doc=Perseus:text:1999.03.0096:part= Schemates%20Rhetorical:subpart=The%20third%20 order:section=Amplification (accessed 17 March 2016).

70 Jonathan Hart, *Reading the Renaissance*, Routledge Revivals: Culture, Poetics, and Drama (London: Routledge, 2015), 141.

71 Herbert Blau, *The Eye of Prey: Subversions of the Postmodern* (Bloomington and Indianapolis: Indiana University Press, 1987), 164.

72 Lutterbie, *General Theory of Acting*, 147.

73 Eugenio Barba, *The Paper Canoe: A Guide to Theatre Anthropology*, trans. Richard Fowler (London and New York: Routledge, 1995), 15.

74 See Tom Bishop, 'Boot and Shtick', for a survey of the feet and walking in early modern theatre.

75 *The Pilgrimage to Parnassus with the Two Parts of the Return from Parnassus: Three Comedies Performed in St. John's College, Cambridge, A.D. 1597–1601*, ed. Rev. W. D. Macray (Oxford: Clarendon Press, 1886), 138.

76 Timothy M. O'Sullivan, *Walking in Roman Culture* (Cambridge: Cambridge University Press, 2011), 7.

77 Ibid., 8.

78 Gallagher, *Body Shapes the Mind*, 37–8.

79 Hubert Godard, quoted in Bolens, *Style of Gestures*, 22.

80 Kerri L. Johnson and Maggie Shiffrar, 'Making Great Strides: Advances in Research on Perceptions of the Human Body', in *People Watching: Social, Perceptual, and Neurophysiological Studies of Body Perception*, ed. Kerri L. Johnson and Maggie Shiffrar (Oxford: Oxford University Press, 2013), 3.

81 Michael J. Richardson and Lucy Johnston, 'Person Recognition from Dynamic Events: The Kinematic Specification of Individual Identity in Walking Style', *Journal of Nonverbal Behavior* 29 (1) (2005): 27.

82 R. E. Gunns, L. Johnston and S. M. Hudson, 'Victim Selection and Kinematics: A Point-Light Investigation of Vulnerability to Attack', *Journal of Nonverbal Behavior* 26 (3) (2002): 129–58.

83 Angela Book, K. Costello and J. A. Camilleri, 'Psychopathy and Victim Selection: The Use of Gait as a Cue to Vulnerability', *Journal of Interpersonal Violence* 28 (11) (2013): 2378.

84 Michel de Montaigne, 'Of Presumption', in *The Complete Works of Montaigne*, trans. Donald M. Frame (Stanford, CA: Stanford University Press, 1957), 479.

85 Edward Connerton, *How Societies Remember* (Cambridge: Cambridge University Press, 1989), 90.

86 Gunns et al., 'Victim Selection and Kinematics', 129–58.

87 See J. Henrich, Steven J. Heine and Ara Norenzayan, 'The Weirdest People in the World', *Behavioral and Brain Sciences* 33 (2–3) (2010): 61–83, for a critique of this practice.

88 Marcel Mauss, 'Techniques of the Body', *Economy and Society* 2 (1) (1973): 73.

89 Baldesar Castiglione, *The Book of the Courtier*, trans. George Bull (Harmondsworth: Penguin Books, 1967), 65.

90 Bryson, *From Courtesy to Civility: Changing Codes of Conduct in Early Modern England* (Oxford: Oxford University Press, 2004), 108.

91 James Cleland, *Hero-Paideia, or the Institution of a Young Man* (Oxford: Ioseph Barnes, 1607), 170.

92 Plutarch, 'The Life of Dion', in *Lives: Dion and Brutus. Timoleon and Aemilius Paulus*, Vol. VI, trans. Bernadotte Perrin, 984–1009 (Cambridge, MA: Harvard University Press, 1918), 3: §958.

93 Unless otherwise stated, all quotations from Shakespeare's plays are from *The Arden Shakespeare Complete Works*.

94 *All's Well That Ends Well*, in *The Norton Shakespeare*, ed. Stephen Greenblatt (New York and London: W. W. Norton and Co., 1997), 2.3.82. fn. 5.

95 Russell Fraser, introduction to *All's Well That Ends Well* (Cambridge: Cambridge University Press, 2004), 13.

96 Thomas Wright, *The Passions of the Mind in General* (London, 1604) ed. William Webster Newbold (New York: Garland, 1986), 174.

97   Mark Rylance doubled Posthumus and Cloten in a 2001
      production of the play at Shakespeare's Globe. See Raphael
      Lyne, 'Recognition in *Cymbeline*', in *Late Shakespeare:
      1608–1613*, ed. Andrew Power and Rory Loughnane
      (Cambridge: Cambridge University Press, 2012), 56–70.

98   In an interesting feedback loop, one of the pointless games
      Jonson makes up is later put in a handbook called *The
      Mysteries of Love and Courtship* (London, 1658), V2r.

Chapter 3: 'Skill of Weapon'

1   Greg Downey, 'Producing Pain', 203.

2   Greg Downey, 'Seeing with a "Sideways Glance"', 223.

3   Marcel Mauss, 'Techniques of the Body', 85.

4   Ibid., 73.

5   See Mauss, *Manual of Ethnography*, ed. N. J. Allen, trans. D.
      Lussier (New York: Dürkheim Press/Berghahn Press, 2007),
      25–6, for a comprehensive list of areas of investigation of
      techniques of the body.

6   See Kathryn Linn Geurts, *Culture and the Senses: Bodily Ways
      of Knowing in an African Community* (Berkeley: University of
      California Press, 2003).

7   Georges Vigarello, 'The Upward Training of the Body from the
      Age of Chivalry to Courtly Civility', in *Fragments for a History
      of the Human Body* II, ed. Michel Feher, Ramona Naddaff and
      Nadia Tarzi (New York: Zone, 1989), 148–99.

8   Michael J. Ryan, 'I Did Not Return a Master, But Well
      Cudgeled Was I: The Role of "Body Techniques" in the
      Transmission of Venezuelan Stick and Machete Fighting',
      Journal of Latin American and Caribbean Anthropology 16 (1)
      (2011): 4.

9   Ibid., 16.

10   Downey, 'Seeing with a "Sideways Glance"', 228.

11   Ibid., 237.

12   Greg Downey, 'Balancing Between Cultures: Equilibrium

in Capoeira', in *The Encultured Brain: An Introduction to Neuroanthropology*, ed. Daniel H. Lende and Greg Downey (Cambridge, MA: MIT Press, 2012), 169.

13 Evelyn B. Tribble, 'Where are the Archers in Shakespeare?', *ELH* 82 (3) (2015): 789–814.

14 George Silver, *Paradoxes of Defence* (1599), A4v.

15 Francis Walsingham, 'Elizabeth: January 1578', in *Calendar of State Papers, Scotland: Volume 5, 1574–81*, ed. William K Boyd (London: His Majesty's Stationery Office, 1907), 268–70. Available online: http://www.british-history.ac.uk/cal-state-papers/scotland/vol5/pp268-27 (accessed 17 March 2016).

16 Jennifer Low, *Manhood and the Duel* (London: Palgrave, 2003).

17 Discussions of the Master of Defence include Jay P. Anglin, 'The Schools of Defense in Elizabethan London', *Renaissance Quarterly* 37 (3) (1984): 393–410; Charles Edelman, *Brawl Ridiculous: Swordfighting in Shakespeare's Plays* (Manchester: Manchester University Press, 1992); Mary McElroy and Kent Cartwright, 'Public Fencing Contests on the Elizabethan Stage', *Journal of Sports History* 13 (3) (1986): 193–211. The existing records of the organization have been compiled by Herbert Berry, *The Noble Science: A Study and Transcription of Sloane Ms. 2530* (London, Newark and Toronto: Associated University Presses, 1991).

18 Berry, *Noble Science*.

19 McElroy and Cartwright, 'Public Fencing Contests', 193, 194 and 200.

20 Berry, *Noble Science*, 3.

21 Ibid., 55.

22 Berry, *Noble Science*, 65; see also 'Event Record: John Devell Barely Passes His Fencing Provost's Prize at the Theatre' (10 August 1582), in *Early Modern London Theatres*. Available online: http://www.emlot.kcl.ac.uk/db/record/event/6532 (accessed 17 March 2016).

23 Berry, *Noble Science*, 87, 89.

24 Ibid., 6.

25   Ibid., 11.

26   Gregory M. Colón Semenza, *Sport, Politics, and Literature in the English Renaissance*, 39.

27   Alexandra Shepard, *Meanings of Manhood in Early Modern England* (Oxford: Oxford University Press, 2006), 147.

28   See, for example, Heith Copes, Andy Hochstetler and Craig J. Forsyth, 'Peaceful Warriors: Codes for Violence Among Adult Male Bar Fighters', *Criminology* 51 (3) (2013): 761–94; E. B. Cohen, 'Once We Put Our Helmets On, There Are No More Friends: The "Fights" Session in the Israeli Army Course for Close-Combat Instructors', *Armed Forces and Society* 37 (3) (2011): 512–33.

29   Will Stokes, 'The Epistle to the Reader', in *The Vaulting-Master, or, the Art of Vaulting Reduced to a Method, Comprized Under Certaine Rules, Illustrated by Examples, and Now Primarily Set Forth by Will. Stokes* ([Oxford]: Printed for Richard Davis in Oxon, 1652).

30   In *Three Elizabethan Fencing Manuals*, ed. James L. Jackson (Delmar, NY: Scholars' Facsimiles and Reprints, 1972).

31   Anglin, 'Schools of Defense', 408.

32   Giacomo di Grassi, 'His True Arte of Defence' (1594), in *Three Elizabethan Fencing Manuals*, A1v; 13.

33   Ibid., Eer: 177, Eev; 178, A2v; 16.

34   Ibid., A2V; 16.

35   Ibid., D4v; 44.

36   Vincentio Saviolo, *His Practice* (1595), in *Three Elizabethan Fencing Manuals*, C3r.

37   Ibid., C3v; 192.

38   Ibid., C1r; 199.

39   Ibid., C4v; 206.

40   Silver wrote a treatise on the art of defence that remained unpublished (Sloane MS No. 376). His *Brief Instructions* is reprinted in *Three Elizabethan Fencing Manuals*, ed. James L. Jackson, 571–634.

41   Ibid., A4v; 494.

42 George Silver, 'Paradoxes of Defence' (1599), in *Three Elizabethan Fencing Manuals*, A5r–v; 495–6.

43 Ibid., B1r; 499.

44 Ibid., B2v; 502.

45 Ibid., 494–5.

46 Ibid., 522–3.

47 Ibid., K4v; 569.

48 Ibid., K3r; 567.

49 Ibid., K3r; 567.

50 George Hale, *The Private Schoole of Defence* (London, 1614), C2v.

51 Edelman, *Brawl Ridiculous*, 7.

52 Alan Dessen, 'The Logic of Elizabethan Stage Violence: Some Alarms and Excursions for Modern Critics, Editors, and Directors', *Renaissance Drama* 9 (1978): 49.

53 Christopher Marlowe, *The Jew of Malta*, 3.2.7.

54 Ian Borden, 'The Blackfriars Gladiators: Masters of Fence, Playing a Prize, and the Elizabethan and Stuart Theater', in *Inside Shakespeare: Essays on the Blackfriars Stage*, ed. Paul Menzer (Selinsgrove, PA: Susquehanna University Press, 2006), 132–46.

55 *Romeo and Juliet*, ed. René Weis, Arden Shakespeare Third Series (London: Bloomsbury, 2012).

56 René Weis, Introduction to *Romeo and Juliet*, 109–10.

57 John Jowett, 'Henry Chettle and the First Quarto of *Romeo and Juliet*', *The Papers of the Bibliographical Society of America* 92 (1) (1998), 72, 54.

58 Weis, Introduction to *Romeo and Juliet*, 115.

59 John Florio, *Florio His Firste Fruites* (London, 1578); quoted in A. L. Soens, 'Tybalt's Spanish Fencing in *Romeo and Juliet*', *Shakespeare Quarterly* 20 (2) (1969): 122.

60 Joan Ozark Holmer, '"Draw, If You Be Men": Saviolo's Significance for *Romeo and Juliet*', *Shakespeare Quarterly* 45 (2) (1994): 163–89.

61 Soens, 'Tybalt's Spanish Fencing', 124.

62 I am indebted to Ian Borden's careful description of the techniques of the duel scene in 'The Blackfriars Gladiators', as well as to his demonstration of the scene at the American Shakespeare Center Blackfriars conference, October 2001.

63 Silver, 'Paradoxes of Defence', C3v; 512.

64 Susan Snyder, '*Romeo and Juliet*: Comedy into Tragedy', *Essays in Criticism* 20 (4) (1970): 391.

65 Ben Jonson, 'Informations to William Drummond of Hawthornden', in *The Cambridge Edition of the Works of Ben Jonson*, ed. David Bevington, et al., V: 359–91, 372.

66 *Cambridge Edition of the Works of Ben Jonson Online*, 'LR15: London Metropolitan Archive. Jail Delivery Roll, October, 40 Elizabeth, for the County of Middlesex, MJ/SR/358/68: Indictment against Ben Jonson for the manslaughter of Gabriel Spencer'. Available online: http://universitypublishingonline.org/cambridge/benjonson/k/life/15_L1598_30_LMA (accessed 17 March 2016).

67 Ben Jonson, *The Case is Altered*, ed. Robert Miola, in *The Cambridge Edition of the Works of Ben Jonson*, I: 1–98.

68 Jennifer Low, *Manhood*, 52.

69 Martin Wiggins and Catherine Richardson, eds, '1250: "The Blind Beggar of Bethnal Green"', in *British Drama 1598–1602: A Catalogue. Volume IV: 1533–1642* (Oxford: Oxford University Press, 2014), 228.

70 John Day and Henry Chettle, *The Blind-Beggar of Bednal-Green* (1659).

71 Silver, *Paradoxes*, 39; 537.

72 Ibid., 38; 536.

73 See Roslyn L. Knutson, *Playing Companies and Commerce in Shakespeare's Time* (Cambridge: Cambridge University Press, 2004), 52. See also Haughton and Day, 'Blind Beggar of Bednal Green (Tom Strowd)', Parts 2 and 3. William Haughton, John Day (1600, 1601) Lost Plays Database. Available online: lostplays.org/index.php/Blind_Beggar_of_Bednal_Green_(Tom_Strowd),_Parts_2_and_3 (accessed 17 March 2016).

74 *King Lear*, Arden Shakespeare Third Series, ed. R. A. Foakes (London: Bloomsbury, 1997), 46.

75 Ibid., 45.

76 An exception is Edelman's discussion in *Brawl Ridiculous*
    (159–60); he too notes the relevance of Silver here.

77 Foakes, ed., *King Lear* (1997), 4.6.231–40n, 345.

78 James S. Cockborn, 'Patterns of Violence in English Society:
    Homicide in Kent 1560–1985', *Past and Present* 130 (1)
    (1991): 83.

79 Foakes, ed., *King Lear* (1997), 5.3.141n, 372.

80 Edelman, *Brawl Ridiculous*, 154–5.

81 Ryan, 'I Did Not Return a Master', 4.

Chapter 4: The Art of Dance

1   Peggy Phelan, 'Thirteen Ways of Looking at Choreographing
    Writing', in *Choreographing History*, ed. Susan Foster
    (Bloomington: Indiana University Press, 1995), 200.

2   Emily Winerock makes this point in 'Reformation and Revelry:
    The Practices and Politics of Dancing in Early Modern
    England, c.1550–c.1640' (unpublished PhD dissertation,
    University of Toronto, 2012), 125.

3   There are no English treatises or manuals on dance between
    the Gresley Manuscript (c. 1500) and John Playford's *English
    Dancing Master* (1651). The consensus among dance historians
    is that whilst there were well-known national variations in
    dance, there nevertheless existed a pan-European vocabulary
    of dance. See Ravelhofer's careful discussion of English
    and continental sources, *Early Stuart Masque*, 27–66. She
    concludes that 'courtly dance culture seems to have been
    cosmopolitan and heteroglot, constituting a legible "kinetic
    vocabulary"' (66). See also Jennifer Nevile's survey on 'Dance
    in Europe 1250–1750', in *Dance, Spectacle, and the Body
    Politick, 1250–1750*, ed. Jennifer Nevile (Bloomington: Indiana
    University Press, 2008), 7–64.

4   Jennifer Nevile, *The Eloquent Body: Dance and Humanist
    Culture in Fifteenth-Century Italy* (Bloomington: Indiana
    University Press, 2004), 2–3.

5   Ibid., 102.

6   Guglielmo Ebreo, *De Pratica Seu Arte Tripudii*, ed. and trans. Barbara Sparti (Oxford: Clarendon Press, 1993), 91.

7   Ibid., 89.

8   Plato, *Timaeus*, trans. Benjamin Jowett, in *Plato: The Collected Dialogues*, ed. Edith Hamilton and Huntington Cairns (Princeton, NJ: Princeton University Press, 1961), 1169 (40c).

9   Lucian, 'The Dance', in *Lucian*, trans. A. M. Harmon, Loeb Classical Library 302 (Cambridge, MA: Harvard University Press, 1936), IV: 221. See Thomas M. Greene, 'Labyrinth Dances in the French and English Renaissance', *Renaissance Quarterly* 54 (2001): 1441–2.

10   Nevile, *Eloquent Body*, 45.

11   Winerock, 'Reformation and Revelry', 134.

12   Anne Daye, 'Skill and Invention in the Renaissance Ballroom', *Historical Dance* 2 (6) (1988): 15.

13   Kate Van Orden, *Music, Discipline, and Arms in Early Modern France* (Chicago: University of Chicago Press, 2005), 7.

14   See William H. McNeill, *Keeping Together in Time: Dance and Drill in Human History* (Cambridge, MA: Harvard University Press, 1997).

15   Guglielmo Ebreo, 103.

16   Ibid., 95.

17   Domenico Pietropaolo, 'Improvisation in the Arts', in *Improvisation in the Arts of the Middle Ages and Renaissance*, ed. Timothy J. McGee (Kalamazoo, MI: Medieval Institute Publications, 2003), 9. Pietropaolo cites Charles Sears Baldwin (15). See also Joe Altman's *The Tudor Play of Mind* (Stanford: University of California Press, 1978).

18   Julia Sutton, 'Late Renaissance Dance', in *'Nobilta di Dame' by Fabritio Caroso*, ed. Julia Sutton (Oxford: Oxford University Press, 1986), 27.

19   Ibid., 27–8.

20   Ibid., 32.

21   Pietropaolo, 'Improvisation in the Arts', 17. On constraints and memory, see David Rubin, *Memory and Oral Traditions:*

The Cognitive Psychology of Epic, Ballads, and Counting-Out Rhymes (New York: Oxford University Press, 1995).

22 Pietropaolo, 'Improvisation in the Arts', 18.

23 Daye, 'Skill and Invention', 13.

24 For a study of verbal wit, see Zucker, *The Places of Wit.*

25 Ravelhofer, *Early Stuart Masque*, 75.

26 Neville quotes this letter from Bussus in *Eloquent Body*, 29.

27 Sutton, 'Dance Types', in *Nobilta di Dame*, 32.

28 Nevile, *Eloquent Body*, 45.

29 Castiglione, *The Book of the Courtier*, 67–8.

30 Ibid., 68.

31 Hoby, trans., *Boke of the Courtier.*

32 Montaigne, 'Of Presumption', *The Complete Works*, 300.

33 Daye, 'Skill and Invention', 12.

34 Nevile, *Eloquent Body*, 29.

35 Van Orden, *Music, Discipline, and Arms*, 92.

36 Frances Ames-Lewis, *The Intellectual Life of the Early Renaissance Artist* (New Haven, CT: Yale University Press, 2000), 74, quoted in Nevile, *Eloquent Body*, 24.

37 Alan Brissenden, *Shakespeare and the Dance* (London and Basingstoke: Macmillan, 1981), 10.

38 Christopher Marsh, *Music and Society in Early Modern England* (Cambridge: Cambridge University Press, 2010), 337. See Ian Archer, *The Pursuit of Stability: Social Relations in Early Modern England* (Cambridge: Cambridge University Press, 1991), 242–3, for a discussion of regulations on dancing schools and bowling alleys. See also Winerock's 'Reformation and Revelry' thesis (University of Toronto, 2012) for a fine survey of attempts to regulate dancing among the lower orders.

39 T. F. (student), *Newes from the North. Otherwise Called the Conference Betvveen Simon Certain, and Pierce Plowman,* faithfully collected and gathered by T. F. (student) (London, 1579). I am indebted to Winerock's thesis for this reference.

40 T. F., *Newes*, E3r.

41 John Marston, *The Malcontent* [1604], ed. Martin L. Wine (Lincoln: University of Nebraska Press, 1964), 77–8 (4.2.6–10).

42 Emily Winerock, 'Staging Dance in English Renaissance Drama', in *Proceedings of the 34th Society of Dance History Scholars Annual Conference (June 23–26, 2011),* compiled by Ken Pierce (Riverside, CA: Society of Dance History Scholars, 2011): 259–66.

43 Jean Howard, 'Dancing Masters and the Production of Cosmopolitan Bodies in Caroline Town Comedy', in *Localizing Caroline Drama: Politics and Economics of the Early Modern English Stage, 1625–1642*, ed. Adam Zucker and Alan B. Farmer (New York: Palgrave Macmillan, 2006), 183–211. For wit and fashion generally in the Caroline drama, see also Zucker, *The Places of Wit.*

44 Howard, 'Dancing Masters', 191.

45 James Shirley, *The Ball* (London, 1639), C2r–v.

46 Ravelhofer, *Early Stuart Masque*, 75.

47 Howard, 'Dancing Masters', 188.

48 Skiles Howard, *The Politics of Courtly Dancing in Early Modern England* (Amherst, MA: University of Massachusetts Press, 1998), 20.

49 Ibid., 22–3.

50 Ibid., 24.

51 Ibid., 24; Howard quotes from Michel Foucault's *Discipline and Punish: The Birth of the Prison*, trans. Alan Sheridan (New York: Vintage Books, 1977).

52 Howard, *Politics of Courtly Dancing*, 24n. 71.

53 Ravelhofer, *Early Stuart Masque*, 99.

54 Ibid.

55 Ibid.

56 Ibid., 108.

57 Ibid.

58 McNeill, *Keeping Together in Time.*

59 Michael Kimmel, 'Intersubjectivity at Close Quarters: How Dancers of Tango Argentino Use Imagery for Interaction and

Improvisation', *Journal of Cognitive Semiotics* 4 (1) (2009): 76–124.

60 Ibid., 76.

61 Ibid., 78.

62 Ibid., 80.

63 Ibid., 79.

64 Ibid., 80.

65 Ibid., 118.

66 Ravelhofer, *Early Stuart Masque*, 67.

67 Nevile, *Eloquent Body*, 85.

68 James Cleland, *Hero-Paideia, or the Institution of a Young Man*, 226.

69 For Inns of Court dancing, see D. R. Wilson, 'Dancing in the Inns of Court', *Historical Dance* 2 (5) (1986–87): 3–16; John Ward, 'Apropos "The Olde Measures"', *Records of Early Drama Newsletter* 18 (1) (1993): 1–21.

70 Dessen and Thomson, *A Dictionary of Stage Directions*, 64.

71 Stern, *Documents of Performance in Early Modern England*, 7.

72 Brissenden, *Shakespeare and the Dance*, 44.

73 Skiles Howard, 'Hands, Feet, and Bottoms: Decentering the Cosmic Dance in *A Midsummer Night's Dream*', *Shakespeare Quarterly* 44 (3) (1993): 334–5. For a recent discussion of dance in the play in light of complexity theory, see Claire Hansen, 'The Complexity of Dance in Shakespeare's *A Midsummer Night's Dream*', *EMLS* 18 (1–2) (2015): 1–26. Available online: https://extra.shu.ac.uk/emls/journal/index.php/emls/article/view/136 (accessed 17 March 2016).

74 Brissenden, *Shakespeare and the Dance*, 44.

75 Howard, *Politics of Courtly Dancing*, 76.

76 Hansen, 'The Complexity of Dance', 16.

77 Jennifer Nevile, 'Dance and Time in Fifteenth-Century Italy', in *Art and Time*, ed. J. Lloyd Jones (Melbourne: Australian Scholarly Publishing, 2007), 305; see also Nevile, *Eloquent Body*, Ch. 3.

78 Nevile, *Eloquent Body*, 86.

79 Daniël Lakens, 'Movement Synchrony and Perceived
Entitativity', *Journal of Experimental Social Psychology*
46 (5) (2010): 701. Lakens's work is discussed by Robert
Shaughnessy, 'Connecting the Globe'.

80 Brissenden, *Shakespeare and the Dance*, 67.

81 Lin, *Shakespeare and Materiality*, 130.

82 Philip D. Collington, '"Stuffed with All Honourable Virtues":
Much Ado About Nothing and *The Book of the Courtier*',
Studies in Philology 103 (3) (2006): 281–312, 283.

83 Stephen Greenblatt, 'Introduction to *Much Ado About
Nothing*', in Greenblatt et al., *The Norton Shakespeare (Digital
Edition)*, 3rd edn (New York: W. W. Norton & Co., 2015),
1396.

84 See Coblentz, 'Killing Time', for a discussion of feints,
counterattacks and tempo between Tamora and Titus in *Titus
Andronicus*.

85 Brissenden, *Shakespeare and the Dance*, 49.

86 Ibid., 49.

87 Collington, 'Stuffed with All Honourable Virtues', 288.

Chapter 5: The Skills behind the Skills: Variety and Overtopping

1 Lois Potter, 'Shakespeare and Other Men of the Theater',
Shakespeare Quarterly 65 (4) (2014): 461.

2 Tribble, *Cognition in the Globe*, 76.

3 McIlwain and Sutton, 'Yoga From the Mat Up', 656.

4 Richard Preiss reviews the evidence for audience reaction in
Clowning and Authorship.

5 Thomas Heywood, *An Apology for Actors*, in *Shakespeare's
Theatre: A Sourcebook*, ed. Tanya Pollard (Oxford and
Malden, MA: Blackwell, 2004), 233–4.

6 Mark Eccles, 'Elizabethan Actors III: K–R', *Notes and Queries*
39 (3) (1992): 293–303.

7   Andrew Gurr, *Playgoing in Shakespeare's London*,
    3rd edn (Cambridge: Cambridge University Press, 2004), 157.

8   Potter, 'Shakespeare and Other Men', 458; James Shapiro, *A
    Year in the Life of William Shakespeare: 1599* (New York:
    HarperCollins, 2005), 36–42.

9   Louise Geddes, 'Playing No Part but Pyramus: Bottom,
    Celebrity and the Early Modern Clown', *Medieval and
    Renaissance Drama in England* 28 (2015): 73.

10 Potter, 'Shakespeare and Other Men', 458.

11 Ibid.

12 Preiss, *Clowning and Authorship*, 4.

13 Ibid., 6.

14 Lois Potter, 'The Director's Tragedy or, Approaches
    to the Really Obscure Play', *The Hare* 1 (1) (2012).
    Available online: http://thehareonline.com/article/directors–
    tragedy–or–approaches–really–obscure–play (accessed 17
    March 2016).

15 Annabel Patterson, Introduction to Thomas Middleton and
    William Rowley, *The Changeling*, ed. Douglas Brewster, in
    Thomas Middleton: The Collected Works, ed. Gary Taylor and
    John Lavagnino (Oxford: Clarendon, 2007), 1636.

16 Roberta Barker and David Nicol, 'Does Beatrice Joanna Have
    a Subtext?: *The Changeling* on the London Stage', *Early
    Modern Literary Studies* 10 (1) (2004): 1–43. Available online:
    http://extra.shu.ac.uk/emls/10-1/barknico.htm (accessed 17
    March 2016).

17 Patterson, Introduction to *The Changeling*, 1636; Bruce
    Boehrer, 'Alsemero's Closet: Privacy and Interiority in *The
    Changeling*', *Journal of English and Germanic Philology* 96
    (1997): 349.

18 N. W. Bawcutt, Introduction to *The Changeling*, by Thomas
    Middleton and William Rowley, xxvii.

19 Thomas Goffe, *The Careless Shepherdess* (London: Richard
    Rogers, 1656), B2v.

20 Bawcutt, Introduction to *The Changeling*, xxvii.

21 William N. West, 'Intertheatricality', in *Early Modern*

Theatricality, ed. Henry S. Turner (Oxford: Oxford University Press, 2013), 151–72.

22 Matthew Steggle, *Laughing and Weeping in Early Modern Theatres* (Aldershot: Ashgate, 2007), 76.

23 Ibid.

24 Ibid., 77.

25 Murray Bromberg, 'Theatrical Wagers: a Sidelight on the Elizabethan Drama', *Notes and Queries* 196 (1951): 533–5.

26 '*MSS 1, Article 6, 01 Recto: Letter from W. P. to Edward Alleyn About a Theatrical Wager, with Six Lines of Verse Beginning "Deny Me Not, Sweete Nedd, the Wager's Downe"*', c. 1590, Henslowe-Alleyn.org.Uk, n.d. Available online: http://www.henslowe-alleyn.org.uk/images/MSS-1/Article-006/01r.html (accessed 17 March 2016).

27 Thomas Dekker and George Wilkins, *Jests to Make You Merrie ... Unto Which is Added the Miserie of a Prison and a Prisoner, and a Paradox in Praise of Saints* (London, 1607).

28 Thomas Dekker, *The Guls Horne–Booke* (London, 1609); Francis Beaumont, *The Knight of the Burning Pestle*, ed. Sheldon Zitner (Manchester: Manchester University Press, 1984), 85–6.

29 Richard Preiss, 'John Taylor, William Fennor, and the *Trial of Wit*', *Shakespeare Studies* 43 (2015): 52. Donald Hedrick describes such moments as instances of the 'sportification' of theatre. See Donald Hedrick, 'Real Entertainment: Sportification, Coercion, and Carceral Theater', 50–66. Preiss takes issue with this characterization, noting that the term posits a 'false distinction ... between theatrical and extratheatrical reception' (54).

30 See Preiss, *Clowning and Authorship*, 90–104.

31 Susan P. Cerasano, 'Edward Alleyn, the New Model Actor, and the Rise of the Celebrity in the 1590's', *Medieval and Renaissance Drama in England* 18 (2006): 48.

32 Andrew Gurr, *The Shakespearean Stage 1574–1642*, 4th edn (Cambridge: Cambridge University Press, 2009).

33 David Mateer, 'Edward Alleyn, Richard Perkins and the

Rivalry Between the Swan and the Rose Playhouses', *Review of English Studies* 60 (243): 70.

34 Christopher Marlowe, *The Jew of Malta*, ed. Richard Van Fossen (London: Edward Arnold Ltd, 1965), 6.

35 Ibid., 6.

36 Ibid., 114.

37 Lucy Munro, 'Marlowe on the Caroline Stage', *Shakespeare Bulletin* 27 (1) (2009): 42.

38 Van Fossen, Introduction to *The Jew of Malta* by Christopher Marlowe (London: Edward Arnold Ltd, 1965), xvii.

39 C. F. Tucker Brooke, ed., *The Works of Christopher Marlowe* (Oxford: Oxford University Press, 1910), 231, quoted in 'The Critical Backstory', Bruce Brandt, in *The Jew of Malta: A Critical Reader*, ed. Robert A. Logan (London: Arden Shakespeare, 2013), 3.

40 Robert A. Logan, Introduction to *The Jew of Malta: A Critical Reader* (London: Arden Shakespeare, 2013), xxiii.

41 Ibid., xxvii.

42 Ibid., xxvii.

43 Roslyn L. Knutson, '*The Jew of Malta* in Repertory', in *The Jew of Malta: A Critical Reader*, 85.

44 Ibid., 85. As Knutson notes, the point about a protaganist being driven by 'criminal passion' was first made by Fredson Bowers.

45 Cerasano, 'Edward Alleyn, the New Model Actor', 49.

46 Edward Guilpin, *Skilalethia* (London, 1598), B2v, quoted in Munro, 'Marlowe on the Caroline Stage', 43.

47 Peter Hyland, *Disguise on the Early Modern Stage* (Aldershot: Ashgate, 2011); Andrew Gurr, *Shakespeare's Opposites: The Admiral's Company, 1594–1624* (Cambridge: Cambridge University Press, 2009).

48 Logan, Introduction to *The Jew of Malta: A Critical Reader*, xxx.

49 Lois Potter, *Shakespeare: A Critical Biography* (London: Wiley-Blackwell, 2012), 281.

50   Margreta de Grazia, 'When Did Hamlet become Modern?',
      Textual Practice 17 (3) (2003): 486.

51   David Wiles, *Shakespeare's Clown: Actor and Text in the
      Elizabethan Playhouse* (Cambridge: Cambridge University
      Press, 1987), 59; Robert Weimann, *Author's Pen and Actor's
      Voice: Playing and Writing in Shakespeare's Theatre*, ed.
      Helen Higbee and William N. West (Cambridge: Cambridge
      University Press, 2000), 28.

52   René Girard, 'Hamlet's Dull Revenge', *Stanford Literature
      Review* 1 (2) (1984): 159–200.

53   William Shakespeare, *Hamlet: The Texts of 1603 and
      1623*, ed. Ann Thompson and Neil Taylor (London: Arden
      Shakespeare, 2007), 2.2.331, 2.2.337, 40.

54   Ibid., 2.2.490–1.

55   See Alison Stone, *'Am I a Clowne?': Clowning in Shakespeare*
      (Otago: MA thesis, 2010), 117ff., for a discussion of Hamlet's
      'annoyingly obstructive cross-talk'.

56   *Hamlet: The Texts of 1603 and 1623*, ed. Thompson and
      Taylor, 4.7.90n.

57   Hoby, trans. *Boke of the Courtier*.

Chapter 6: Conclusions: Reconstructing Skill

1   Paul Menzer, 'Something Wanting: The Actor, the Critic, and
      Histrionic Skill', *Shakespeare Studies* 43 (2015): 80.

2   Ibid., 81.

3   Kevin Ewert, 'The Thrust Stage is Not Some Direct Link to
      Shakespeare', *Shakespeare Bulletin* 29 (2) (2011): 165, 168.

4   Ibid., 172.

5   On the question of repertory, see Weingust, 'Authentic
      Performances or Performances of Authenticity? Original
      Practices and the Repertory Schedule', *Shakespeare* 10 (4)
      (2014): 402–10. See also W. B. Worthen, 'Reconstructing the

Globe: Constructing Ourselves', *Shakespeare Survey* 52 (1998): 175–88. I have a brief consideration of the cognitive ecologies of reconstructed theatres in the conclusion to *Cognition in the Globe*.

6 Jackie Snow, *Movement Training for Actors* (London: Methuen, 2012), xiii.

7 Richard Ouzounian, 'Stratford Festival: A Tragic Mounting of *Romeo and Juliet*: Review'. Available online: http:// www.thestar.com/entertainment/stage/2013/05/28/stratford_ festival_a_tragic_mounting_of_romeo_and_juliet_review. html (accessed 17 March 2016). J. Kelly Nestruck, the *Globe and Mail* reviewer, conducted an extremely hostile interview with Carroll, comparing original practices to religious fundamentalism and smallpox: http://www.theglobeandmail. com/arts/theatre-and-performance/stratford-goes-back-in-time-with-original-practices-shakespeare/article12133556/?page=all (accessed 17 March 2016).

8 Chet Greason, 'Comedy of Romeo and Juliet Eclipses the Drama'. Available online: http://www.southwesternontario. ca/whats-on/comedy-of-romeo-and-juliet-eclipses-the-drama (accessed 17 March 2016).

9 Penelope Woods, 'Skilful Spectatorship? Doing (or Being) Audience at Shakespeare's Globe Theatre', *Shakespeare Studies* 43 (2015): 99–113.

10 Brad Ruby, interview by Evelyn B. Tribble, 25 September 2013.

11 Geoff Scoville, interview by Evelyn B. Tribble, 25 September 2013. The Stratford Festival has a long lineage in stage combat; Paddy Crean was fight director there for twenty years. The current Head of Combat is John Stead; Geoff Scoville was Assistant Head in 2013.

12 Rapier Wit, 'Rapier Wit: Combat for Stage and Screen'. Available online: http://www.rapierwit.com (accessed 17 March 2016).

13 The Shakespeare and Dance Project, 'The Shakespeare and Dance Project'. Available online: http://shakespeareandance. com (accessed 17 March 2016).

14 Ken Pierce, 'Using a Dance Historian's Approach as a Guiding
    Concept in Stage Direction', *Proceedings of the Society of
    Dance History Scholars* (2011): 191–9.

15 Ibid., 192.

16 Kendra Preston Leonard, 'Hearing the Scene: Approaches to
    Live Music in Modern Shakespearean Productions', *Early
    Modern Studies Journal* 5 (2013): 22–40.

17 Veronica Horwell, 'The Jig is Up: Shakespeare Globe Sends
    Them Out Dancing', *Guardian*, 1 October 2014. Available
    online: http://www.theguardian.com/stage/2014/oct/01/
    shakespeare-jig-music-choreography-globe-theatre (accessed 17
    March 2016).

18 Ibid., 82.

19 For a discussion of attempts to distinguish Falstaff from
    Oldcastle, see Peter Corbin and Douglas Sedge, eds, *The
    Oldcastle Controversy: Sir John Oldcastle, Part I and The
    Famous Victories of Henry V*, by Michael Drayton, Richard
    Hathwaye, Anthony Munday and Robert Wilson (Manchester:
    Manchester University Press, 1991), 10–11.

20 William N. West, 'When is the Jig Up – and What is it Up to?',
    in *Locating the Queen's Men*, ed. Andrew Griffin, Holger Schott
    Syme and Helen Ostovich (Aldershot: Ashgate, 2009), 214.

21 Roger Clegg and Lucie Skeaping, *Singing Simpkin and Other
    Bawdy Jigs: Musical Comedy on the Shakespearean Stage*
    (Exeter: University of Exeter Press, 2014), 1.

22 Ibid.

23 Clegg and Skeaping, *Singing Simpkin*, 24. See Gustav Binz,
    'Londoner Theater und Schauspiele im Jahr 1599', *Anglia* 22
    (1899): 458.

24 Clegg and Skeaping, *Singing Simpkin*, 24.

25 Claire van Kampen, 'Music and Aural Texture at Shakespeare's
    Globe', in *Shakespeare's Globe: A Theatrical Experiment*,
    ed. Christie Carson and Farah Karim-Cooper (Cambridge:
    Cambridge University Press, 2008), 86.

26 Ibid., 87.

27 Veronica Horwell, 'The Jig is Up: Shakespeare Globe Sends
    Them Out Dancing', *Guardian*, 1 October 2014.

28 Robert Shaughnessy, 'Connecting the Globe: Actors,
    Audiences, and Entrainment', *Shakespeare Survey* 68 (2015):
    295–305.

BIBLIOGRAPHY

Altman, Joe. *The Tudor Play of Mind*. Stanford: University of
California Press, 1978.

Ames-Lewis, Frances. *The Intellectual Life of the Early Renaissance
Artist*. New Haven, CT: Yale University Press, 2000.

Anglin, Jay P. 'The Schools of Defense in Elizabethan London'.
Renaissance Quarterly 37 (3) (1984): 393–410.

Archer, Ian. *The Pursuit of Stability: Social Relations in Early
Modern England*. Cambridge: Cambridge University Press, 1991.

Ascham, Roger. *Toxophilus: The Schole of Shootinge Contayned
in Tvvo Bookes. To all Gentlemen and Yomen of Englande,
Pleasaunte for Theyr Pastyme to Rede, and Profitable for Theyr
Use to Folow, Both in War and Peace* [Londini: In aedibus
Edouardi VVhytchurch. Cum priuilegio ad imprimendum solum,
1545]. Early English Books Online (EEBO).

Ascham, Roger. *Toxophilus*. Edited by Peter Medine. Tempe, AZ:
ACMRS, 2002.

Astington, John H. *Actors and Acting in Shakespeare's Time: The Art
of Stage Playing*. Cambridge: Cambridge University Press, 2010.

Astington, John H. 'Actors and the Body: Meta-Theatrical Rhetoric
in Shakespeare'. *Gesture* 6 (2) (2006): 241–59.

Barba, Eugenio. *The Paper Canoe: A Guide to Theatre
Anthropology*. Translated by Richard Fowler. London and New
York: Routledge, 1995.

Barker, Roberta and David Nicol. 'Does Beatrice Joanna Have a
Subtext?: *The Changeling* on the London Stage'. *Early Modern
Literary Studies* 10 (1) (May 2004): 1–43. Available online:
http://extra.shu.ac.uk/emls/10-1/barknico.htm (accessed 17
March 2016).

Bawcutt, N. W. Introduction to *The Changeling* by Thomas
Middleton, xv–lxviii. London: Methuen, 1958.

Beaumont, Francis. *The Knight of the Burning Pestle*. Edited by
Sheldon Zitner. Manchester: Manchester University Press, 1984.

Berry, Cicely. *The Actor and the Text*. London: Virgin Books, 2000.

Berry, Herbert. *The Noble Science: A Study and Transcription of Sloane Ms. 2530*. London, Newark and Toronto: Associated University Presses, 1991.

Bevington, David M. *Action is Eloquence: Shakespeare's Language of Gesture*. Cambridge, MA: Harvard University Press, 1984.

Binz, Gustav. 'Londoner Theater und Schauspiele im Jahr 1599'. *Anglia* 22 (1899): 456–64.

Bishop, Tom. 'Boot and Shtick'. *Shakespeare Studies* 43 (2015): 35–49.

Blau, Herbert. *The Eye of Prey: Subversions of the Postmodern*. Bloomington and Indianapolis: Indiana University Press, 1987.

Bloom, Gina. *Voice in Motion: Staging Gender, Shaping Sound in Early Modern England*. Philadelphia: University of Pennsylvania University Press, 2007.

Bloom, Gina. 'Games'. In *Early Modern Theatricality*, edited by Henry S. Turner, 189–211. Oxford: Oxford University Press, 2013.

Boehrer, Bruce. 'Alsemero's Closet: Privacy and Interiority in *The Changeling*'. *Journal of English and Germanic Philology* 96 (1997): 349–68.

Bolens, Guillemette. *The Style of Gestures: Embodiment and Cognition in Literary Narrative*. Baltimore, MD: Johns Hopkins University Press, 2012.

Book, Angela, K. Costello and J. A. Camilleri. 'Psychopathy and Victim Selection: The Use of Gait as a Cue to Vulnerability'. *Journal of Interpersonal Violence* 28 (11) (2013): 2368–83.

Borden, Ian. 'The Blackfriars Gladiators: Masters of Fence, Playing a Prize, and the Elizabethan and Stuart Theater'. In *Inside Shakespeare: Essays on the Blackfriars Stage*, edited by Paul Menzer, 132–46. Selinsgrove, PA: Susquehanna University Press, 2006.

Bourdieu, Pierre. *Outline of a Theory of Practice*. Cambridge and New York: Cambridge University Press, 1977.

Bradbrook, M. C. *Elizabethan Stage Conditions: A Study of Their Place in the Interpretation of Shakespeare's Plays*. Cambridge: Cambridge University Press, 1932.

Brandt, Bruce. 'The Critical Backstory'. In *The Jew of Malta: A Critical Reader*, edited by Robert A. Logan, 1–26. London: Arden Shakespeare, 2013.

Brissenden, Alan. *Shakespeare and the Dance*. London and
   Basingstoke: Macmillan, 1981.

Bromberg, Murray. 'Theatrical Wagers: A Sidelight on the
   Elizabethan Drama'. *Notes and Queries* 196 (1951): 533–35.

Bryson, Anna. *From Courtesy to Civility: Changing Codes of
   Conduct in Early Modern England*. Oxford: Oxford University
   Press, 2004.

Bulwer, John. *Chirologia: Or the Natural Language of the Hand
   and Chironomia: Or the Art of Manual Rhetoric* (1644). Edited
   by James W. Cleary. Carbondale and Edwardsville: Southern
   Illinois Press, 1972.

Burton, Hal. *Great Acting*. London: British Broadcasting
   Corporation, 1967.

Butterworth, Philip. *Magic on the Early English Stage*. Cambridge:
   Cambridge University Press, 2005.

Calendar of State Papers, Venetian, 1617–19. Edited by Allen B.
   Hinds. London: His Majesty's Stationery Office, 1909; Nendlen,
   Liechtenstein, Kraus Reprint, 1970.

Carson, Christie and Farah Karim-Cooper, eds. *The Globe: A
   Theatrical Experience*. Cambridge: Cambridge University Press,
   2008.

Castiglione, Baldassarre. *The Courtyer of Count Baldessar Castilio
   Diuided into Foure Bookes. Very Necessary and Profitatable
   [sic] for Yonge Gentilmen and Gentilwomen abiding in Court,
   Palaice or Place, / Done into Englyshe by Thomas Hoby.*
   Translated by Thomas Hoby. London: Wyllyam Seres at the
   Signe of the Hedghogge, 1561.

Castiglione, Baldassarre. *The Book of the Courtier [by Baldesar
   Castiglione]* (1528). Translated by George Bull. Harmondsworth:
   Penguin Books, 1967.

Cerasano, Susan P. 'Edward Alleyn, the New Model Actor, and the
   Rise of the Celebrity in the 1590s'. *Medieval and Renaissance
   Drama in England* 18 (2006): 47–58.

Chambers, E. K. *The Elizabethan Stage*, vols 1 and 2. Oxford:
   Clarendon Press, 1923.

Charlton, Kenneth. *Education in Renaissance England*. London:
   Routledge and Kegan Paul, 1965.

Christensen, Wayne, John Sutton and Doris J. F. McIlwain.
   'Cognition in Skilled Action: Meshed Control and the Varieties
   of Skill Experience'. *Mind and Language* 31 (1): 37–66.

Available online: http://philpapers.org/rec/CHRCIS (accessed 17 March 2016).

Clark, Andy. 'Gesture as Thought?' In *The Hand, an Organ of the Mind: What the Manual Tells the Mental*, edited by Zdravko Radman, 255–68. Cambridge MA: MIT Press, 2013.

Clegg, Roger and Lucie Skeaping. *Singing Simpkin and Other Bawdy Jigs: Musical Comedy on the Shakespearean Stage.* Exeter: University of Exeter Press, 2014.

Cleland, James. *Hero-Paideia, or the Institution of a Young Man.* Oxford: Ioseph Barnes, 1607.

Coblentz, Dori. 'Killing Time in *Titus Andronicus*: Timing, Rhetoric, and the Art of Defense'. *Journal for Early Modern Cultural Studies* 15 (4) (2015): 52–80.

Cockborn, James S. 'Patterns of Violence in English Society: Homicide in Kent 1560–1985'. *Past and Present* 130 (1) (1991): 70–106.

Cohen, E. B. 'Once We Put Our Helmets On, There Are No More Friends: The "Fights" Session in the Israeli Army Course for Close-Combat Instructors'. *Armed Forces and Society* 37 (3) (2011): 512–33.

Collington, Philip D. '"Stuffed with All Honourable Virtues": *Much Ado About Nothing* and *The Book of the Courtier*', *Studies in Philology* 103 (3) (2006): 281–312.

Connerton, Edward. *How Societies Remember.* Cambridge: Cambridge University Press, 1989.

Copes, Heith, Andy Hochstetler and Craig J. Forsyth. 'Peaceful Warriors: Codes for Violence Among Adult Male Bar Fighters'. *Criminology* 51 (3) (2013): 761–94.

Csordas, Thomas. 'Somatic Modes of Attention'. *Cultural Anthropology* 8 (2) (1993): 135–56.

Day, John and Henry Chettle. *The Blind-Beggar of Bednal-Green.* 1659.

Daye, Anne. 'Skill and Invention in the Renaissance Ballroom'. *Historical Dance* 2 (6) (1988): 12–15.

Daye, Anne. '"Youthful Revels, Masks, and Courtly Sights": An Introductory Study of the Revels within the Stuart Masque'. *Historical Dance* 3 (4) (1996): 5–22.

Dekker, Thomas. *The Guls Horne-Booke.* London, 1609.

Dekker, Thomas and George Wilkins. *Jests to Make You Merrie … Unto Which is Added the Miserie of a Prison and a Prisoner, and a Paradox in Praise of Saints.* London, 1607.

Dessen, Alan. 'The Logic of Elizabethan Stage Violence: Some Alarms and Excursions for Modern Critics, Editors, and Directors'. *Renaissance Drama* 9 (1978): 36–69.

Dessen, Alan and Leslie Thomson. *A Dictionary of Stage Directions in English Drama 1580–1642*. Cambridge: Cambridge University Press, 1999.

Di Grassi, Giacomo. 'His True Arte of Defence' (1594). In *Three Elizabethan Fencing Manuals*, edited by James L. Jackson. Delmar, NY: Scholars' Facsimiles and Reprints, 1972.

Downey, Greg. 'Educating the Eyes: Biocultural Anthropology and Physical Education'. *Anthropology in Action* 12 (2) (2005): 56–71.

Downey, Greg. 'Producing Pain: Techniques and Technologies in No-Holds-Barred Fighting'. *Social Studies of Science* 37 (2) (2007): 201–26.

Downey, Greg. 'Seeing with a "Sideways Glance": Visuomotor "Knowing" and the Plasticity of Perception'. In *Ways of Knowing: New Approaches in the Anthropology of Experience and Learning*, edited by Mark Harris, 222–41. Oxford: Berghahn Books, 2007.

Downey, Greg. '"Practice Without Theory": A Neuroanthropological Perspective on Embodied Learning'. *Journal of the Royal Anthropological Institute* 16 (2010): S22–S40.

Downey, Greg. 'Balancing Between Cultures: Equilibrium in Capoeira'. In *The Encultured Brain: An Introduction to Neuroanthropology*, edited by Daniel H. Lende and Greg Downey, 169–94. Cambridge, MA: MIT Press, 2012.

Drayton, Michael, Richard Hathwaye, Anthony Munday and Robert Wilson. *The Oldcastle Controversy: Sir John Oldcastle, Part I and The Famous Victories of Henry V* (1599). Edited by Peter Corbin and Douglas Sedge. Manchester: Manchester University Press, 1991.

Dreyfus, Hubert L. 'Overcoming the Myth of the Mental'. *Topoi* 25 (1–2) (2006): 43–9.

Ebreo da Pesaro, Guglielmo. *De Pratica Seu Arte Tripudii: On the Practice or Art of Dancing*. Edited and translated by Barbara Sparti. Oxford: Clarendon Press, 1993.

Eccles, Mark. 'Elizabethan Actors III: K–R'. *Notes and Queries* 39 (3) (1992): 293–303.

Edelman, Charles. *Brawl Ridiculous: Swordfighting in Shakespeare's Plays*. Manchester: Manchester University Press, 1992.

Egan, Gabriel. 'Elizabethan Acting'. In *The Oxford Companion to Shakespeare*, edited by Michael Dobson and Stanley Wells, 1–3. Oxford: Oxford University Press, 2001.

Ericsson, K. Anders and Robert Pool. *Peak: Secrets from the New Science of Expertise*. New York: Houghton Mifflin, 2016.

Eustis, Morton. 'The Actor Attacks His Part: Lyn Fontanne and Alfred Lunt'. In *Theatre Arts: On Acting*, edited by Laurence Senelick, 287–95. London and New York: Routledge, 2008.

Evans, G. Blakemore. *Elizabethan Jacobean Drama: The Theatre in its Time*. London: A&C Black, 1989.

Evans, Mark. *Movement Training for the Modern Actor*. London and New York: Routledge, 2008.

'Event Record: John Devell Barely Passes His Fencing Provost's Prize at the Theatre' (10 August 1582). In *Early Modern London Theatres*. http://www.emlot.kcl.ac.uk/db/record/event/6532 (accessed 17 March 2016).

Ewert, Kevin. 'The Thrust Stage is Not Some Direct Link to Shakespeare'. *Shakespeare Bulletin* 29 (2) (2011): 165–76.

Ewing, Sherman. 'Wanted: More Stars, Less "Method"'. In *Theatre Arts: On Acting*, edited by Laurence Senelick, 280–4. London and New York: Routledge, 2008.

Fay-Thomas, Miranda. 'King's College London: Gesture Lab'. Available online: https://www.kcl.ac.uk/cultural/-/Current-projects/Gesture-Lab.aspx (accessed 17 March 2016).

Feltovich, Paul J., Michael J. Prietula and K. Anders Ericsson, 'Studies of Expertise from Psychological Perspectives'. In *The Cambridge Handbook of Expertise and Expert Performance*, edited by K. Anders Ericsson, Neil Charness, Paul J. Feltovich and Robert R. Hoffman, 41–68. New York: Cambridge University Press, 2006.

Florio, John. *Florio: His Firste Fruites*. London, 1578.

Foucault, Michel. *Discipline and Punish: The Birth of the Prison*. Translated by Alan Sheridan. New York: Vintage Books, 1977.

[Gainsford, Thomas.] *The Rich Cabinet Furnished with Varietie of Excellent Descriptions*. London: I. B. for Roger Jackson, 1616.

Gallagher, Shaun. *How the Body Shapes the Mind*. Oxford: Clarendon Press, 2005.

Geddes, Louise. 'Playing No Part but Pyramus: Bottom, Celebrity and the Early Modern Clown'. *Medieval and Renaissance Drama in England* 28 (2015): 70–85.

Geeves, Andrew, Doris McIlwain, John Sutton and Wayne Christensen. 'To Think or Not to Think: The Apparent Paradox of Expert Skill in Music Performance'. *Educational Philosophy and Theory* 46 (6) (2013): 674–91.

Geurts, Kathryn Linn. *Culture and the Senses: Bodily Ways of Knowing in an African Community*. Berkeley: University of California Press, 2003.

Girard, René. 'Hamlet's Dull Revenge'. *Stanford Literature Review* 1 (2) (1984): 159–200.

Goffe, Thomas. *The Careless Shepherdess*. London: Richard Rogers, 1656.

Goldin-Meadow, Susan and Sian Beilock. 'Action's Influence on Thought: The Case of Gesture'. *Perspectives on Psychological Science* 5 (6) (2010): 664–74.

Goldin-Meadow, S., H. Nusbaum, Spencer D. Kelly and Susan Wagner. 'Explaining Math: Gesturing Lightens the Load'. *Psychological Science* 12 (6) (2001): 516–22.

Gosson, Stephen. *Plays Confuted in Five Actions*. London, 1582.

Grasseni, Christina. 'Skilled Vision: An Apprenticeship in Breeding Aesthetics'. *Social Anthropology* 12 (1) (2004): 41–55.

Grazia, Margreta de. 'When Did Hamlet Become Modern?' *Textual Practice* 17 (3) (2003): 485–503.

Greason, Chet. 'Comedy of Romeo and Juliet Eclipses the Drama'. Stratford Gazette, 11 June 2013. Available online: http://www. ourperth.ca/news-story/6023961-comedy-of-romeo-and-juliet-eclipses-the-drama/ (accessed 17 March 2016).

Greenblatt, Stephen. Introduction to *Much Ado About Nothing* (1396). In *The Norton Shakespeare* (Digital Edition), 3rd edn. Edited by Stephen Greenblatt, Walter Cohen, Jean E. Howard, Katharine Eisaman Maus et al. New York: W. W. Norton & Co., 2015. VitalSource Bookshelf Online.

Greene, Thomas M. 'Labyrinth Dances in the French and English Renaissance'. *Renaissance Quarterly* 54 (2001): 1403–66.

Greg, W. W. *Two Elizabethan Stage Abridgements: The Battle of Alcazar and Orlando Furioso*. Oxford: Oxford University Press, 1922.

Guilpin, Edward. *Skilalethia*. London, 1598.

Gunns, R. E., L. Johnston and S. M. Hudson. 'Victim Selection

and Kinematics: A Point-Light Investigation of Vulnerability
to Attack'. *Journal of Nonverbal Behavior* 26 (3) (2002): 129–58.

Gurr, Andrew. *Playgoing in Shakespeare's London*. 3rd edn.
Cambridge: Cambridge University Press, 2004.

Gurr, Andrew. *The Shakespearean Stage 1574–1642*. 4th edn.
Cambridge: Cambridge University Press, 2009.

Gurr, Andrew. *Shakespeare's Opposites: The Admiral's Company,
1594–1624*. Cambridge: Cambridge University Press, 2009.

Hale, George. *The Private Schoole of Defence*. London, 1614.

Hanabusa, Chiaki. 'The Will of Simon Jewell and the Queen's Men
Tours in 1592'. *Early Theatre* 16 (1) (2013): 11–30.

Hansen, Claire. 'The Complexity of Dance in Shakespeare's *A
Midsummer Night's Dream*'. *EMLS* 18 (1–2) (2015): 1–26.
Available online: https://extra.shu.ac.uk/emls/journal/index.php/
emls/article/view/136 (accessed 17 March 2016).

Harbage, Alfred. 'Elizabethan Acting'. *PMLA* 54 (1939): 685–708.

Hardwicke, Cedric. 'The Moribund Craft of Acting'. In *Theatre
Arts: On Acting*, edited by Laurence Senelick, 360–5. London
and New York: Routledge, 2008.

Hart, Jonathan. *Reading the Renaissance*. Routledge Revivals:
Culture, Poetics, and Drama. London: Routledge, 2015.

Hattaway, Michael. *Elizabethan Popular Theatre: Plays in
Performance*. London: Routledge, 1982.

Haughton, William and John Day. *Blind Beggar of Bednal Green
(Tom Strowd), Parts 2 and 3*. Lost Plays Database. Available
online: lostplays.org/index.php/Blind_Beggar_of_Bednal_Green_
(Tom_Strowd),_Parts_2_and_3 (accessed 17 March 2016).

Hedrick, Donald. 'Real Entertainment: Sportification, Coercion,
and Carceral Theater'. In *Thunder at a Playhouse: Essaying
Shakespeare and the Early Modern Stage*, edited by Peter
Kanelos and Matt Kozusko, 50–66. Selinsgrove, PA:
Susquehanna University Press, 2010.

Hedrick, Donald. 'Distracting Othello: Tragedy and the Rise of
Magic'. *PMLA* 129 (4) (2014): 649–71.

Henrich, J., Steven J. Heine and Ara Norenzayan. 'The Weirdest
People in the World'. *Behavioral and Brain Sciences* 33 (2–3)
(2010): 61–83.

Heywood, Thomas. *An Apology for Actors* (1612). In *Shakespeare's
Theater: A Sourcebook*, edited by Tanya Pollard, 213–54.
Oxford and Malden, MA: Blackwell Publishing, 2004.

Holmer, Joan Ozark. '"Draw, If You Be Men": Saviolo's Significance for *Romeo and Juliet*'. *Shakespeare Quarterly* 45 (2) (1994): 163–89.

Honigmann, E. A. J. and Susan Brock. *Playhouse Wills 1558–1642*. Manchester: Manchester University Press, 1993.

Horwell, Veronica. 'The Jig is Up: Shakespeare Globe Sends Them Out Dancing'. *Guardian*, 1 October 2014. Available online: http://www.theguardian.com/stage/2014/oct/01/shakespeare-jig-music-choreography-globe-theatre (accessed 17 March 2016).

Howard, Jean E. 'Dancing Masters and the Production of Cosmopolitan Bodies in Caroline Town Comedy'. In *Localizing Caroline Drama: Politics and Economics of the Early Modern English Stage, 1625–1642*, edited by Adam Zucker and Alan B. Farmer, 183–211. London: Palgrave Macmillan, 2006.

Howard, Skiles. 'Hands, Feet, and Bottoms: Decentering the Cosmic Dance in *A Midsummer Night's Dream*'. *Shakespeare Quarterly* 44 (3) (1993): 325–42.

Howard, Skiles. *The Politics of Courtly Dancing in Early Modern England*. Amherst, MA: University of Massachusetts Press, 1998.

Hutchins, Edwin. 'The Cultural Ecosystem of Human Cognition'. *Philosophical Psychology* 27 (1) (2014): 34–49.

Hyland, Peter. '"A Kind-of-Woman": The Elizabethan Boy-Actor and the Kabuki Onnagata'. *Theatre Research International* 12 (1) (1987): 1–8.

Hyland, Peter. *Disguise on the Early Modern English Stage*. Studies in Performance and Early Modern Drama. Aldershot: Ashgate, 2011.

Ingold, Tim. *Making: Anthropology, Archaeology, Art and Architecture*. London: Routledge, 2013.

James, Heather. *Shakespeare's Troy: Drama, Politics, and the Translation of the Empire*. Cambridge: Cambridge University Press, 1997.

Johnson, Kerri L. and Maggie Shiffrar. 'Making Great Strides: Advances in Research on Perceptions of the Human Body'. In *People Watching: Social, Perceptual, and Neurophysiological Studies of Body Perception*, edited by Kerri L. Johnson and Maggie Shiffrar, 3–10. Oxford: Oxford University Press, 2013.

Jonson, Ben. *The Case is Altered*. Edited Robert Miola. In *The Cambridge Edition of the Works of Ben Jonson,* edited by David Bevington, Martin Butler and Ian Donaldson, vol. 1, 1–98. Cambridge: Cambridge University Press, 2012.

Jonson, Ben. *Bartholomew Faire*. In *The Cambridge Edition of the Works of Ben Jonson*, edited by David Bevington, Martin Butler and Ian Donaldson, vol. 4, 253–428. Cambridge: Cambridge University Press, 2012.

Jonson, Ben. *Every Man in His Humour*. In *The Cambridge Edition of the Works of Ben Jonson*, edited by David Bevington, Martin Butler and Ian Donaldson, vol. 4, 619–728. Cambridge: Cambridge University Press, 2012.

Jonson, Ben. 'Informations to William Drummond of Hawthornden'. In *The Cambridge Edition of the Works of Ben Jonson*, edited by David Bevington, Martin Butler and Ian Donaldson, vol. 5, 359–91. Cambridge: Cambridge University Press, 2012.

Jowett, John. 'Henry Chettle and the First Quarto of *Romeo and Juliet*'. *The Papers of the Bibliographical Society of America* 92 (1) (1998): 53–74.

Karim-Cooper, Farah. *The Hand on the Shakespeare Stage: Gesture, Touch and the Spectacle of Dismemberment*. London: Bloomsbury, 2016.

Kathman, David. 'Grocers, Goldsmiths, and Drapers: Freemen and Apprentices in the Elizabethan Theater'. *Shakespeare Quarterly* 55 (2004): 1–49.

Kathman, David. 'Players, Livery Companies, and Apprentices'. In *The Oxford Handbook of Early Modern Theatre*, edited by Richard Dutton, 413–28. Oxford: Oxford University Press, 2011.

Keenan, Siobhan. *Acting Companies and their Plays in Shakespeare's London*. London: Bloomsbury, 2014.

Kemp, Rick. *Embodied Acting: What Neuroscience Tells Us About Performance*. London: Routledge, 2012.

Kimmel, Michael. 'Intersubjectivity at Close Quarters: How Dancers of Tango Argentino Use Imagery for Interaction and Improvisation'. *Journal of Cognitive Semiotics* 4 (1) (2009): 76–124.

Knutson, Roslyn L. *Playing Companies and Commerce in Shakespeare's Time*. Cambridge: Cambridge University Press, 2004.

Knutson, Roslyn L. '*The Jew of Malta* in Repertory'. In *The Jew of Malta: A Critical Reader*, edited by Robert A. Logan, 79–105. London: Bloomsbury, 2013.

Lakens, Daniël. 'Movement Synchrony and Perceived Entitativity'. *Journal of Experimental Social Psychology* 46 (5) (2010): 701–8.

Lawrence-King, Andrew. 'Historical Action for Early Opera and Theatre'. *The Harp Consort*. Available online: http://www.theharpconsort.com/#!historical-action/c12q3 (accessed 17 March 2016).

Leonard, Kendra Preston. 'Hearing the Scene: Approaches to Live Music in Modern Shakespearean Productions'. *Early Modern Studies Journal* 5 (2013): 22–40.

Lin, Erika. *Shakespeare and the Materiality of Performance*. New York: Palgrave, 2012.

Logan, Robert A. Introduction to *The Jew of Malta: A Critical Reader*, xix–xxxiv. London: Bloomsbury, 2013.

Low, Jennifer. *Manhood and the Duel*. London: Palgrave, 2003.

Lucian. 'The Dance'. In *Lucian*, vol. IV, translated by A. M. Harmon, 209–90. Loeb Classical Library (LCL 302). Cambridge, MA: Harvard University Press, 1936.

Lutterbie, John H. *Toward a General Theory of Acting: Cognitive Science and Performance*. New York: Palgrave Macmillan, 2011.

Lyne, Raphael. 'Recognition in *Cymbeline*'. In *Late Shakespeare: 1608–1613*, edited by Andrew Power and Rory Loughnane, 56–70. Cambridge: Cambridge University Press, 2012.

Macknik, Stephen L., Susana Martinez-Conde and Sandra Blakeslee. *Sleights of Mind: What the Neuroscience of Magic Reveals About our Everyday Deceptions*. London: Macmillan, 2010.

Mallin, Eric S. *Inscribing the Time: Shakespeare and the End of Elizabethan England*. Berkeley: University of California Press, 1995.

Manley, Laurence and Sally-Beth McLean. *The Lord Strange's Men and their Plays*. Cambridge: Cambridge University Press, 2014.

Marlowe, Christopher. *The Works of Christopher Marlowe*. Edited by C. F. Tucker Brooke. Oxford: Oxford University Press, 1910.

Marlowe, Christopher. *The Jew of Malta*. Edited by Richard Van Fossen. London: Edward Arnold Ltd, 1965.

Marsh, Christopher. *Music and Society in Early Modern England*. Cambridge: Cambridge University Press, 2010.

Marston, John. *The Malcontent* (1604). Edited by Martin L. Wine. Lincoln: University of Nebraska Press, 1964.

Massinger, Philip. 'The Roman Actor' (1626). In *Drama of the English Renaissance II: The Stuart Period*, edited by Russell

Fraser and Norman Rabkin, 716–42. New York: Macmillan, 1976.

Mateer, David. 'Edward Alleyn, Richard Perkins and the Rivalry Between the Swan and the Rose Playhouses'. *Review of English Studies* 60 (243): 61–77.

Mauss, Marcel. 'Techniques of the Body'. *Economy and Society* 2 (1) (1973): 70–88.

Mauss, Marcel. *Manual of Ethnography*. Edited by N. J. Allen. Translated by D. Lussier. New York: Dürkheim Press/Berghahn Press, 2007.

McElroy, Mary and Kent Cartwright. 'Public Fencing Contests on the Elizabethan Stage'. *Journal of Sports History* 13 (3) (1986): 193–211.

McIlwain, Doris and John Sutton. 'Yoga From the Mat Up: How Words Alight on Bodies'. *Educational Philosophy and Theory* 46 (6) (2014): 655–73.

McIntyre, Jean. *Costumes and Scripts in the Elizabethan Theatres*. Edmonton: Alberta University Press, 1992.

McMillin, Scott. 'Simon Jewell and the Queen's Men'. *Review of English Studies* 27 (106) (1976): 174–7.

McMillin, Scott and Sally-Beth McLean. *The Queen's Men and their Plays*. Cambridge: Cambridge University Press, 1998.

McNeil, David. *Hand and Mind: What Gestures Reveal About Thought*. Chicago: University of Chicago Press, 1992.

McNeill, William H. *Keeping Together in Time: Dance and Drill in Human History*. Cambridge, MA: Harvard University Press, 1997.

Menzer, Paul. 'That Old Saw: Early Modern Acting and the Infinite Regress'. *Shakespeare Bulletin* 22 (2) (2004): 27–44.

Menzer, Paul. *Anecdotal Shakespeare: A New Performance History*. London: Bloomsbury, 2015.

Menzer, Paul. 'Something Wanting: The Actor, the Critic, and Histrionic Skill'. *Shakespeare Studies* 43 (2015): 79–86.

Middleton, Thomas and William Rowley. *The Changeling* (1636). In *Thomas Middleton: The Collected Works*, edited by Gary Taylor and John Lavagnino, 1632–78. Oxford: Clarendon, 2007.

Montaigne, Michel de. *The Complete Works of Montaigne: Essays, Travel Journal, Letters*. Translated by Donald M. Frame. Stanford, CA: Stanford University Press, 1957.

Montero, Barbara. 'Practice Makes Perfect: The Effect of Dance Training on the Aesthetic Judge'. *Phenomenology and the Cognitive Sciences* 11, 1 (2012): 59–68.

Munday, Anthony. 'Players Incline their Audience to Wickedness'. In *English Professional Theatre*, edited by Glynne Wickham, Herbert Berry and William Ingram, 162–4. Cambridge: Cambridge University Press, 2000.

Munro, Lucy. *Children of the Queen's Revels*. Cambridge: Cambridge University Press, 2005.

Munro, Lucy. 'Marlowe on the Caroline Stage'. *Shakespeare Bulletin* 27 (1) (2009): 39–50.

Nashe, Thomas. *The Unfortunate Traveller and Other Works*. Edited by J. B. Steane. Harmondsworth: Penguin, 1972.

Nestruck, J. Kelly. 'Stratford Goes Back in Time with "Original Practices" Romeo and Juliet'. *The Globe and Mail*, 24 May 2013. Available online: http://www.theglobeandmail.com/arts/theatre-and-performance/stratford-goes-back-in-time-with-original-practices-shakespeare/article12133556/?page=all (accessed 17 March 2016).

Nevile, Jennifer. *The Eloquent Body: Dance and Humanist Culture in Fifteenth-Century Italy*. Bloomington: Indiana University Press, 2004.

Nevile, Jennifer. 'Dance and Time in Fifteenth-Century Italy'. In *Art and Time*, edited by J. Lloyd Jones, 299–313. Melbourne: Australian Scholarly Publishing, 2007.

Nevile, Jennifer. 'Dance in Europe 1250–1750'. In *Dance, Spectacle, and the Body Politick, 1250–1750*, edited by Jennifer Nevile, 7–64. Bloomington: Indiana University Press, 2008.

Noble, Greg and Megan Watkins. 'So, How did Bourdieu Learn to Play Tennis? Habitus, Consciousness and Habituation'. *Cultural Studies* 17 (3–4) (2003): 520–38.

O'Sullivan, Timothy M. *Walking in Roman Culture*. Cambridge: Cambridge University Press, 2011.

Ouzounian, Richard. 'Stratford Festival: A Tragic Mounting of Romeo and Juliet: Review'. *Toronto Star*, 28 May 2013. Available online: http://www.thestar.com/entertainment/stage/2013/05/28/stratford_festival_a_tragic_mounting_of_romeo_and_juliet_review.html (accessed 17 March 2016).

Palfrey, Simon and Tiffany Stern. *Shakespeare in Parts*. Oxford: Oxford University Press, 2007.

Parviainen, Jaana. 'Bodily Knowledge: Epistemological Reflections on Dance'. *Dance Research Journal* 34 (1) (2002): 11–26.

Patterson, Annabel. 'Introduction to Thomas Middleton and William Rowley, *The Changeling*'. Edited by Douglas Brewster, 1632–6. In *Thomas Middleton: The Collected Works*, edited by Gary Taylor and John Lavagnino. Oxford: Clarendon, 2007.

Peacham, Henry. *The Garden of Eloquence* (1593). New York: Scholars' Facsimiles and Reprints, 1977.

Pearson, Roberta E. *Eloquent Gestures: The Transformation of Performance Style in the Griffith Biograph Films*. Berkley: University of California Press, 1992.

Phelan, Peggy. 'Thirteen Ways of Looking at Choreographing Writing'. In *Choreographing History*, edited by Susan Foster, 200–10. Bloomington: Indiana University Press, 1995.

Pierce, Ken. 'Using a Dance Historian's Approach as a Guiding Concept in Stage Direction'. *Proceedings of the Society of Dance History Scholars* (2011): 191–9.

Pietropaolo, Domenico. 'Improvisation in the Arts'. In *Improvisation in the Arts of the Middle Ages and Renaissance*, edited by Timothy J. McGee, 1–28. Kalamazoo, MI: Medieval Institute Publications, 2003.

The Pilgrimage to Parnassus with the Two Parts of the Return from Parnassus: Three Comedies Performed in St. John's College, Cambridge, A.D. 1597–1601. Edited by Rev. W. D. Macray. Oxford: Clarendon Press, 1886.

Plato. 'Timaeus'. Translated by Benjamin Jowett. In *Plato: The Collected Dialogues*, edited by Edith Hamilton and Huntington Cairns, 1151–211. Princeton, NJ: Princeton University Press, 1961.

Plett, Heinrich F. *Rhetoric and Renaissance Culture*. Berlin and New York: Walter de Gruyter, 2004.

Plutarch. 'The Life of Dion'. In *Lives: Dion and Brutus. Timoleon and Aemilius Paulus*, vol. VI, translated by Bernadotte Perrin, 984–1009. Loeb Classical Library (LCL 98). Cambridge, MA: Harvard University Press, 1918.

Polyani, Michael. *The Tacit Dimension*. Chicago: University of Chicago Press, 1966.

Potter, Lois. 'The Director's Tragedy or, Approaches to the Really Obscure Play'. *The Hare* 1 (1) (2012). Available online: http://thehareonline.com/article/

directors-tragedy-or-approaches-really-obscure-play (accessed 17 March 2016).

Potter, Lois. *The Life of William Shakespeare: A Critical Biography*, 2nd edn. Blackwell Critical Biographies. London: Wiley-Blackwell, 2012.

Potter, Lois. 'Shakespeare and Other Men of the Theater'. *Shakespeare Quarterly* 65 (4) (2014): 455–69.

Pouw, Wim. T., Jacqueline A. de Nooijer, Tamara van Gog, Rolf A. Zwaan and Fred Paas. 'Toward a More Embedded/Extended Perspective on the Cognitive Function of Gestures'. *Frontiers in Psychology* 5 (359) (2014): 1–14.

Preiss, Richard. *Clowning and Authorship in Early Modern Theatre*. Cambridge: Cambridge University Press, 2014.

Preiss, Richard. 'John Taylor, William Fennor, and the *Trial of Wit*'. *Shakespeare Studies* 43 (2015): 50–78.

Prest, Wilfrid. 'Legal Education of the Gentry at the Inns of Court, 1560–1640'. *Past and Present* 38 (1967): 20–39.

Rackin, Phyllis and Evelyn Gajowski, eds. 'Introduction: A Historical Survey'. In *The Merry Wives of Windsor: New Critical Essays*. London: Routledge, 2015.

Ramsey, John. 'Practise for Dauncinge'. Oxford, Bodleian Library, MS Douce 280, folio 66av–66bv.

Rapier Wit. 'Rapier Wit: Combat for Stage and Screen'. Available online: http://www.rapierwit.com (accessed 17 March 2016).

Ravelhofer, Barbara. *The Early Stuart Masque: Dance, Costume, and Music*. Oxford: Oxford University Press, 2006.

Richardson, Michael J. and Lucy Johnston. 'Person Recognition from Dynamic Events: The Kinematic Specification of Individual Identity in Walking Style'. *Journal of Nonverbal Behavior* 29 (1) (2005): 25–44.

Roach, Joseph R. *The Player's Passion: Studies in the Science of Acting*. Ann Arbor: University of Michigan Press, 1985.

Rosenberg, Marvin. 'The Myth of Shakespeare's Squeaking Boy Actor – or Who Played Cleopatra?' *Shakespeare Bulletin* 19 (2) (2001): 5–6.

Rubin, David. *Memory and Oral Traditions: The Cognitive Psychology of Epic, Ballads, and Counting-Out Rhymes*. New York: Oxford University Press, 1995.

Ruby, Brad. Interview by Evelyn B. Tribble. In discussion with the author. Stratford, Ontario, 25 September 2013.

Ryan, Michael J. 'I Did Not Return a Master, But Well Cudgeled Was I: The Role of "Body Techniques" in the Transmission of Venezuelan Stick and Machete Fighting'. *Journal of Latin American and Caribbean Anthropology* 16 (1) (2011): 1–23.

Saviolo, Vincento. *His Practice* (1595). In *Three Elizabethan Fencing Manuals*, edited by James L. Jackson. Delmar, NY: Scholars' Facsimiles and Reprints, 1972.

Scoville, Geoff. Interview by Evelyn B. Tribble. In discussion with the author. Stratford, Ontario, 25 September 2013.

Semenza, Gregory M. Colón. *Sport, Politics, and Literature in the English Renaissance*. Cranbury, NJ: Associated University Press, 2003.

Shakespeare, William. *All's Well That Ends Well*. In *The Norton Shakespeare*, edited by Stephen Greenblatt. New York and London: W. W. Norton and Co., 1997.

Shakespeare, William. *King Lear*. Edited by R. A. Foakes. Arden Shakespeare Third Series. London: Bloomsbury, 1997.

Shakespeare, William. *Troilus and Cressida*. Edited by Anthony B. Dawson. New Cambridge Shakespeare. Cambridge: Cambridge University Press, 2003.

Shakespeare, William. *All's Well That Ends Well*. Edited by Russell Fraser. Cambridge: Cambridge University Press, 2004.

Shakespeare, William. *Hamlet*. Edited by Ann Thompson and Neil Taylor. London: Arden Shakespeare, 2007.

Shakespeare, William. *Hamlet: The Texts of 1603 and 1623*. Edited by Ann Thompson and Neil Taylor. London: Arden Shakespeare, 2014.

Shakespeare, William. *The Arden Shakespeare Complete Works*. Edited by Richard Proudfoot, Ann Thompson and David Scott Kastan. London: Arden Shakespeare, 2011.

Shakespeare, William. *Romeo and Juliet*. Edited by René Weis. Arden Shakespeare Third Series. London: Bloomsbury, 2012.

Shakespeare, William. *Troilus and Cressida*. Edited by David Bevington. Arden Shakespeare Third Series. London: Bloomsbury, 2015.

The Shakespeare and Dance Project. 'The Shakespeare and Dance Project'. Available online: http://shakespeareandance.com (accessed 17 March 2016).

Shapiro, James. *A Year in the Life of William Shakespeare: 1599*. New York: HarperCollins, 2005.

Shaughnessy, Robert. 'Connecting the Globe: Actors, Audiences, and Entrainment'. *Shakespeare Survey* 68 (2015): 295–305.

Sheets-Johnstone, Maxine. 'Embodied Minds or Mindful Bodies? A Question of Fundamental, Inherently Inter-Related Aspects of Animation'. *Subjectivity* 4 (4) (2011): 451–66.

Shepard, Alexandra. *Meanings of Manhood in Early Modern England*. Oxford: Oxford University Press, 2006.

Shirley, James. *The Ball*. London, 1639.

Silver, George. *Paradoxes of Defence* (1599). In *Three Elizabethan Fencing Manuals*, edited by James L. Jackson. Delmar, NY: Scholars' Facsimiles and Reprints, 1972.

Smithson, Lisa and Elena Nicoladis. 'Lending a Hand to Imagery? The Impact of Visuospatial Working Memory Interference Upon Iconic Gesture Production in a Narrative Task'. *Journal of Nonverbal Behaviour* 38 (2) (2014): 247–58.

Snow, Jackie. *Movement Training for Actors*. London: Methuen, 2012.

Snyder, Susan. '*Romeo and Juliet*: Comedy into Tragedy'. *Essays in Criticism* 20 (4) (1970): 391–402.

Soens, A. L. 'Tybalt's Spanish Fencing in *Romeo and Juliet*'. *Shakespeare Quarterly* 20 (2) (1969): 121–7.

Spolsky, Ellen. 'Elaborated Knowledge: Reading Kinesis in Pictures'. *Poetics Today* 17 (2) (1996): 157–80.

Steggle, Matthew. *Laughing and Weeping in Early Modern Theatres*. Aldershot: Ashgate, 2007.

Sterelny, Kim. *The Evolved Apprentice: How Evolution Made Humans Unique*. Cambridge, MA: MIT Press, 2012.

Sterelny, Kim. 'Language, Gesture, Skill: The Co-Evolutionary Foundations of Language'. *Philosophical Transactions of the Royal Society of London: B Biological Sciences* 367 (1599) (2012): 2141–51.

Stern, Tiffany. *Rehearsal from Shakespeare to Sheridan*. Oxford: Oxford University Press, 2000.

Stern, Tiffany. *Documents of Performance in Early Modern England*. Cambridge: Cambridge University Press, 2009.

Stern, Tiffany and Farah Karim-Cooper, eds. *Shakespeare's Theatre and the Effects of Performance*. London: Bloomsbury, 2014.

Stokes, James and Ingrid Brainard. '"The Olde Measures" in the West Country: John Willoughby's Manuscript'. *Records of Early English Drama Newsletter* 17 (2) (1992): 1–10.

Stokes, Will. 'The Epistle to the Reader'. In *The Vaulting-Master, or, the Art of Vaulting Reduced to a Method, Comprized Under Certaine Rules, Illustrated by Examples, and Now Primarily Set Forth by Will. Stokes.* [Oxford]: Printed for Richard Davis in Oxon, 1652.

Stone, Alison. *'Am I a Clowne?': Clowning in Shakespeare.* MA thesis, University of Otago, 2010.

Sutton, John, Doris McIlwain, Wayne Christensen and Andrew Geeves. 'Applying Intelligence to the Reflexes: Embodied Skills and Habits Between Dreyfus and Descartes'. *Journal of the British Society for Phenomenology* 42 (1) (2011): 78–103.

Sutton, Julia, ed. *'Nobilta di Dame' by Fabritio Caroso.* Oxford: Oxford University Press, 1986.

Sutton, Julia. 'Late Renaissance Dance'. In *'Nobilta di Dame' by Fabritio Caroso*, edited by Julia Sutton, 21–30. Oxford: Oxford University Press, 1986.

T. F. (student). *Newes from the North. Otherwise Called the Conference Betvveen Simon Certain, and Pierce Plowman,* Faithfully Collected and Gathered by T. F. (Student). London, 1579.

Three Elizabethan Fencing Manuals. Edited by James L. Jackson. Delmar, NY: Scholars' Facsimiles and Reprints, 1972.

Toft, Robert. *With Passionate Voice: Re-Creative Singing in Sixteenth-Century England and Italy.* Oxford: Oxford University Press, 2014.

Tribble, Evelyn B. 'Distributing Cognition in the Globe'. *Shakespeare Quarterly* 56 (2) (2005): 135–55.

Tribble, Evelyn B. *Cognition in the Globe: Attention and Memory in Shakespeare's Theatre.* Houndmills, Basingstoke: Palgrave Macmillan, 2011.

Tribble, Evelyn B. and John Sutton. 'Cognitive Ecology as a Framework for Shakespearean Studies'. *Shakespeare Studies* 39 (2011): 94–103.

Tribble, Evelyn B. 'Where are the Archers in Shakespeare?' *ELH* 82 (3) (2015): 789–814.

Van Fossen, Richard. Introduction to *The Jew of Malta.* Edited by Richard Van Fossen, xii–xxv. London: Edward Arnold, 1965.

Van Kampen, Claire. 'Music and Aural Texture at Shakespeare's Globe'. In *Shakespeare's Globe: A Theatrical Experiment*, edited by Christie Carson and Farah Karim-Cooper, 79–89. Cambridge: Cambridge University Press, 2008.

Van Orden, Kate. *Music, Discipline, and Arms in Early Modern France*. Chicago: University of Chicago Press, 2005.

Vigarello, Georges. 'The Upward Training of the Body from the Age of Chivalry to Courtly Civility'. In *Fragments for a History of the Human Body II*, edited by Michel Feher, Ramona Naddaff and Nadia Tarzi, 148–99. New York: Zone, 1989.

Villiers, George, Duke of Buckingham. *The Rehearsal*. London: Printed for R. Bentley and S. Magnes, 1683. Available online: http://eebo.chadwyck.com/search/full_rec?SOURCE=config. cfg&ACTION=SINGLE&ID=13672708 (accessed 17 March 2016).

Walsingham, Francis. Letter. 'Elizabeth: January 1578'. In *Calendar of State Papers, Scotland: Volume 5, 1574–81*, edited by William K. Boyd, 268–70. London: His Majesty's Stationery Office, 1907. Available online: http://www.british-history.ac.uk/cal-state-papers/scotland/vol5/pp268-27 (accessed 17 March 2016).

Ward, John. 'The English Measure'. *Early Music* 14 (1) (1986): 15–21.

Ward, John. 'Apropos "The Olde Measures"'. *Records of Early Drama Newsletter* 18 (1) (1993): 1–21.

Weimann, Robert. *Author's Pen and Actor's Voice: Playing and Writing in Shakespeare's Theatre*. Edited by Helen Higbee and William N. West. Cambridge: Cambridge University Press, 2000.

Weingust, Don. 'Authentic Performances or Performances of Authenticity? Original Practices and the Repertory Schedule'. *Shakespeare* 10 (4) (2014): 402–10.

Weis, René. 'Introduction to *Romeo and Juliet*'. Arden Shakespeare Third Series. London: Bloomsbury, 2012.

West, Michael. 'Spenser, Everard Digby, and the Renaissance Art of Swimming'. *Renaissance Quarterly* 26 (1) (1973): 11–22.

West, William N. 'When is the Jig Up – and What is it Up to?' In *Locating the Queen's Men*, edited by Andrew Griffin, Holger Schott Syme and Helen Ostovich, 201–15. Aldershot: Ashgate, 2009.

West, William N. 'Intertheatricality'. In *Early Modern Theatricality*, edited by Henry S. Turner, 151–72. Oxford: Oxford University Press, 2013.

Wickham, G., H. Berry and W. Ingram, eds. *English Professional*

Theatre, 1530–1660. Cambridge: Cambridge University Press, 2000.

Wiggins, Martin and Catherine Richardson, eds. *British Drama 1598–1602: A Catalogue. Volume IV: 1533–1642*. Oxford: Oxford University Press, 2014.

Wiles, David. *Shakespeare's Clown: Actor and Text in the Elizabethan Playhouse*. Cambridge: Cambridge University Press, 1987.

Wilson, D. R. 'Dancing in the Inns of Court'. *Historical Dance* 2 (5) (1986–7): 3–16.

Wilson, T. *The Passions of the Mind in General*. London, 1604.

Winerock, Emily. 'Staging Dance in English Renaissance Drama'. In *Proceedings of the 34th Society of Dance History Scholars Annual Conference (June 23–26, 2011)*, compiled by Ken Pierce, 259–66. Riverside, CA: Society of Dance History Scholars, 2011.

Winerock, Emily. 'Reformation and Revelry: The Practices and Politics of Dancing in Early Modern England, c.1550–c.1640'. Unpublished PhD dissertation, University of Toronto, 2012.

Woods, Penelope. 'Skilful Spectatorship? Doing (or Being) Audience at Shakespeare's Globe Theatre'. *Shakespeare Studies* 43 (2015): 99–113.

Worthen, W. B. 'Reconstructing the Globe: Constructing Ourselves'. *Shakespeare Survey* 52 (1998): 175–88.

W. P. *MSS 1, Article 6, 01 Recto: Letter from W. P. to Edward Alleyn About a Theatrical Wager, with Six Lines of Verse Beginning 'Deny Me Not, Sweete Nedd, the Wager's Downe'* (c. 1590). Henslowe-Alleyn.org.uk, n.d. Available online: http://www.henslowe-alleyn.org.uk/images/MSS-1/Article-006/01r.html (accessed 17 March 2016).

Wright, L. B. 'Variety Entertainment by Elizabethan Strolling Players'. *Journal of English and Germanic Philology* 26 (3) (1927): 294–303.

Wright, Thomas. *The Passions of the Mind in General* (1604). Edited by William Webster Newbold. New York: Garland, 1986.

Youth's Behaviour: or Decencie in Conversation Amongst Men. Composed in French by Grave Persons, for the Use and Benefit of their Youth; Now Newly Turned into English, by Francis Hawkins; with the Addition of Twenty Six New Precepts which are Marked Thus (*) and Some More Additon, Added 1651. Translated by Francis Hawkins. London: W. Lee, 1661.

Zucker, Adam. *The Places of Wit in Early Modern English Comedy*. Cambridge: Cambridge University Press, 2011.

INDEX